MIDDLE CHILD 2

Better Than Good

Historical Drama

Novel

By

Taj Shotwell

Middle Child2: Better Than Good

Library of Congress 2015910275

ISBN-10:0692472312
ISBN-13:978-0-692-47231-6

Author: Taj Shotwell

Website: www.tajshotwell.com
Email: taj.shotwell@outlook.com

Cover Design: Taj Shotwell
Cover Graphics: Fiverr Webmark

Printed in the United States of America
This is a work of historical drama, and some ADULT LANGUAGE AND SITUATIONS ARE INCLUDED. This collection of historical drama stories is based on true stories beginning in the mid-1950s. Fictional names are used for privacy and security reasons.

In Loving Memory of

Godfrey Fulton James
(Dec. 6, 1914-Feb. 24, 1996)

Maggie Ella Douglass James
(Aug. 11, 1920-Nov. 18-2009)

Acknowledgments

First, I give honor and praise to God for allowing me to take a journey that has given me peace and gratitude.

Many thanks to my editors and reviewers for their unwavering dedication to my work: Rose Jackson Ford from Memphis, TN; Harold James from Reno, NV; Fatmah Saidah Radovich from Costa Rica; Jenifer Peckoo from Tallahassee, FL.; and Daniel Miller from Memphis, TN.

Furthermore, thanks to my family members and friends who provided me with unbroken encouragement. My special acknowledgment and gratitude to Lilieth Peckoo and her loving family in Tallahassee for their spiritual uplifting and thoughtfulness.

To all who read my first novel "Middle Child: Build A Fence All Around Me", thank you for your kind support.

Finally, thanks to the staff at My Provider Productions LLC for their trust in my work.

Prologue

Annie Fowler Hightower was the middle child of eleven children. Her father, Jessie Jacob Fowler, was a career Army sergeant, and her mother, Margaret Elaine McGwin Fowler, was a homemaker. During the mid-fifties and through the sixties, Annie lived in Europe and a few states. Annie's transition from military life to living in Memphis was difficult as she developed a strong fear of specific southern people. Annie participated in the civil rights movement. Yet, her family environment was hostile, and she survived molestation as a young girl. While still in high school, she found work to help support herself and the family.

When Annie became pregnant, she dropped out of college and married an abusive man who oppressed her in every aspect of life. At the age of twenty-one, Annie's mother, Margaret, helped her to escape her brutal marriage. Annie divorced her husband, but his threats to her and her parents forced her to move to St. Louis, Missouri, with her maternal grandmother and uncle.

Annie found a happy life and a new love interest in St. Louis—only to see it all quickly vanish before her. Again, in fear, Annie packed up and sought a new start somewhere safe. Her mother, once more, helped Annie to find shelter with a relative in San Francisco.

Sixty-four-year-old Annie spent the early part of the day alone on her birthday. She sat in her comfortable large wing chair and persisted to turn pages in the family photo albums that were stacked on the floor next to her chair and her lap. Her eyes focused on a photo taken in 1973 of her with her Aunt Olivia and other family members in San Francisco.

Annie arrived in San Francisco with her eyes wide open. With tenacity and endurance, she was determined to make a good life for herself and her daughter. Always with a song and prayer in her heart, "Lord, build a fence all around me, as I travel on my way," Annie continued to recollect her life's journeys.

CHAPTER 1

The Golden State

Once Annie stepped on the soil of San Francisco, she felt both liberated and safe. She knew it would not be easy. Hard work was a natural part of her being. Annie was willing to do whatever it took to make a good life for her and her daughter.

Annie received a warm welcome to the home of her maternal Aunt Olivia and her husband Uncle Larry, as well as, their five children. Aunt Olivia was the youngest child of the eleven McGwin siblings. She left Memphis during the fifties to start a new life with her husband. Their house was located in a small town on the east bay of San Francisco called San Pablo. The house was built on a steep hill and a clear day, there was a striking view of the San Francisco landscapes and the Bay Bridge.

Annie called her mother as soon as she got settled in.

"Hello, Mother, I'm at Aunt Olivia's house."

"That is great, Annie, so glad you made it safely."

Margaret shared terrible news with Annie about her paternal great uncle, Theodore Fairweather.

"Your Uncle Ted passed away."

Annie was shocked by the news. She had not seen any of her family for over a year and now she would never see Uncle Ted again.

"Oh, my goodness! When did he die?"

"He passed away about three weeks ago, but I didn't tell you because I didn't want you to return to Memphis. It's not safe for you now."

Annie couldn't restrain her tears, but she understood her mother's decision. She had fond memories of Uncle Ted, especially his good cooking.

"Mother, how is Granny handling it?"

"Oh, she is better now, you know how close she was to her brother. She will be fine," Margaret responded.

"I miss you all so much. I wish I could be there."

"I know, but we're fine, you just get your life straighten out and write us to let us know you are okay."

"I will, and thank you, Mother, for everything. Is Daddy there?"

"Yes, do you want to talk to him?"

"Yeah"

"Hello," Jessie answered.

"Hey, Daddy, how you doing?"

"Hey, Annie, I'm good. Are you at the bus stop?" They laughed.

That is what Jessie always asked when Annie called.

"I'm sorry to hear about Uncle Ted, I know you two were close."

"Yeah, we were. I'll miss him. Well, you come home – when you can."

"I will, Daddy, take care. I love you."

****

3

Although Annie was truly grateful to her aunt and uncle for their hospitality, she felt the living arrangement was not suitable for her and her daughter, Whitney. There were five males living in the home and privacy was very limited. Aunt Olivia had only one daughter who was sixteen years old.

Until Annie was able to get her apartment, she decided to take Whitney to the home of her oldest sister, Elaine, who lived in Washington. Elaine's daughter, Alisa, was about eleven-years-old and an only child. She was a precocious and nurturing little girl and loved younger children. At four-years-old, Whitney was articulate and independent. Annie believed that it was a great opportunity for the two cousins to bond, and it would allow Annie time to obtain suitable living space.

Annie caught a flight with Whitney to Washington. After they arrived, Annie felt welcomed by Elaine and her husband. They took Annie and the children on a tour of the local areas, Seattle, and a boat cruise where they toured several attractions in Victoria, Canada.

Annie observed the interactions between Alisha and Whitney and felt that she had made a good decision to leave her with Elaine. But most importantly, Annie felt little Whitney would be safe and have the proper care.

CHAPTER 2

New Job

Annie was grateful to start working immediately after her return from Washington. Her heart and mind had been filled with confusion over the recent occurrence in St. Louis. Dmitri's death was devastating and she didn't know why it happened or by whom. She knew leaving was best, and she pondered if Floyd was involved in the murder. Annie decided not to share her experience in St. Louis with anyone and to have a fresh beginning in San Francisco. She, once again, placed herself in "survival mode" and stopped dwelling on the matter. Annie's main objective was to find a nontoxic environment for her and her daughter.

Annie had contacted the Executive Director for the San Francisco branch of the nonprofit organization that she had worked for in St. Louis. Annie was excited about working as a bookkeeper and was determined to impress them with her skills. She used public transportation until her car arrived about two weeks later. Then, she drove her car to the BART station and rode the rapid train to San Francisco. She walked about six blocks to the office.

When she arrived at the office, she met with the director, Ralph Carter, to talk about her duties and responsibilities. He was a short heavy statue man, with a receding hairline, and wore thick glasses. Carter was pleasant but for an instant, Annie felt uncomfortable alone with him. Annie was introduced to her supervisor, DeAndra Woods, who showed Annie her workspace and gave her instructions to work on a project. Although the project had nothing to do with bookkeeping, Annie was happy to have a job.

After about three weeks on the job, Annie became curious and asked DeAndra about the work she was doing and what were the plans for her position in accounting. DeAndra was a bit annoyed by the questioning.

"I don't know why you were hired and there is no position available for a bookkeeper," she told Annie.

Annie was confused but didn't want to cause any problems. So, she continued to do the work that was given to her. Fortunately, there was enough work to keep Annie busy. She didn't have much time to socialize with the coworkers, but she overheard gossip from them about Cora who was Ralph Carter's administrative assistant. It was rumored that Cora had a baby with Carter.

On a Friday afternoon, about six weeks from the day Annie started to work, Ralph Carter called her into his office. Annie was surprised and worried that she might be laid off from work. She didn't see DeAndra anywhere around the office to get some idea about why Mr. Carter personally summoned her to his office.

Annie walked into his office.

"Hello, Mr. Carter, how may I help you?" She asked him.

He got up from his desk to close the door.

"Have a seat," he told Annie. Annie sat down.

"How have you been doing?" He stood near her.

"Great, I enjoy working here," said Annie.

He touched her on her shoulder. Annie flinched.

"Well, I think you and I should get together sometimes."

"What do you mean, Mr. Carter?"

"Well, you are so pretty … it's been hard seeing you and not …" He stepped closer to Annie.

"I did you a favor and now it's time for you to do me one."

"I don't know what you mean." Annie leaned away from him and felt repelled.

He touched her again on her shoulder and made rubbing movements towards her breast. Annie jumped up and pushed him back. He was blocking the door. She felt trapped.

"What do you want, Mr. Carter?" Annie shouted.

"I just want you to be nice to me," he walked toward her.

"If you have an ounce of sense, you would get back off of me or I will scream for help!" Annie shouted louder.

"After all, I've done for you," he said.

"What have you done? I come to work, I do my job, and there've been no complaints. Let me out," she pushed him again.

Carter stepped back. Annie rushed to the door and exited it. She grabbed her belongings from her desk and tearfully ran to the BART station for home.

"Lord, build a fence all around me." Annie prayed. Like a fish, she swam away and never returned.

CHAPTER 3

Job Search

Within a few days, Annie landed a consultant job with a small corporation in San Francisco. She worked in the accounting department. It was the first job she worked where she was the only black person. It surprised Annie that she felt comfortable and the environment was non-threatening. Her supervisor and coworkers were very nice to her.

The office workers were really into sports. Gambling pools were going on all the time for various sports. Annie decided to participate in one of the games that cost a minimum of $5 to enter. Five dollars was a day's transportation cost to work. She really couldn't afford it but to be sociable, she gave it a try. Annie went back to her duties and had forgotten all about the game until one of the coworkers rushed to her desk.

"Annie, you are the winner." She handed Annie $85 in cash. Annie was beside herself because she had never won anything before. She thanked everyone. Annie did notice that there was one guy that was a bit annoyed by her winning the money, but he soon got over it.

Annie clearly understood why many of her relatives left the south after graduating from high school and chose to move to the west coast. The area and weather were resplendent, but most importantly, the fear of white people subsided tremendously in her spirit. Annie quickly learned that it wasn't the entire race of people to fear. Instead, it was the ignorance within a culture and its environment. She held on with the hope and dream of Martin Luther King, when he said, "… children will one day live in a nation where they will not be judged by the color of their skin, but by the content of their character."

Annie fully realized that racism existed everywhere, but it appeared not as brutal and pronounced as she had experienced in the Deep South.

A month later, Annie found a two-bedroom apartment in Richmond, California. She purchased one full-size bed and one twin-size bed without headboards, a card table, and two folding chairs from Goodwill. She bought bed sheets and towels and then, she got the apartment ready for Whitney's arrival.

As she walked through the new apartment, she felt her father, Jessie's presence. She recalled the last time he first visited her in her apartment when she was a newlywed. Annie worked for hours getting the apartment ready for her parents' visit. Very pregnant, she got on her knees to scrub the baseboards and floors. She washed the door panels and around the doorknobs and cleaned the kitchen. When Jessie and Margaret arrived, Annie, feeling proud, gave them a tour of the small apartment. Jessie observed her place as if he was supervising his staff at the mess hall. He pointed at the stove.

"You missed the drip pans." He said.

Annie was devastated that she didn't receive a one-hundred percent approval. But from that experience, she never forgot to clean the drip pans. Annie hoped that Whitney will enjoy the new space.

Annie flew to Washington to pick up Whitney, who looked fit and content. They were so happy to see one another. Annie expressed sincere gratitude to Elaine and Alisa for taking such good care of Whitney. She would never forget their love and generosity.

It felt wonderful to have her daughter with her once again, and Annie hoped it would be their last separation. She found a nice daycare center near the apartment that operated from 7:00 a.m. – 6:00 p.m. Whitney loved her bedroom and the daycare center.

The following summer, Annie's niece, Alisa, from Washington, came to visit for two weeks. Whitney and Alisa got along wonderfully.

Annie had worked with the corporation for about six months when she landed a full-time accounting position with a subsidiary of a large corporation located in one of the San Francisco financial district's famous landmarks, "The Transamerica Pyramid." The financial district was so exciting and different from Annie's. Although it was the seventies, many wore conservative business attire. The .area was very colorful. There were hippies and people wore wide-leg pantsuits, ethnic garb, and natural and disco looks.

This time, Annie was one of two black people who worked in the office, but she had a great rapport with all her coworkers. Annie felt so blessed to have a job with medical and educational benefits.

Annie couldn't believe how affordable it was to get an education in California. Since her employer paid educational benefits after ninety days of employment, Annie enrolled in evening classes at a well-known prestigious business and law university in San Francisco. It wasn't far from the financial district. Annie's neighbor picked up Whitney on those evenings and watched her until she arrived home.

Little Whitney also started kindergarten that fall, in 1974. She was so excited on her first day. Whitney was a bit shy but soon gravitated to a little girl and sat down next to her. The girl showed Whitney where the crayons and paper were located. Annie arranged for Whitney to be bused to the afterschool program near the apartment. Annie became tearful when she realized that her baby was growing up so fast.

CHAPTER 4

Check-Up

About six months later, Annie was feeling much rundown and thought she had better go for a physical, especially since she hadn't had an exam in three years. After the exam and blood tests, Annie received a call from her doctor's office for her to come in for her blood test results. The doctor looked at Annie with concern.

"Ms. Hightower, how do you do it?"

Annie wasn't sure what he meant.

"You have chronic anemia. We should hospitalize you."

"You are scaring me, doctor. What is anemia? This is the second time I heard the term," Annie asked.

"It should scare you because it is serious… Anemia is when your red blood cell count is lower than normal and or when a person's red blood cells do not include enough hemoglobin. In both situations, you are far below normal," the doctor explained.

"How can you help me, doctor? I just started a new job."

"We can try you as an outpatient and get you started on scheduled appointments to come into this office for iron injections and supplements. We will also set up a dietary plan. You are thin, but your weight is fine. You must eat the right foods and remember to eat a few meals a day."

Annie went to the doctor's office twice a week during her lunch break for her injections. From that incident, Annie began to take charge of her eating habits and researched more about healthy choices.

She had learned a lot early on about good food choices and preparation from her father. He didn't like his vegetables

11

overcooked and didn't eat much fat and sweets. Her mother, Margaret, was the total opposite, she ate almost anything. She loved fried foods, starchy carbohydrates, the skin on the meats, and desserts. When Annie was younger, she recalled the times her parents argued about the food and its preparation.

Annie had been eating one meal a day for quite a while. She loved a hefty lunch. Eating to her was like a job. She didn't enjoy food and ate only when she was hungry. Although the doctor recommended red meat like liver, she had already removed all red meats from her diet because she didn't like them. Instead, she took iron supplements and ate more vegetables that contained iron. She mostly ate green leafy vegetables, beans, fish, and poultry white meat. When she remembered, she ate more small meals throughout the day and didn't eat after six o'clock, because she didn't sleep well when she did. Annie had never cared for meat. She had stopped eating pork after she left Memphis and moved to St. Louis. She had never given her daughter pork and allowed very little sugar. Although Annie's healthy food choices had been influenced by her father, who managed a Mess Hall during his military career, she also was influenced by Dick Gregory, who was a comedian and civil rights activist and remained a vegetarian.

It was a very slow process, but Annie gradually started to feel stronger and was thankful to learn ways that would improve her health.

CHAPTER 5

San Francisco

Working in San Francisco's financial district had been a gratifying experience for Annie. She was able to hop on a cable car or bus and visit all the popular attractions, entertainment, and sites.

There were so many different cultures represented in the bay area. Annie ate at her favorite spots every opportunity she could— China Town, Thai restaurants, the Ghirardelli Square, Japanese Tea Garden, and Fisherman's Wharf. The popular Haight-Ashbury area included hippies and was a melting pot of cultural and social views. It lacked drugs and sexual and social inhibitions. Annie only visited the area once and passed through it when she had to. She didn't feel comfortable with some of the social views and peculiar behaviors.

It was the seventies and people talked about free love. They smoked and snorted drugs. Annie had heard about pot or grass in high school but had not personally known anyone that used it. While living in St. Louis, she was around some cigarette smokers and was not aware of anyone smoking pot or using drugs. This was a cultural shock for her.

Annie's father, two of her sisters, and a brother were cigarette smokers. Annie couldn't understand the need for the disgusting habit. She tolerated their choices but tried to avoid the smoke whenever she could.

Annie discovered, in San Francisco and the Bay Area, that the people were very open about smoking pot. She was first introduced to the pot by a first cousin in the bay area. Annie had visited her cousin's home several times and noticed that when her cousin smoked the pot around her, Annie became hungry and craved snacks. It was referred to as a "contact high." Although the smell was terrible and the smoke irritating, Annie did not complain. Several times Annie was invited to take a hit, she refused, except once she tried it. She tried to inhale the disgusting smoke but choked and it soon gave her a headache. That experience was a confirmation of what she already knew. She didn't want it, didn't like it, and didn't need it. So she didn't smoke it.

Sometimes Annie's coworkers smoked in their cars during lunch break. Once she drove to lunch with a coworker. The person lit up a joint in Annie's car while she drove back to work. The scent of the joint was all in Annie's hair and clothes. She ran to the bathroom and sprayed herself down with the bathroom spray.

Although Annie tried to avoid those who partook in the drugs, it would be a few years before she finally learned to stop associating with and accommodating others with bad habits.

Annie had many maternal first cousins living in the San Francisco Bay Area including El Cerrito, Vallejo, and Union City. There were also some in Palencia, Los Angeles, and Sacramento. Her cousins represented six of the eleven McGwin siblings. Occasionally, she and Whitney would visit them on weekends. It gave Annie a nostalgic feeling being around family and she encouraged more gatherings.

Napa Valley was not too far from San Francisco. Annie made a few trips there with friends for wine and cheese tastings. She developed a taste for white cheese, sparkling wines that were not too sweet, and extra dry champagnes. Annie didn't have a special brand and she drank sparingly. She never purchased any of the high price items but enjoyed the scenic and peaceful rides to the valley.

San Francisco was unquestionably a place where Annie wanted to plant roots for a new life with her daughter.

CHAPTER 6

Hanging Out

Annie had not dated anyone since she left St. Louis, over two years before. She was too busy and had no interest. Besides, she still felt a deep loss from the death of her "would-be lover," Dmitri. The image of him lying on the ground, dead, remained so vivid in her mind and heart. Her primary goals were to secure a job, find a safe home, and earn a college degree.

With all she had on her plate, Annie did find little time to hang out with a few friends. Since Annie loved to dance and used it as a form of exercise, she looked for spots that would give her a good workout. On Wednesdays, there was Salsa dancing in the Marina, and on some Fridays, there was Reggae dancing in Oakland. She was a fast learner and soon felt comfortable with the styles of dancing.

During the fall of 1975, an agent for a major insurance company came into the accounting department where Annie worked. He was in his late thirties, six feet tall, and about twenty pounds overweight, but a nice-looking man. He was talking to another employee but noticed Annie working at her desk. Annie had not noticed him. She got up to take some invoices to another employee when he moved toward her to say hello.

Annie smiled and said, "Hello."

He introduced himself.

"I'm Frankie Watson."

"Hi, I'm Annie."

Annie was not impressed but listened for a moment.

"I've been here a few times and noticed you but didn't have the nerves to speak to you," he told her.

15

"Oh, really. Why not?" She asked him.

"Because I thought someone as cute as you must be attached to some lucky man." He gave Annie his business card.

"Please, call me sometimes for a drink or lunch."

Annie took his card.

A week later, Frankie was in the office again. Annie had not called him. He asked Annie out for dinner. She declined his offer. So he suggested lunch. Annie accepted.

The next day, Annie and Frankie met at a Thai restaurant. She learned that Frankie had been in the insurance business for several years and that he lived in Oakland. He also told her that he was in divorce proceedings and had a nine-year-old daughter from a previous relationship. This didn't bother Annie because she wasn't feeling a possible love connection.

Annie continued to meet Frankie on periodic lunch dates and a few times for drinks before she went to class. He drank gin and tonic and she had ginger ale with lime. Afterward, Frankie gave Annie a lift to school.

Annie began to like Frankie, he was down-to-earth and pleasant to be around. She especially enjoyed his strong laugh. He invited her and Whitney to go camping at a nearby lake. Annie thought that would be fun for her and Whitney.

Frankie had invited his daughter but told Annie that his daughter's mother had made other plans. He found a nice private spot with only one other camper present. He set up two tents, one for Annie and Whitney, and the other for him. Frankie spoke gently to Whitney and showed her a few fishing tips. Whitney told him, "I know how to fish because my uncle in Indiana already showed me."

The lake was low and the fish were not biting. However, later that evening, there was a striking sunset, and soon the sky was filled with shiny stars. Frankie pointed at the big dipper and a few other stars. He started a small fire inside a large metal pan. The three of them sat around the fire eating sandwiches, chicken, fruits, veggies, and cookies. Annie was glad that there was no alcohol but there was plenty of water and Seven-up. They also roasted marshmallows. Annie and Whitney appreciated the outing and were thankful that there were no mosquitoes. Frankie made sure that Annie and Whitney were tucked in and he kissed Annie on the forehead.

"Sleep tight and have a good night." He smiled and went to his tent.

Despite no fish, the camping trip was exciting. Annie and Whitney relished the time spent with Frankie.

A couple of weeks later, Frankie took Annie for a visit to meet his Aunt Betty and Uncle Rufus's house in Oakland. He told Annie that he had planned to live with them until after his divorce. They were very pleasant people and Uncle Rufus was a jokester. He shared many jokes and sayings. One of his favorite sayings, after he made a statement, was, "Am I right or Am-I-rilla?"

After a few visits, they nicknamed Annie, "Hollywood." Annie wasn't sure where they were coming from with the nickname or even if it was a compliment. Nevertheless, Frankie and his relatives made Annie feel welcome.

CHAPTER 7

New Plan

Towards the end of the school year in 1975, Whitney's kindergarten teacher asked Annie to meet with her for Whitney's progress report. During the meeting, the teacher recommended to Annie that Whitney be held back a year because of her low achievement scores. Annie didn't agree with the assessment and told the teacher that she would personally work with Whitney to raise her scores.

The school year 1975-76 was a very challenging period for Annie. She was working full-time and she took twelve credit hours of classes towards her degree. Whitney was in the first grade and Annie worked hard with her to raise her scores. On many occasions, Annie took Whitney with her to class at the university. This allowed Annie to oversee Whitney's homework assignments as she completed them in the classroom. Fortunately, Whitney was a perfect angel and the professors didn't mind her there. The hard work paid off as Whitney completed the first grade in the ninety-eight percentile. Whitney's teacher told Annie that she made the right decision to let Whitney go forward.

During the same period, Annie received a letter from her mother, Margaret. She informed Annie that Whitney's paternal Aunt Ruby wanted to talk to Whitney. Annie had not made any contact with her ex-husband, Floyd Hightower, and his family since her divorce in 1972. He had not made any payments for child support that were ordered by the court. Annie was still concerned about both her and Whitney's safety. She didn't know how dangerous Floyd was. After all, Floyd had threatened to harm Annie and her parents if she pursued getting child support. So she decided she would not.

It was rumored that Floyd had set fires and Annie wanted nothing to happen to her parents in Memphis.

Annie thought long and hard about contacting Ruby and decided it would be safe to just call her.

It had been about four years since anyone in Memphis had seen Annie and Whitney, so during the Christmas holidays, Annie called Ruby. She put Whitney on the phone to talk with her. Annie and Ruby talked for a long time, but Annie never asked about Floyd.

"Hey, Sister, I was hoping that you would let Whitney come to Memphis for a visit during one of her school breaks. You know between me and the Twins, we will take good care of Whitney. She needs to know her relatives," Ruby expressed to Annie.

Annie wanted to say no, but not right away.

"I will think about it and get back to you."

A few months after that conversation in the spring of 1976, on a late afternoon, Annie's supervisor called her into his office. Annie had worked for the company for over two years and such a request was not unusual. But this visit was different.

"Annie, we have enjoyed you and your work. However, I'm sorry to tell you that due to budget cuts, your position has been eliminated. You have only two more weeks remaining here. The company will pay for the current courses you are taking at the university—after you complete them."

Annie was in shock, but she maintained her cool. Her mind immediately went into survival and planning mode.

At that time Annie needed forty-eight credits to complete her bachelor's degree in accounting. She realized that to get a more stable job and earn a decent income, she would have to complete the degree. After a thorough detailed planning analysis, Annie decided to apply for financial aid and to finish the credits within one year. Although a bit ambitious, she would have to take nine credits in the summer, eighteen credits in the fall, and twenty-one credits in the spring. This would allow her to graduate by May of 1977. Annie also knew she would not be able to afford the rent on the apartment. She had considered asking one of her cousins to rent her a room temporarily, at least until she completed her degree.

Annie called her ex-sister-in-law, Ruby, to talk to her about letting Whitney spend the entire school year with her. Ruby thought it would be good for Whitney, but because of the length of stay, she thought that Floyd would have to be involved. She explained that he had an extra bedroom and that he and his girlfriend, Rena, had married. Rena didn't have any children but always wanted them. Ruby assured Annie that she and her twin sisters would keep a close watch over Whitney and that they would be active in her life. Ruby suggested that she would first talk with Floyd and Rena to get a feel of the situation. Annie gave Ruby her phone number and asked her to call her back as soon as possible.

Annie was conflicted on whether to let Whitney stay with Floyd and Rena. She strongly felt that Floyd would not hurt Whitney and that who he wanted to hurt was her instead.

Annie was also torn about the statement Ruby made about Whitney getting to know her relatives. – *'Even her "low-life—dead-beat" father.' Annie thought.*

During her thought process, Annie shared her plans with her friend, Frankie. He thought it was a great idea. He also surprised Annie with the option to move in with him. He would get an apartment in San Francisco where she would not have to commute too far to school. Annie told Frankie that she would consider it.

A few days later, Ruby called Annie. She told Annie that Floyd and Rena were excited about Whitney coming and that he wanted to talk to Annie. Annie immediately flinched at the idea of ever talking to Floyd again, but she knew it was only fair to Whitney

that she gets to know her father through her own eyes. Annie agreed
to talk with Floyd. He was at Ruby's house and he took the phone
from Ruby.

"Hey, Annie, are you okay?"

"I'm fine, and you?"

"I'm okay. When do you want Whitney to come to
Memphis?"

"It will be in about two months from now—at the end of
her school term."

"What grade is Whitney now?"

Annie felt proud of Whitney's last progress report.

"She will be finishing the first grade, but she is doing so
well that her teacher had to give her second-grade work to keep
Whitney busy."

"Well, I will look for an airplane ticket. Since she will turn
seven, she can travel alone with the airline staff."

"Oh, I didn't think about that… Then, I rather it is a direct
flight."

"That should be no problem since they are too major
cities."

"Okay."

"Well, I will let you know. Is it okay to have your phone
number?"

"Yes."

"Okay, talk to you later."

"Bye," Annie concluded.

The conversation was intense for Annie, but she thought it
went well. Floyd sounded the same and she hoped he wasn't the
same monster she had left and that he had changed for the better.

The plan was in motion. About two months later, Frankie
drove Annie and Whitney to the airport. Whitney had spoken to her

father twice. She was so excited and fearless about riding the airplane and seemed to understand where she was going.

Frankie had his camera and snapped a picture as tearful Annie lifted Whitney into her arms to hug and kiss her. Annie felt so guilty about sending Whitney away again but thought she had made the right decision.

About a month later, Annie moved in with Frankie in an apartment located in San Francisco not too far from the university. They got along very well. They laughed a lot and spent time together sharing stories about themselves. They became very close and sexually compatible.

Annie spent a lot of time traveling to classes and to the library to complete her assignments. She took part-time jobs to help with her expenses. Such jobs included selling "Weber Grills" and food demonstrations in grocery stores. She also sold hair and body products for a company. Annie was determined to meet her goals. She was especially grateful for Frankie's patience and understanding.

CHAPTER 8

Frankie

In the following year, in May 1977, Annie graduated with a B.S. degree in accounting. Whitney had not yet returned from Memphis because her school did not end until later that month. Annie had not sent out any formal invitations. She just wanted it to be over. So, no one attended Annie's graduation, except Frankie.

Floyd had enrolled Whitney into the third grade, instead of the second. Annie was worried that it would be too much pressure on Whitney to keep up. She had preferred to see Whitney leading in her class, instead of struggling to keep up.

Shortly after graduation, Annie knew she would have to find a job and an apartment before Whitney came home. Frankie's attitude seemed to have changed towards Annie. Then at forty-one years old, he had not finished college but was a certified insurance agent. His income was based on commissions only. As Annie was going to job interviews, she noticed Frankie stayed home more. Sometimes she would come into the apartment to find him playing dominoes with a few buddies. Once, he was gone overnight.

Early one morning, Annie was awakened by a phone call. It was Frankie's, Aunt Betty.

"Sorry to call so early in the morning, but thought you should know that Frankie is in the hospital."

"Is he okay?" Annie asked her.

"He was shot."

Annie panicked and thought to herself, "Oh, My God, not again, did I cause this? First Dmitri—and now Frankie."

"What happened?" Annie asked.

"I don't have the whole story, but this is my understanding: Frankie was trying to get back with his ex-wife. But she had moved on with another man who was living with her. Frankie went over to the house and tried to break down the door and her boyfriend shot him. Frankie had a gun, too."

"Is he going to be okay?"

"They say he is stable and they believe he is going to be okay."

"When can I see him?"

"He's under a lot of drugs now but later today should be fine."

"Thanks for calling me and I'm sorry that you are going through this."

"I'm sorry for all of us. Take care and I'll see you soon," Aunt Betty ended.

Annie got out of bed and began to pace the floor. Again, she had to make a plan. She knew it was over between her and Frankie.

On that same day, Annie interviewed for a position with a certified public accounting firm. She felt the interview went well and thought she might be hearing from them soon.

After the interview, Annie went to the hospital to visit Frankie. He was awake and there were no visitors in his room. She entered his room and saw his frailness. He gave Annie a weak smile and she smiled back.

"How are you doing?" Annie asked.

"I'm okay."

"They say you are going to be fine."

"I know and I feel so stupid," Frankie said but couldn't look at Annie.

"It was a stupid thing you did," I spoke frankly.

"I know."

"I just wanted to check on you and hope that you will fully recover soon," I said.

"Thanks, so what is next?" Frankie asked Annie.

"Well, I will be moving out of the apartment and getting a job."

"There is still a few weeks left on the lease. You can stay. I plan to go back to my aunt and uncle's to recover." Frankie said.

"I appreciate that, I probably won't need the place that long, but we'll see."

Annie chose not to go into the discussion of why Frankie did what he did because she already knew. It was because she was moving forward and advancing in life and he was not.

Annie said her goodbyes knowing it would be the last time she would see Frankie.

CHAPTER 9

A Bad Place

It was early June 1977 and Annie had gotten the job with the CPA firm in Oakland. She rented a two-bedroom house in Oakland and removed all of her items from Frankie's apartment. Annie knew she had a short time to get the house ready for Whitney's arrival.

One evening after work, Annie was home decorating the front room and Whitney's bedroom. Someone knocked on the door. Annie didn't think to look out first, so she just opened the door. There stood Frankie and he stepped inside before she could say anything.

"Frankie, what are you doing here?"

"We need to talk." He pulled out a gun from his jacket and pointed it at Annie.

Annie backed away. Frankie followed her and closed the door behind him. She could smell the strong scent of alcohol on him and became frantic but did not want to show it. "Lord, build a fence all around me," she sang in her heart.

"What do you want, Frankie?"

"I want you – I need you in my life now. If I can't have you, then we will both die tonight"

Annie could see the desperation in his face and tried to calm the situation.

"Okay, Frankie, let's talk about it. Why don't we sit down calmly and talk about it? I think you are right, we should be together. We had some fun times."

Annie could see that Frankie was calming down when he lowered his gun. Annie continued to talk to him.

"But right now, I just started a new job and I have to get a report out tonight or I could lose my job. Can we have lunch tomorrow? I can meet you anywhere. We can plan where to go from here," Annie pleaded.

Skeptical, Frankie placed his gun back in his jacket.

"Okay, tomorrow at 1:00 p.m. Is that good for you?" Annie nodded.

"Okay, that sounds like a good idea. I'll be at my aunt's house." Frankie told Annie.

Frankie kissed Annie on her forehead. So relieved, Annie walked Frankie to the door. When he walked down the steps, Annie locked the front door and checked the entire house to see if it was secured. She thought about calling the police, but instead, she chose to call Frankie's aunt and uncle the following morning.

When Annie got to work, she immediately called Frankie's Aunt Betty and told her what had transpired the night before. Aunt Betty was surprised and disappointed.

"Don't you worry, Annie, I will take care of the situation and the only call you'll ever get from Frankie will be an apology."

"That is not necessary. I just want Frankie out of my life." Annie told his aunt.

Sure enough, Frankie called Annie.

"Annie that was a good move to call my aunt and uncle because they are all I have left in this world. I apologize and promise you that I will not bother you again. Thank you, Annie, for not calling the police because what I did was wrong and I was in *a bad place* in my head, but I will be okay."

Annie never heard from Frankie again.

27

CHAPTER 10

Hawaii

After the drama with Frankie, Annie focused on her duties at her new job. The CPA firm that she worked for was a well-known firm in the area and Annie was very impressed with the organization and professionalism of the partners. It was owned and managed by two black men. The firm had been built by them over several years of hard work and public respect. Annie learned a lot from them. She audited governmental agencies, university and school programs, and medical facilities.

The CPA partners were strictly all about business and making a profit. They were both married with a family. Not once did Annie encounter any impropriety. It was a relief for her to see that there were real men who respected women and their wives.

Annie wanted to spend some fun and special time with Whitney and to show her how much she appreciated her endurance and acceptance during complicated times. She found a special deal on a one-week vacation to Hawaii for two and paid for it on a credit card. It would also be a celebration of Annie's recent accomplishments — a bachelor's degree and a new job. The trip would be a surprise to Whitney who was then eight-years-old. Annie had informed her new employer of her plans and they approved her time off.

When Whitney came home a few days before the planned trip to Hawaii, Annie was so happy to have her back. Whitney updated Annie on her version of what happened during her one-year stay in Memphis. She had a lot to tell.

One story Whitney shared that was unsettling to Annie:

28

"Aunt Samantha told me that you married Daddy because you were pregnant and that you thought about getting an abortion."

Annie was very surprised by the statement and upset that her sister would say such a thing to her eight-year-old daughter.

"I was pregnant when I got married, but I've never told anyone that I wanted to get an abortion. If I wanted one, I would have gotten one. That was a difficult time for me—you are here and I have no regrets."

Whitney seemed to be satisfied with Annie's response, but the most important thing that came out of the conversation was that Whitney had not been hit or abused during her stay in Memphis.

During the year that Whitney was away in Memphis, Annie received a phone call from Floyd and was taken aback, especially since he called to give her praises on how well she'd done on raising Whitney.

"Whitney is such a good girl—very polite and she doesn't cry as she used to and she is easygoing. Everyone thinks you have done a good job."

Such words coming from Floyd were colossal to Annie. She was so relieved that he and Whitney had enjoyed each other. Although she called to check on Whitney as often as she could, Annie still wondered what was going on in the minds of Floyd and Rena and how they were treating Whitney. Annie believed that every child, when possible, should see their parents through their own eyes. Yet, Annie still questioned her decision to let Whitney visit Memphis.

A day before the trip, Annie told Whitney to pack her bags for a trip to Hawaii. Whitney squealed with excitement about the trip. Annie received joy from seeing her daughter's pleasure.

The view from the sky was breathtaking during the flight to the big island of Hawaii. When they landed, Annie and Whitney got settled into the hotel and immediately began to explore the hotel and its surroundings.

Annie met a woman named Sarah at the hotel who was also on vacation with her teenage daughter. Sarah was a cute redhead with green eyes. Her daughter, Britney, was a cute blond with brown eyes who was thirteen-years old. They went on some of the same tours with Annie and Whitney, including the trip to Oahu Island. After a few days, Sarah suggested to Annie that they go out one evening together and that her daughter would watch Whitney. The children had no problem with the arrangement, especially since they could order anything from the hotel menu.

Annie and Sarah went to a couple of hotels to check out the music. They listened for a while but decided to walk through the mall. Annie was very star shy and surprised when she saw Muhammad Ali in the shopping mall. He and his security guard were cruising alone looking in store windows. Annie was too shy to say anything to Ali so she kept staring at him. A moment later, Ali saw Annie and walked up to her and said, "You are a pretty red thang," and gave Annie a little hug.

Annie recalled him having bad breath, but she didn't mind because she was standing next to "The Greatest." She asked him where was Mrs. Ali. He told her that Veronica was somewhere shopping and that they were on their honeymoon. Annie congratulated him and asked Ali if she could take a picture with him." He told her it was okay. Annie turned to Sarah, who was observing and asked her to take a picture, but Ali's security guard volunteered to do it. He snapped a picture and returned the camera to Annie. Annie thanked Ali and walked away.

Annie had forgotten Sarah was with her and remained on clouds for the rest of the evening. She couldn't wait to get home to develop the film. Instead, on the next day, she stopped in a one-hour Kodak photo shop to have the film developed. Annie was so excited when she received the developed pictures that she ripped open the envelope. She flipped through the pictures and there before her was another lesson learned: Don't let the security guard snap a picture because all she got was a finger over the lens. It was heartbreaking but a lesson learned.

Seven days in Hawaii were filled with enjoyment and lots of memories. The tours and island hops were breathtaking. Whitney and Annie truly loved their time together.

CHAPTER 11

911

The Hawaiian trip was a wonderful experience and Annie was grateful for the opportunity to get away with Whitney. Before school started, Whitney spent a few days with one of Annie's cousins in the Bay Area. Her cousin, Sherry, had an eleven-year-old daughter, Gloria. Sherry had been very kind to Annie and Whitney and years before, had opened her home to them when Annie was searching for an apartment. Gloria and Whitney got along well and planned several activities together. Sometimes during school breaks, Annie would drop Whitney off in the mornings and collect her in the evenings. There were times when Whitney spent the night.

One evening after work, Annie went to her cousin's house to pick up Whitney. Annie decided to visit awhile to hear how the girls' day went. They were all sitting in the living room.

"We went to the park today," Whitney told her mother.

"Oh, you did. Did you have fun?" Annie asked.

"Yeah, but we saw a crazy man."

"You did? Why was he crazy?"

"He took his penis out."

"He did what?" Annie panicked.

"Yeah, he took it out and it was this long…" Whitney showed the length with both index fingers which was about a foot long and laughed.

"Did anyone call the police?" Annie asked Sherry.

Her cousin shook her head no. Annie became upset because it brought back the painful memories of a similar incident when she was walking home alone at the age of twelve in Memphis. Now her

32

eight-year-old daughter and eleven-year-old cousin had been subjected to the same disrespectful and perverted act of a low-life human being. Annie grabbed the nearest phone and dialed 9-1-1.

"Hello, I would like to make a report on a pervert in the park who flashed his penis at children."

Annie continued to talk with the operator, and she had the children give her the details. Annie wanted to make sure the children knew how serious the matter was and to let them know that such acts are unacceptable and definitely not funny.

****

The summer seemed to pass by fast to Annie. After Whitney got settled in, she adjusted well to the school and the new neighborhood. Annie enrolled in the MBA program at a university in San Francisco for three nights a week.

One night, several months later, Annie and Whitney had gone to bed when there was hard banging on the front door. Annie wasn't expecting anyone, so she didn't answer. Whitney jumped out of the bed and followed Annie to the front door. The front yard was well lit with a street lamp that reflected a shadow of a tall man through the window. He kept banging on the door without saying anything. He knocked harder each time. Annie grabbed her phone, held Whitney close to her, and sat down on the floor beside the sofa. She dialed 9-1-1.

"9-1-1."

"Some man is banging on my front door. Please send someone out here." Annie whispered on the phone.

"Is your door locked?"

"Yes, but he is banging hard."

"What is he saying?"

"Nothing, just banging on the door. I'm afraid to say anything. He's been beating on the door for a while. I am here alone with my young daughter."

"You said he is outside?"

"Yes. Can you send someone?"

"I will put a call in for an officer to come by your place."

"Thank you," Annie then hung up the phone."

Annie sat on the floor holding Whitney.

"Lord, build a fence all around me. Protect us." Annie prayed.

The man kept banging on the door for another five minutes, then walked away. Annie peeped out the crack of the window curtain and saw the man standing next to the light pole. After several minutes, the man walked away. The police never called Annie and they didn't bother to come by to check on her.

Annie had not paid close attention to the residents in her neighborhood before, but she soon became aware that the majority of the residents were Black and Hispanic. She felt the police were prejudiced on which calls they responded to. Annie knew then, that she would have to move again to feel safe for her and her daughter.

A few months later, Annie put a small deposit down on the purchase of a duplex also located in Oakland. It was her first purchase as a homeowner. It needed a little work, but the roof and the exterior paint were in good condition. She planned to live downstairs and rent the upstairs for a couple of years and then, flip it for a nicer home in the suburbs.

The neighborhood where Annie purchased the duplex wasn't much better than the one she left. It was located on a corner lot. It also stood on a small hill and the backyard was not fenced on the street side. Annie decided to purchase a gun. Her ex-husband, Floyd, a police officer, had taught Annie how to shoot and care for a revolver when they were married. She hated guns but thought it was necessary at the time.

After Annie moved into the duplex, she found a renter in a short time. The renter was a lady in her late forties. She was very neat and pleasant to be around. She worked in a tailor shop and specialized in embroidery. Importantly, she paid her rent on time.

The school year went by without any more problems in the hood. Whitney wanted to spend a few weeks in Memphis during the summer. Floyd arranged for her flight and Whitney was off again.

CHAPTER 12

Granny

Annie decided to take only one course for the summer. Her goal was to complete the MBA degree by May 1979, the following year. Her job did not require any travel or overtime during the summer. Therefore, it allowed time for Annie to do some repairs on the house while Whitney was away.

A couple of weeks after Whitney had left, Annie received a call from her mother, Margaret.

"Granny is in poor condition, Annie, maybe you should think about visiting home."

Annie immediately made plans for the flight to Memphis. The earliest she could get a flight was on the 4th of July. Annie wanted to hear granny's voice, but there were no cordless or cell phones during that time. The nearest phone in the house was in the front of the house, while Granny's bedroom was in the rear. Annie gave Margaret messages to give Granny.

"Mother, tell Granny, I will be there soon and that I love her."

"I will," said Margaret.

Margaret had kept Granny's wish to stay home throughout her illnesses. Granny died on July 2, 1978. Annie was devastated. She had not seen Granny since 1972 when she was in Memphis for her divorce hearing. Annie vividly remembered Granny who had once weighed as much as two-hundred and ninety pounds, but the last time Annie saw her, she was a bit frail and had lost over ninety pounds.

When Annie arrived in Memphis, her father, Jessie, was at the airport to greet her. Annie was so happy to see her father, that she hugged him hard. Jessie smiled and welcomed her home. He took her to the house where Margaret was busy making Granny's funeral arrangements. When she saw Annie, she cried. Margaret had always been a crier. She cried when she was happy and she cried when there was sadness. Annie knew, in this situation, that her tears were for a little of both. She ran to her mother and hugged and kissed her. Annie was so happy to be home.

All eleven siblings were home for the funeral. Jessie had made arrangements for a professional photographer to take a family portrait. But this time, the family had grown much larger. Jessie and Margret had eight grandchildren.

Annie was so happy to see all of her sisters and brothers. She was eager to get updates and to get to know them better.

The firstborn, Elaine, still lived in Washington and had only one child. Her husband had passed away and she remarried. She worked in her husband's business.

The second born, Junior, had two sons out of wedlock. He had been working on an offshore oil rig on the Atlantic Ocean and had been passing for an Irishman. His skin was so pale white and he wore his hair long and straight.

"So you spent all that time and money getting a degree. I could have gotten you as many degrees as you wanted. It's just a piece of paper," Junior told Annie.

"I rather earn my degrees." Annie rebutted.

No other sibling acknowledged Annie's accomplishment. She was the first in the Fowler family to earn a college degree.

The third child, Samantha, was still in Memphis and married. She was working at a grocery store and doing homecare work.

The fourth born, Robert Lee, also lived in Washington and had one daughter. He was enrolled at a university.

The fifth born, Claudine, still lived in Indiana. She had two sons and worked as a nurse's aide.

Annie, the sixth child, had only one child and lived in California.

The seventh child, Donny, was still in the Navy and lived in San Diego with one child and one on the way.

The eighth child, Daisy, had dropped out of college and gave birth to the newest grandchild, a beautiful baby girl named Ebony.

The ninth born, Aaron, had just finished his first year in college and was home for the summer.

The tenth and eleventh children, Janis and Martha, were both in high school.

Jessie had been busy harvesting his vegetable gardens that were located in a rural town outside the city. Aaron had helped with the planting and harvesting of crops during his school breaks.

Margaret continued her volunteer work with the Parent and Teacher Association. She had recently returned from Washington, D.C. with a group of advocates for the Title III Program.

The evening before Granny's funeral, several of the siblings got together and drove to "Beale Street" in downtown Memphis. It was a long time since Annie had been downtown. As a National Historic Landmark, "Beale Street" and its surrounding area had nice small parks, restaurants, shops, stores, nightclubs, and great entertainment. The siblings walked along the street and stopped in several places before they ended up in a nightclub that played the best blues. They ordered drinks and Annie, Samantha and Daisy danced the night away.

Granny, Candice Fairweather Fowler, was survived by three sons, seventeen grandchildren, and eight great-grandchildren. Annie remembered all the family stories Granny told her and the homemade cake patties she shared during her visits to Granny's room. Annie could visualize Granny working in the flower beds and dragging her cane and stool to sit on. Annie also recalled the times she just sat with Granny, in her room—sometimes not saying a word. But feeling the comfort of her presence.

The funeral was beautiful. As the family stood to give their last respects to Granny in the open casket, Annie felt weak and feared she was not able to look at Granny. As she got closer to the casket, Annie focused on Granny's face. She stared at Granny and thought, *"Where is my Granny? This looks nothing like her." This body is only about ninety pounds, her face so thin, and her skin much darker."*

The Granny who Annie remembered, had a smooth golden brownish complexion and a full round face, and she was almost two hundred pounds.

Annie could not grieve for the body in the casket. But she was badly grieved for the loss of her grandmother in her heart and mind that she would never see on earth again.

All the Fowler relatives got together at Jessie's house after the funeral. There was plenty of food and everyone seemed to enjoy each other.

"Take what you want, but eat what you take." Jessie always said after blessing the food. He didn't like wasting any food.

Annie had made several calls to Floyd to bring Whitney over to the house. Whitney had already been in Memphis for over a month. Now Annie was waiting for Whitney to take the family photo. The photographer could not wait any longer. Jessie's family lined up in the front yard where there were a few chairs in front of those who were standing. Annie took her usual position and sat next to her father. She could not relax or smile during the process. She was upset that Whitney was not present.

Floyd eventually brought Whitney to the house. Annie was shocked to discover that Whitney's hair had been cut off above her shoulders. When Whitney left California, her hair was midway through her back. While very upset, Annie remained calm and gladly greeted Whitney. She learned later that Floyd had given Whitney a perm and left it on her hair too long.

Annie was happy to learn that Whitney had visited Granny several times before her death. Whitney told wonderful stories about her visit with Granny. Margaret shared with Annie how Whitney helped feed Granny during her illness.

That night, Daisy invited Annie and other relatives to her apartment. When Annie entered she saw weed, paper wraps, and a pipe on the coffee table. Daisy offered Annie some of the weed. Annie declined, but Daisy persisted.

"This is not what you think. It's hash, not marijuana."

Annie had never heard of it. The room was filled with funky smoke.

"No, thanks."

"Just take a small hit, Annie." Daisy persisted. Annie took one buff.

"This is nasty," Annie said with a frown on her face.

Daisy laughed and continued to entertain. About an hour later, she suggested to everyone, "Let's go dancing at Floyd's new club." Everyone agreed.

Floyd was one of the owners of a very nice club. It had an upstairs area for dining and downstairs for dancing. The family group found tables downstairs and ordered drinks and snacks. Annie stayed on the floor dancing. Even when the music stopped, she still stood.

Later that evening, Floyd approached Annie, who was still standing.

"Hey, Annie, how are you?

"I'm fine."

"Do you want a drink?"

"No, I'm good."

"Why are you standing?" Floyd asked.

"I do enough sitting when I'm working."

He leaned closer to Annie.

"Why did you leave me?" Floyd asked.

Annie stepped back and stared at him in disbelief as she contemplated her response. She thought *This fool dares to ask me such an absurd question. How does he explain his vicious acts against me? He beat me, verbally and emotionally abused me, threaten to kill me and my parents, cheated on me, gave me an STD, kept me away from my family and church, and worst of all, he could have been responsible for the death of my boyfriend, Dmitri, whose death is still a cold case. Why am I here? I can barely look at him. Now, this chump stands before me like he's been hurt and asks me why I left him.*

Annie stared directly into Floyd's eyes. She knew that she should hate him, but amazingly, she felt sorry for him.

"You were a lousy lover—and you should be paying child support." She walked away.

Usually, by eleven p.m., Annie would become so sleepy that she couldn't stay awake. But that night, she never got sleepy. She was still awake at six a.m. and it frightened her. It was then she realized that it must be from the effects of the "hash."

"Lord, forgive me for my sins. If you bring me down from this high, I will never get high again." Annie prayed.

The effects did eventually wear off and Annie kept her promise. Furthermore, that experience impelled Annie to distance herself from any drug users and she stopped tolerating their habits.

The next day, Floyd called Annie at her parent's home.

"Your family worked my waitresses real hard last night and didn't tip them."

"Sorry to hear that, I didn't eat or drink," Annie said.

"I know. I took care of the waitresses," Floyd said.

"That's good, but you should let them know how you feel. I don't plan to say anything to them about it."

"Thought you should know that—uh—you have a close enemy among you," Floyd whispered.

"Who and why are you telling me this?"

"You are still so naïve—you'll find out."

Annie was annoyed by Floyd's call and thought perhaps it was his way of getting even, especially after their previous discussion.

During that visit, Annie realized that she had not heard her family use the words "I love you." Her parents had not said it to each other or the children. Although she felt she was loved by her parents, Annie decided after Granny's funeral that she would start telling them that she loved them.

The next day, Annie said her goodbyes. It was so hard for Annie to leave Jessie and Margaret. She knew she would have to come home more often. Her parents aging and weariness were apparent and she didn't want to stay away from them too long.

"Goodbye, Daddy." Annie hugged her father. "I love you."

Jessie was caught off guard.

"Okay... you have a safe trip back and call us."

"Goodbye, Mother." Annie hugged her mother. "I love you."

"Love you, too." Her mother responded.

CHAPTER 13
Oakland

When Annie landed in Oakland, she took off running. She went back to her job and after work and on weekends, Annie worked on remodeling projects at the house. Annie pulled from her personal skills that she learned by watching and helping her father as he made repairs around the house. She began stripping the paint off the kitchen cabinets. Then, she painted a clear varnish on the bare wood. That was a difficult and laborious task, but Annie was able to finish it before the end of the summer. Annie also repainted the walls and laid new linoleum in the kitchen and bathroom. The upstairs apartment was in good condition, but Annie had decided she would repaint it if or when the tenant moved out. Annie also purchased on credit, a new stove, washer, and dryer.

At the end of the summer, when Whitney returned home, she was again surprised at the new changes to the house. Annie learned from Whitney that Floyd was no longer with the police force and was working for a manufacturing company. Along with the nightclub, he also had a small clothing business. Nine-year-old Whitney made a comment to Annie that made her feel discombobulated.

"I don't see what you saw in Daddy."

"Did anyone hurt you, Whitney?"

"No, but Rena is stupid, she lets Daddy hit her. She shows me the bruises on her head and stuff."

Annie recalled the conversation with Rena when they first met while working together at a job many years ago in Memphis. Rena was in a relationship with a guy named "Peanut." A few times, she came into the office and shared with Annie the beatings she received from him. Rena thought it was a game and believed that it was his way to express his love for her. To Annie, it was pathetic, and now Rena was playing the same game with Floyd.

Annie didn't want to get Whitney in trouble for telling her about the situation, but Annie was concerned for Whitney's safety.

"Are you afraid of your father?" She asked Whitney.

"No," Whitney replied.

"Do you want to visit him again?"

"Yes. Uuughhh, Mom, they think that you are talking about them to me. But I told them that you don't ever say anything about them— and you don't even care. You have moved on."

"Well, that's okay. You are right." Annie reassured her.

Annie noticed that Whitney called her Mom instead of Mommie. She asked Whitney why she changed.

"Uncle Aaron said I sounded like a baby and he teased me every time I said Mommie."

Annie also noticed that Whitney's eating changed. She asked for more processed and junk foods.

Annie began to distrust her decision to let her little girl visit Memphis. It would be about another year before Whitney's next visit to Memphis, so Annie felt she had time to think more on the matter.

CHAPTER 14

Angel Candice

Despite all the losses and abusive, life threatening events that had occurred in Annie's life, she often wondered why and how she survived them. She realized that, although "humans" can plan for some life occurrences such as a career, family, marriage, what they eat, say and do, etc., she believed it was truly "God's Plan" that controlled a person's destiny. Annie supposed that God had little helpers that carried out his plan, and his helpers were angels that prepared and protected. Usually, Annie's angel prepared her through dreams or incidents.

Although many of the horrific events Annie experienced occurred long before Annie's paternal grandmother passed away in 1978, in memory of "Granny," she named her angel, Candice.

Annie remembered before her actual sexual experience, she had not read about intercourse or had any clue about it. Yet, she had a dream that felt like a real painful act that she later experienced.

In 1972, while Annie lived in St. Louis and desperately looked for work, she read a newspaper ad: "Seeking models over eighteen-years old at $10 an hour."

The applicant had to apply in person at a suite located in a very nice well-known hotel. Therefore, Annie thought she should apply. She asked her friend, Kenny, to drive her there.

Annie dressed up in a yellow blouse and green mini-skirt and entered the hotel suite, where there were several cute young women of many ethnicities. The greeter smiled and handed Annie an application. Annie completed the application and returned it. Within minutes, an older blond-headed woman came over to Annie.

"Oh, my goodness, you are so beautiful, you can make a lot of money... an easy $500."

The woman ran her hand up and down Annie's upper arm and walked around Annie to get a total view of Annie's body. In a split second, Annie recalled a conversation she had with her best friend, Valencia, not too long ago. Valencia told Annie about a modeling scam that was a prostitution setup.

"I need to go to the restroom, and I'll be right back." Annie lied to the lady and grabbed her purse.

"You can leave your purse with me, it will be safe."

"Thank you, but I have things that I need," Annie lied again.

Annie left the suite and went straight to the hotel lobby. She called her friend, Kenny.

"Come get me, now! This is a prostitution ring."

Annie thanked God for sending his angel to give her the wisdom to walk away from the situation.

Another incident Annie remembered was the unexpected death of her maternal grandmother in 1971, while living in St. Louis. The night before her death, Annie dreamt that her sister, Claudine, passed away. She was sitting on the bench in church with her family. Annie looked at the beautiful white casket and began to weep uncontrollably. She wished she and her sister had spent more time together. When Annie looked to the right of her and saw Claudine sitting next to her, the ringing of the phone awoke Annie. It was her Uncle Shooey calling to let Annie know that Grandma McGwin had died. Annie believed the dream was intended to prepare her for the loss of her grandmother.

Nevertheless, there had been several incidents in that Annie felt in her heart that God intervened and sent Angel Candice. Maybe not always when Annie expected her to come but always on time.

46

CHAPTER 15

A Friend

Working as an accountant and auditor allowed an individual to meet people of various professions. Due to the nature of the client's needs, the most common profession an accountant interacted with was an attorney. Annie met many attorneys during her job performances.

While having lunch with a coworker, Annie was approached by a man who was in his late twenties. He introduced himself as Joey Howell. Joey was average looking but had a contagious smile and a personality that drew attention. He was about six feet-one, slim, and had a dark complexion. He told Annie that he remembered her at one of his client's offices when she was performing an audit. Annie remembered Joey. He was an attorney and in partnership with two other attorneys. Annie introduced Joey to her coworker and asked if he would like to join them. Joey accepted and pulled up a chair. The three of them talked throughout lunch. Joey asked Annie to have lunch with him the following week. She accepted.

Annie went on a few lunch outings with Joey. He was single and had never been married. When time permitted, they went out dancing and soon became enthralled with one another. They loved to laugh and share special moments. After about a year, Annie realized that Joey wanted more in their relationship. She, again, was in the same situation as her previous relationships. A perfect man with ambition and who liked her and her child. Joey wanted marriage and children, but Annie did not.

Annie and Joey remained friends over the years. She was grateful that he was in her life because she could pick up the phone or drop by his office to get a candid perspective on issues—and always a good laugh.

Once Joey became married and had several children, they didn't talk as much. But Annie would never forget his kindness and friendship.

CHAPTER 16

Margaret in Hawaii

In May 1979, Annie completed her MBA degree and later passed the certified public accounting exam. She continued to work for the same CPA firm.

Whitney flew to Memphis again for the summer. To celebrate another accomplishment, Annie found a discounted deal on a trip to Hawaii for two. This time she decided to take her mother, with her. Margaret had never been to Hawaii and was very excited about it. Whitney was already in Memphis for the summer with her father.

Once in Hawaii, fifty-nine-year-old Margaret was eager to see everything. The only problem was that Margaret had not been accustomed to walking any distance. She had only walked from the house to the driveway. Every time Margaret asked Annie, "How far?"

Annie replied, "One more block."

Annie had bought two tickets to the luau party that was about four blocks from the hotel. Annie and Margaret got dressed and started walking along the strip. After the first block, Margaret stopped to catch her breath.

"Take deep, slow breaths, Mother."

"How far?" Margaret asked.

"Just another block."

They walked to the next block when Margaret stopped again and took deep breaths. Without a word she continued. She knew Annie was not telling her the truth. Margaret seemed to get a little stronger by the fourth block.

They entered the gates to the event. Everyone was greeted by a pretty or handsome native who placed fresh colorful flowers, called leis, around each guest's neck. Annie and Margaret found a table and sat down. The space was brilliantly decorated and the entertainment was fantastic. There were singers, hula dancers, as well as male sword dancers.

Margaret lit up when she saw a few of the natives carrying two large pigs. The pigs had been prepared for the underground roast pit and intended to be fully cooked by the end of the entertainment.

Annie had worn some green contact lenses that caught the attention of the MC. He pointed at Annie.

"Love those eyes, come on up here." Annie walked on stage.

"Are you married?" He asked.

"No," Annie replied.

"Well, as cute as you are, you won't be single for long."

The audience laughed. He walked Annie over to one of the male dancers on the stage and walked away to recruit other guests. He coupled men with the lady dancers and vice versa. Once all selected guests were on stage, the dancers demonstrated how to do the hula dance. When the music started, Annie and the other guests on stage danced... and danced their version of the hula. Margaret was laughing so hard, that she was holding her stomach and soon tears ran down her face. Everyone applauded and cheered for the guest. When the music stopped, the guests left the stage. Annie joined Margaret who was still laughing.

A little later, the pigs were dug up from the pit. Annie had no interest in tasting the pork, but Margaret wanted some. Once they reached the food table, Annie got fresh fruit and veggies. Margaret placed a slice of the pork, bread, fruit, and veggies on her plate. They sat down to eat. Surprisingly, Margaret barely touched the pork.

"This is not good, it is the worst pork I ever tasted." Disappointed, Margaret frowned.

Annie laughed at Margaret's facial expressions. They enjoyed the remaining entertainment and interacted with other guests at the table. Afterward, they took a cab back to the hotel.

In addition to Oahu, Annie and Margaret toured the Big Island and Maui. They relished the sites and the weather. Annie felt so good being with her mother and sharing such special moments.

When they returned to Memphis, Margaret had a lot to share with her friends and relatives. Annie said her goodbyes and flew back to California.

CHAPTER 17

Moving On Again

In addition to working full-time for the CPA firm, Annie accepted teaching assignments on some evenings and weekends at a community college. She taught accounting and computer, and software classes. Annie discovered that she truly enjoyed teaching and thought that when she was older, she would teach full-time.

Annie's younger brother, Donny, visited her one day. He was in the Navy and stationed in Long Beach, California. He came to return the $500 that he borrowed from Annie. Instead of cash, he dropped off a large waterbed and a bicycle. Annie was disappointed because she needed the cash and didn't like waterbeds—even though they were popular during that time. She thought maybe Donny was having a hard time but wished he had given her notice. Yet, Annie never complained.

Not too long after that, Donny called Annie and asked her to come to Long Beach. He had witnessed the murder of one of his fellow officers and wanted a family member there for support. Annie didn't hesitate, she made arrangements and headed to Long Beach.

When she arrived, Donny was a bit out of sorts. It was apparent to Annie that he was frightened by the situation. Donny thought someone wanted to hurt him if he testified, but he was determined to do so. Annie wanted to be strong for Donnie and to help as much as she could. She watched Donny on the witness stand as he testified about the murder and what he saw that night. His story was horrific. Annie hoped that he felt her presence and support. Donny managed to do well and seemed to be relieved that it was over. Annie spent a day with him and toured the submarine that he lived on.   Although he did not say so, she believed that Donny had appreciated her being there.

****

Sometime during that summer, Annie's renter in the duplex submitted a termination notice to her. The tenant was moving east to be closer to her family. Immediately after she moved out, Annie quickly repainted the apartment in time for another interested tenant. The new tenant was a single mom with a twelve-year-old son. Athea and her son, Calvin, were very kind and generous individuals. Athea played an active role in Whitney's life. She sometimes offered to babysit her and invited Whitney to different activities. Annie also discovered the talented angelic singing voice of Athea. They became very close and lifelong friends.

One weekend, when Annie came home from visiting one of her cousins, she discovered that her house had been raided. She immediately called the police. The thief had taken Annie's gun and Whitney's toys. Nothing else of value was taken. Therefore, the police speculated that it must have been a child who broke into the house. Fortunately, there was a witness who was a little boy about ten-years old. He showed the police where the other kid had hidden the gun and was supposed to come back to retrieve it. The little boy claimed he didn't know the thief. The police officer gave Annie the gun and suggested that she put better locks on the doors. He also told her that she should invest in a fence.

Annie completed all the work that the officer had suggested to her. But within a few months, she put the house on the market for sale. It did not take long for an interested buyer. After living in the duplex for about two years, Annie sold the property for more than twice the amount that she had paid for it. The sale incurred a nice down payment on a single-family home in a small suburban city about twenty minutes east of San Francisco.

The buyer of the duplex was a forty-two-year-old man, named Peter. He was about five-feet-eight, thin, medium brown skin, and was in the construction business. Peter was divorced and had three children, one son was a pre-teen, and a daughter and son were adults. He was very attracted to Annie and pursued her. About a month later, Peter called Annie a few times and soon, they went out to eat and dance.

CHAPTER 18

Bahamas

A few months later, Annie's younger sister, Daisy, called to invite Annie to go on a summer trip with her and their brother, Robert Lee, to the Bahamas. She found a great deal on a five-day trip to Freeport. Annie thought it was a wonderful idea to celebrate her recent thirtieth birthday and for earning her MBA degree the year before. She also looked forward to spending time with her sister and brother.

Annie made plans to fly to Memphis to visit her parents. From there, Daisy and Robert Lee would fly to the Bahamas. It had been two years since Annie had seen her parents and siblings. Jessie was waiting for Annie at the airport and smiled as he greeted Annie with a hug. Annie was so happy to see him. She noticed that Jessie had put on a few pounds, but he looked well.

When they arrived at the house, Annie jumped out of the car and ran to greet her mother. Margaret cried. Annie knew it was all good and hugged her mother. Margaret was sitting at the table in the kitchen picking greens. Aaron, Janis, and Martha greeted Annie. She hugged them all. Margaret gave Annie an update on things that had happened since the last time Annie was in Memphis.

"Jessie has been in a couple of car accidents but won't give up driving. He is a little different in the head, but he doesn't drink much anymore," Margaret confided in Annie.

Annie wasn't sure what her mother meant. Jessie was only sixty-six years old and seemed fine when he picked her up from the airport.

Annie visited and called several relatives and friends while she was there. Several of them came by the house to visit with her. The next day, Annie, Daisy, and Robert Lee headed to the Bahamas.

The sights and weather were beautiful in the Bahamas. The three of them went on tours and spent a lot of time on the beach. Annie and Daisy walked through the village to shop. Annie had a native braid her hair, but the braids felt so tight and painful on her scalp that Annie had to take them out the next day.

One day, on the beach, the three were lying under an umbrella. Annie realized that she didn't bring her wallet. She wanted to buy a bottle of water that cost eighty cents. Daisy didn't have her wallet either.

"Hey, Robert Lee, would you lend me eighty cents for some water until I get back to the room?"

"If you were out in a desert, dying of thirst, I would walk right over you," he said to Annie.

Annie was in shock. Daisy was lying next to Robert Lee with no reaction to what he had said. Since there had been practically no conversation between Annie and Robert Lee, Annie couldn't imagine what she had said or done to Robert Lee for him to make such a cruel remark. She could only speculate that it was something much deeper within him that she could not understand.

Annie managed the remaining stay without any further negative interactions. But she felt relieved, on the last day, to return to the states. Robert Lee's comment stayed in Annie's heart and mind for many years. Yet, she never let him know how badly it hurt her.

CHAPTER 19

Peter

Annie returned to her new home in the East Bay in a city called Pleasant Hills. It had three bedrooms, and two baths, and was a single-story dwelling. It had a two-car garage, and a nice size backyard, and was built out of wood and stucco. She decorated the house nicely with the current trend of an earth tone. She also decided to add a room off the kitchen and garage for a den.

Eleven-year-old Whitney decorated her room. Annie enrolled her in the nearest middle school. The neighborhood was nice and quiet. The residents were racially diverse and friendly.

Annie continued to date Peter. He invited her to his church in Oakland. She met a few of Peter's sisters, brothers, and their children. Peter had eight sisters and brothers. One of Peter's nephews was in church with his girlfriend. After church, she approached Annie with a friendly and beautiful smile.

"Hey, I'm Kathy Wallace, how are you?" She addressed Annie in a very soft, little girl voice.

"Hi, Kathy, I'm Annie Hightower. I'm fine and you?"

Kathy was a pretty woman. She had the smoothest honey complexion. She wore long hair that reached her waist and she was five-feet-five. She was wearing a formfitting dress that showed her tiny waistline. But when the eyes traveled downward— "Bam— there it is". She had a large shapely butt and legs that drew the attention of everyone. Kathy was from the east coast and had earned a Ph.D. She had worked as a professor at an HBCU.

Annie accepted Kathy's invitation to her house for a small social gathering. She was impressed with Kathy's beauty and accomplishments. Since Annie loved to sew, she was particularly impressed that Kathy was also a seamstress and could make a cute outfit in a matter of minutes. They hit it off immediately and they became lifelong friends. Annie wasn't aware at the time, of how much of a positive impact Kathy would have on her life. They visited each other and went out dancing as often as they could.

Annie had turned thirty years old earlier that year. The number three-zero hit her in a way she didn't expect it would. She felt satisfied with her life and the things she had accomplished, but she believed it wasn't normal to be thirty and not have a serious man in her life.

Annie had had several wedding proposals but felt she could not deliver what her pursuers wanted from her – a child. She was certain that she didn't want any more children. After only three months of dating and a simple kiss, one of her pursuers was very pissed off with her when she said no to his wedding proposal.

"Do you know who I am? I have a Ph.D. and a scholar professor. I make a very good living and I could give you a very nice life. You must not be as smart as I thought you were."

He went on and on but his tantrum didn't impress Annie. Instead, it only confirmed that she had made the right decision.

Annie had prevented any man from getting too close to her. But, now at thirty years old, she decided to allow the next good man who would love her and her child to become a part of her life. She often wondered what it would be like to have a 'sole' or even a 'soul' mate.

About a year after dating, Annie accepted Peter's invitation for a Caribbean cruise. They toured five islands during the nine-day cruise. The islands were the Nassau Bahamas, Martinique, Barbados, Grenada, and St. Vincent.

Annie decided to let her guard down with Peter. She had become very attracted to him and cared a lot for him. She wasn't sure if she was truly in love, but she felt good being with him. He was a very affectionate lover.

The cruise was a mesmerizing experience for Annie. Soon afterward, she and Peter decided to elope. He placed a tenant in his place and moved in with Annie.

Annie and Peter enjoyed each other very much. The den was added to the house for more space. Whitney seemed to be okay with the marriage and with Peter. Sometimes Peter invited his son Patrick to stay over. It was fine until one day, Peter asked Annie if she would talk to Whitney about hitting Patrick. Annie decided to closely observe the interaction between the two children when Patrick visited. She saw Whitney hit Patrick once on the arm. She thought it was just a little girl's crush on a boy. But Patrick didn't like it. Later, the four of them were sitting in the living room and Annie saw Whitney hit Patrick again on his shoulder.

"Whitney, keep your hands to yourself. If you hit him again, I am going to allow him to hit you back," Annie demanded.

Annie realized that perhaps her daughter had inherited the hitting and hoped that she would be able to break Whitney from the bad habit. Annie had stopped spanking Whitney by the age of eight because Annie didn't like hitting and thought the punishment was more effective with Whitney.

As several months passed, Annie began to notice that Peter drank a lot and sometimes came home drunk. His slurred speech and smell of alcohol had become annoying and disrespectful. But most importantly, Annie did not want such behavior around her child. She tried to talk to Peter about it because it brought bad memories and made Annie feel very uncomfortable. Sometimes they would argue about it. Finally, Annie had had enough and asked Peter to move out.

The next day, Whitney was in Oakland for her regular dance class and Annie was home alone. Peter came home drunk again. This time, he had his gun in his hand. Annie was scared when she saw the gun. Her life began to flash before her eyes, and she wondered how it had come to this again. Peter pointed his thirty-two caliber handgun at Annie. He slapped Annie on her face with such force that he stumbled.

"So you want me to leave," he said with each word slurred.

Annie was in shock and she held her face where he had hit her. Now she was angry.

"You hit me Peter and I will never forgive you for it. What do you want, Peter?" Annie asked in a calm, yet, fearful voice.

"Well... I don't want to go and we belong together... augh... I guess... Nothing."

"Then stop pointing that damn gun at me," Annie demanded.

Peter stumbled as he moved towards the bedroom door. He lowered the gun and walked into the bedroom. He laid down on the bed and fell asleep as soon as his head hit the pillow.

Instead of running out the door to get help, Annie got mad.

I am tired of living in fear. This is my home. I will take charge. Annie thought.

As Peter slept, Annie picked up the gun he had dropped on the floor beside the bed. As she held the gun, for an instant, Annie stared at Peter and thought, *If I was not a God-fearing woman, I could blow you away.*

Annie left the bedroom and placed the gun in the washing machine. She knew he had another twenty-two caliber handgun that he kept in one of the dresser drawers. She removed it and put it also in the washer. She removed her gun from her closet and placed it in the washer with the other guns. Annie then got trash bags and began to fill Peter's items in them. She grabbed his keys and took the bags outside and placed them in his truck.

Annie looked in the phone book for a locksmith. She dialed the number and asked him to come out right away. When the man arrived, Annie asked him to work quietly because her husband was trying to sleep. She knew if Peter woke up while the man was working, she would have to call the police. Within an hour, all the door locks had been changed.

Peter slept through the night and got up early to go to work. Annie slept very lightly in the third bedroom. Peter didn't say anything to her. But when Annie heard the front door close behind him, she jumped up to make sure it was locked.

Later that day on her job, Annie received a phone call from Peter. He was aware of the bags that she put in his truck.

"So you kicked me out. Where are my guns?" He demanded.

"I threw them away."

"I guess it's over."

"Yes, it is!"

The marriage lasted only ten months, but it was another life lesson learned for Annie about the consequences of feeling desperate to be with a man—or not wanting to be alone.

CHAPTER 20

When It Rains

Annie continued her routine at work and she taught a course at the college. She and Kathy continued to go out and they visited different churches together. Kathy loved to party but one thing she was persistent about was that she had to be in a church on Sunday morning. It didn't matter what church as long as it was a Christian church.

Annie didn't receive many communications from her siblings. But periodically, Daisy would call Annie only to share bad news and gossip. Daisy never failed to remind Annie how much their other siblings didn't like Annie.

"Why do you even talk to her? She doesn't do anything but talk bad about you and she doesn't like you." Daisy told Annie about another sister.

Unfortunately, there was no caller ID during that time. Each phone call from Daisy was always emotionally draining to Annie. She believed that it was Daisy who was initiating the conflicts. But Annie listened without making comments.

****

Annie resigned from the CPA firm and decided to start her firm. Although she could possibly make more money, the downside was she didn't have dental and healthcare plans. Her goal was to work independently for about five years and revisit her options. She was still young and both she and Whitney were in very good health. The major benefit was that she could control her work hours and the type of work.

During the same year, Annie received a phone call from a former coworker, Michelle, who was having hard times and needed temporary shelter. Annie thought about how her parents opened their home when people were in need. However, in this case, Michelle had three young boys, ages five, seven, and eight. Annie couldn't say no to her, so they moved in. Two of the boys slept in the den, on the floor, in sleeping bags. Michelle and her youngest boy slept in the third bedroom with twin beds. Annie was aware that Michelle smoked pot but insisted that she did not smoke in her house or around the children.

A few months later in 1982, while Whitney was in Memphis, Annie received a call from her brother, Aaron, who had just finished college but was unemployed. He asked if he could stay with her while he looked for work. Since Aaron had a business degree, Annie felt that he could work for her until he found something permanent. She agreed that he could stay with her.

About two days later, Aaron called Annie again to let her know that Daisy wanted to come, too. Daisy had only completed two years of college, but Annie thought if Daisy was serious, she could find a job while she finished her degree. Annie agreed to let Daisy and her seven-year-old daughter, Ebony, come along with Aaron.

Daisy decided to drive her car, so Annie sent a credit card to Daisy to pay for the gas cost. This gesture was with the understanding that they would pay off the credit card when they got a job.

Annie informed Michelle that her family was coming and that she would need to look for another place to live. Michelle had been living in the house rent-free for six months.

Aaron, Daisy, and Ebony arrived about two weeks later. Michelle and her kids had left only a day before. Michelle left the house without a thank you. She told Annie that she would call her later.   Annie got her siblings and niece settled in.   Aaron immediately started working with Annie. She taught him how to post entries to clients' ledgers and prepare financial reports.

In contrast, Daisy's work ethic was different. She didn't have much drive in getting a job. Annie noticed that Daisy had gained even more weight since she saw her two years prior in the Bahamas. She was about sixty pounds overweight. She drank alcohol and smoked cigarettes and pot. Daisy left the house several times to meet up with former classmates and to party at the club. She also told Annie that she would like to lose a few pounds while she was there and wanted to join a gym.   Annie purchased a membership for Daisy at a nearby Health Club. Daisy never went to the gym. It was money wasted.

Michelle had called the house and had conversations with Daisy. Unbeknownst to Annie, whatever they discussed upset Daisy. Shortly after their conversation, Daisy, while away from the house, called Annie. She cursed Annie while making several false allegations against her.

"You are no Saint. I know you use drugs. You are a hypocrite!" Daisy shouted at Annie.

Annie had no idea what was going on. But later that day, Michelle called the house again and was surprised when Annie answered the phone. Annie asked Michelle what she said to Daisy. Michelle mentioned that Daisy had asked her for some weed. It was apparent to Annie that Michelle was upset about having to leave the house on short notice. Annie quickly cut off the discussion with Michelle because she knew that it would be impossible to get the whole truth from either Michelle or Daisy. To Annie, they were lazy deadbeats.

Annie was relieved when Daisy decided to go back to Memphis. But several days later, Annie received a call from Daisy.

"Guess where I am, bitch? Right here in your ex's house with Whitney. Yeah, and they needed to know the person you are."

Aaron overheard Annie's reaction on the phone and assumed it was Daisy on the other end. He whispered to Annie.

"Tell her that you are on your way to Memphis to kick her ass, and then hang up."

Annie repeated what Aaron had said and hung up the phone.

"She is a coward. She will be out of Floyd's house before the end of the day," Aaron told Annie.

Aaron was right. Daisy was out of the house. She packed her items so fast in her car trunk that she literally packed the cat, too. The beautiful Siamese cat belonged to Athea, who was a former tenant but had become a very close friend. Whitney had fallen in love with the male cat and asked Athea if she could take him to Memphis for the summer. Before the cat was discovered in the trunk, he had died. Whitney, as well as Althea, was devastated by the loss.

Daisy had moved out of Floyd's house, but the damage was done. Annie was puzzled by the entire situation. She wondered how anyone could tell her daughter (a hormonal teenager) awful lies about her mother and expect the child to get over it. Furthermore, Daisy contributed to the death of the beloved cat. Whitney was only thirteen-years old and going through, not only, the typical teenage rebellion and crisis, but also dealing with divorced parents.

Whitney later called to share with her mother a little of what her Aunt Daisy had told her, "Your mother doesn't love you... your mother uses drugs."

"Do you believe your Aunt?" Annie asked her daughter.

"No," Whitney replied.

"Have you ever seen me use drugs or had any questions about whether I use drugs?" Annie asked

"No," Whitney replied.

"Do you believe I love you? Annie asked.

"Yes, " Whitney replied.

"That is all that is important to me," Annie replied.

But Annie knew that her thirteen-year-old daughter would always remember those cruel statements and perhaps someday might question them or use them against her mother.

"I do feel sorry for my cousin, Ebony," Whitney said.

"Why is that?" Annie asked Whitney.

"Well, because Ebony and I talked a few times and she told me that Aunt Daisy curses her and calls her a bitch and whore. She said she couldn't wait to be old enough to leave home."

Whitney knew that Annie would never use such language with her.

Annie knew that her sister was always an evil person, even as a child, but Annie did not understand Daisy's hatred and the mean acts against her or to others—even to her daughter. Annie recalled a statement Daisy had made to her a few years before. "I wanted to do everything you did, and to have what you have."

Annie had thought of her sister's statement as an inspiration for Daisy to achieve, but instead, it was a mission to destroy. These actions confirmed Floyd's comments that he made to Annie a few years before. "You have an enemy among you." Daisy was definitely an enemy.

When Annie received an invoice for her credit card that Daisy used to purchase gas during the travel from Memphis to California, she was shocked when the balance was about $800. Annie read each transaction and discovered that some of the transactions included souvenirs and personal items.

****

Several months later, Annie became disappointed when her dear friend, Kathy, decided to move to the east coast to teach at a well-known university. Annie decided to host a farewell party for Kathy. She prepared finger foods and a large salad. Kathy did not drink, so Annie made a large bowl of natural fruit punch. About twenty people gathered at Annie's house for the event. A few brought bottles of spirits. Her brother, Aaron, helped with music and was great at entertaining the guest.

About an hour into the party, Annie became very drowsy. She couldn't understand why she felt that way. She thought if she drank another sip of the fruit punch it would help to energize her. She had been sipping on the punch throughout the party.

Annie became so drowsy that she could barely stand. She decided to sneak away from the party and go to her bedroom to lie down for a moment until she felt a little better. But when she entered her bedroom, she saw the guests' items on her bed. Annie took a blanket, folded it, and laid it in the master bathtub. She then hopped in the tub, laid down, and fell asleep.

What seemed forever, was about thirty minutes later, she woke up and went back to the party.

"Where you been?" Aaron asked Annie.

"I had to take a nap. I don't know why I felt so drowsy."

"Oh, well, maybe it was because I spiked the punch with this." Aaron showed Annie a bottle of vodka.

Aaron was always a jokester, but Annie was a bit pissed at him, yet she didn't show it. However, she did warn the guests of the prank and fortunately, Kathy, who didn't drink alcohol, hadn't drunk any of the punch.

A couple of days before she left, Kathy drove her Jaguar to Annie's house and parked it in front of her garage. Kathy left the keys with Annie and told her that she would have someone pick up the Jaguar and have it shipped to her. The Jaguar sat there for a few months.

One day, Annie came home and discovered a large dent in the two-car garage door and that the Jaguar had been moved. Annie parked her car next to the Jaguar and got out to assess the damages. The Jaguar barely had a scratch, but the garage door was practically hanging off its hinges. Annie went into the house where fourteen-year-old Whitney was sitting in the living room with guilt written all over her face.

"What happened to the car, Whitney?"

"It rolled into the garage."

"So after all this time the car had been sitting out there, it just decided to roll itself into the garage."

"No, I moved it."

"You moved it where?"

"Down the street, and when I came back to park it, it wouldn't stop."

"You don't have a driver's license and you're too young to drive, so what possessed you to drive the car?"

"I don't know, something just told me to."

"Whitney, you will come straight home from school and will not participate in activities for a month, including the weekends. Do you understand me?" Annie asked, now upset.

"Yes... A month? Just whip me!" Whitney begged her mother.

Whitney knew that when her mother dished out punishments, she stuck with it to the end. A month meant a month. There was no early release for good behavior.

Thanks to homeowner's insurance, most of the cost to repair the garage door was covered, and eventually, the Jaguar was picked up.

Not too long after that incident, Whitney brought home a school photo. Whitney looked cute, but Annie noticed that she didn't have a normal smile. When she asked Whitney about it, Whitney replied, "I have a crooked front tooth and it looks bad. Can I get it fixed?" Whitney asked her mother.

Annie knew how important self-image was to preteens and teenagers and how it affected their confidence. She didn't have dental insurance, but Annie didn't hesitate to take Whitney to the dentist for cosmetic repair.

What Annie didn't realize at that time was—the rain of issues was just a shower and that she soon would be faced with thunderstorms of issues.

CHAPTER 21

European Adventure

The summer of 1983 came quickly. Whitney was off to Memphis, and Aaron had found a full-time management position at a top chain store.

Sherman Stanford was a successful automobile dealership owner. He specialized in Cadillac and international cars, such as Rolls Royce, Bentley, Lamborghini, Jaguar, and Ferrari.

Annie had met Sherman through her friend, Kathy, about a year before. He was eighteen years older than Annie, but he was quickly attracted to her. Sherman was a distinguished-looking man. He was six-feet-two, about thirty pounds overweight, with thinning curly hair, and had a light brown smooth complexion. He was always dressed in business attire.

They had met on several occasions for lunch, dinner, and also at special events. Sherman would sometime pick up Annie in his Rolls Royce and would drive along the coastline for lunch or dinner.

One time, Annie called Athea to join them along with one of Sherman's male friends. It was like a blind date setup. Athea reluctantly agreed. It was a beautiful cool day as they traveled through San Francisco and along the Pacific coast. Sherman had his camera and snapped several pictures of Annie sitting in front of his Rolls Royce and of Annie and Althea together. Athea had a wonderful time and was jovial throughout the trip. But there wasn't a love connection with her blind date.

One day, after a nice drive, Sherman stopped at an exclusive designer store and told Annie to pick out two suits for her. Each suit cost more than Annie's car note. She was very surprised and grateful to him for the luxurious suits.

What was amazing to Annie was that Sherman did not pressure her for sex. He truly enjoyed being with her. Although Annie was not sexually attracted to him, she too enjoyed the excitement he brought into her life.

Sometime later, Annie received a call from Sherman. He invited her to travel with him to several countries in Europe. Sherman was going on business to purchase new cars and thought he would also make it a pleasure trip. Annie graciously accepted the invitation.

Annie quickly completed all of her clients' financial reports and let them know that she would be away for a while. She had not been to Europe since she was very young. She also contacted Whitney who was in Memphis to let her know about the trip.

They first traveled to London, England. When he returned from his business meeting, Sherman and Annie toured the sights, such as the Tower of London, Buckingham Palace, Winsor Castle, Tower Bridge, and more.

A few days later, they flew to Paris, France, where they stayed at a five-star hotel. They toured the Eiffel Tower and other beautiful sights. Sherman and Annie dined in the finest restaurants. Although Annie didn't care for European food, she enjoyed every moment with Sherman.

Three days later, they took a train to Monaco, France. The hotel was on a beach that consisted of black pebbles. The beach wasn't too comfortable to walk on or sit on. But many people managed to sunbathe. The casinos were near the hotel and beach.

One day after walking along the beach, Annie suggested to Sherman that they go to the casino. She was wearing shorts and tennis shoes and he wore a shirt and jeans. When they tried to enter, they were turned away because of the required dress code. Annie was very surprised at the restriction in France, especially since some people were naked on the beach across from the casino. However, the next day, they visited the casino properly dressed.

A couple of days later, they flew to Rome, Italy. They stayed in a very old and well-known hotel near some of the tourist sights. Annie was fascinated with the tours of the Vatican City and the Colosseum. They also toured St. Peter's Basilica, the Sistine Chapel, and the Vatican Museums. The architecture of each site was spectacular.

Sherman and Annie spent three days in Rome. Annie was surprised that the pizzas weren't as good as those she tasted in the USA. But the people were nice and the service was good. She enjoyed the laughter and conversations with Sherman.

When they arrived in Vienna, Austria, there was a little drizzle and overcast, but the next day was clear and beautiful. They took a canoe ride down the canal. It was better than Annie had seen in the movies.

They rode overnight on a train to Frankford, Germany. As a young girl, Annie had lived in Germany, but she had not visited Frankford. The landscapes and buildings looked similar to the places she remembered in Germany.

Annie had noticed that throughout their travels, Sherman tired easily. When they went to bed, he kissed her and touched her body so gently. Although there was no sexual intercourse, he laid beside her and held her close to him throughout the night. It was such a comforting feeling for Annie. He was the second man that had made her feel truly safe and loved. Dmitri, who was killed several years before, was the first to make her feel loved.

When they arrived at the Amsterdam, Holland airport, one of Sherman's best friends pulled up at the curb and jumped out of the taxi he was driving. Annie was surprised to see Robert again. Sherman had introduced them a couple of years ago in San Francisco when Robert was in the states visiting his relatives.

Robert was originally born in Ethiopia, Africa, and was married to a native of Amsterdam. They had a son and a daughter, both of who were very cute kids. Robert drove Annie and Sherman to the hotel and promised he would check in on them a little later.

After Annie and Sherman got settled in, they went downstairs to the restaurant. Annie noticed Sherman looked very peaked.

"Sherman, are you okay?" Annie asked him.

"I'm fine. But I want you to know that I have to go back to the states."

"Is everything okay?"

"Of course, everything is fine. I want you to know that I truly enjoyed the trip with you. You have been so wonderful and patient with me."

"I've enjoyed every moment with you, Sherman. When do we leave?"

"I am leaving. I've planned for Robert to take you around and you still have one more trip to Switzerland. The tickets and hotel are already paid for."

"You want me to go alone?"

"No, I will rather be with you, but an emergency has come up and I don't want to cut the trip short for you. Please stay and enjoy the rest of the trip. Do that for me."

"I guess I can. When are you leaving?"

73

"In the morning."

"In the morning?" Annie asked, surprised.

"So let's eat and enjoy the time while I'm here."

After eating dinner, they decided to get some fresh air and took a little walk outside of the hotel for a couple of blocks and then returned to the hotel. They showered together. Sherman held Annie's body close to him and kissed her under the running shower. Annie held him tight. They stood in the shower without talking for just taking at the moment. They dried off, sat on the bed, and chatted for a few minutes. Sherman got in bed. This time Annie scooted behind Sherman and held him tightly against her body all night.

Annie didn't want Sherman to leave, but she knew it must have been important for him to go. They had spent over a month together and it had been a wonderful experience for Annie.

Robert was at the hotel bright and early to pick up Sherman. Annie rode to the airport with them. She kissed Sherman goodbye and felt tearful as he disappeared through the terminal.

Robert asked Annie, "What do you want to do?"

"First, I would like to eat a little and then later perhaps, tour some of the sights."

"I would like for you to meet my wife and children."

"Thank you, Robert, it would be an honor to meet your family."

Annie didn't want to be alone during the remainder of her trip.

Robert drove for a while and finally parked at an apartment building. Annie followed him up two flights of stairs. He took his keys and opened the door. His wife, Irina, was in the kitchen.

Although the native language was Dutch, she greeted Annie with a hug and spoke in English.

"Hello, welcome to our home."

Annie truly felt welcome. To Annie, the Dutch were similar to the German *Deutsch* that she learned as a child, but it sounded a little different. Irina had a nice face with a pretty smile. Her hair was shoulder length and light brown. She was about five-feet-three, with just a little baby fat. The children were at home. The boy, David, was eight-years old, and the cute little sandy brown-headed girl, Natasha, was five-years old. They were both so nice to Annie. Little Natasha greeted Annie in Dutch and David spoke in English and Dutch. Robert was fluent in his native African language, Dutch, and English.

Annie had breakfast with them and ate eggs and toast with butter. They offered her some type of beef sausages, but she declined. She also drank a cup of tea. By habit, when she finished eating, Annie picked up her dishes and placed them in the sink.

The apartment was very small. The bathroom had a toilet similar to that in the USA, but it didn't have a tub. The shower was not enclosed around the floor, but it did have a curtain.

Robert was ready to take Annie to a few tourist sights. Irina told Annie that she should stay with them. Annie looked around and wondered where would she sleep, but she also remembered how her parents always found a space for visitors.

"That is very nice of you, but I don't want to be a problem."

"You will be no problem. The sofa is also a bed. You will have your own space," Irina insisted.

"Well, I guess. If you are okay with it, I will stay."

Annie knew she always had an option to go back to the hotel if things got uncomfortable.

"Well, okay, we will go back to the hotel and get your luggage, and then I will show you a little of Amsterdam," Robert said.

It was a wonderful day, Robert drove through the Jordann area, and Annie was able to tour some of the canals. That day, Annie was also able to see The Magere Brug (Skinny Bridge) and a few other popular landmarks.

Annie stayed four days with Robert and Irina. She and Irina went to a few shopping malls and museums. They also took Annie to a park with the kids. She had a lot of fun.

On her last night of stay, Annie asked Robert where was a fun place to dance. Robert had been a taxi driver for several years and was familiar with the area. He told Annie that since it was a weekday, it would be difficult to find a good dance spot, but he took her by a couple of places. The first club had only about four couples sitting at tables, and they were all women. He said it was a Lesbian hang out, but they usually had great music on the weekend. Robert asked Annie did she want a drink but she declined. They left that club and he drove to another place he knew would be open during the week. When they stepped into the place, it was all men coupled at the tables. Annie guessed it was a Gay bar. Again, Annie declined Robert's offer to have a drink.

Instead, she asked Robert to take her through the Red Light District. She didn't want to get out of the cab, but she had heard a lot about it.

Fortunately, it was a weekday and there weren't many people on the streets or in the show windows. Annie observed the windows where ladies sat or stood in various positions, and they were dressed in very little clothing. Robert didn't have to explain to Annie the women's profession. She already knew. She was ready to go back to the apartment.

The trip to Amsterdam had been a great experience. Annie was satisfied with all the tours and truly enjoyed her stay with Irina, Robert, and their beautiful children. They all rode with Annie to the airport the next morning. Each hugged Annie goodbye as she headed to Geneva, Switzerland.

Annie stayed in a very nice hotel in Geneva. After taking a nap and eating a light lunch, she began her tours. Over two days, she visited the Place of Nations, St. Pierre Cathedral, and Victoria Hall. This ended Annie's European adventure. She packed up her belonging and returned to the USA.

Annie's European adventure with Sherman and her new acquaintances left a lifetime of great memories. She was so grateful for the opportunity and wished that Sherman had been able to stay throughout the trip. Annie caught an early flight out of Switzerland and headed back to the USA.

CHAPTER 22

The Letter

It took Annie about three days to overcome the jet lag from her European travel. Aaron was still working at his new job and was looking for an apartment. Whitney was expected to return to Memphis in about a week.

Annie had called Sherman to let him know that she had returned home, but his phone was not working. She called his dealership and left a message on his phone service. She still had not heard anything.

Aaron had collected all the mail and placed it in a large box and set it on the kitchen counter. Annie fixed a cup of hot tea and set the box on the floor next to the wingchair where she sat in the den. There was a lot of junk mail, and bills. She also saw a letter with no return address. But the handwriting looked familiar. Annie tore open the letter and began to read.

Dear Annie:

I am still on the airplane, heading back home. Hope you can read my terrible handwriting. As I write this letter to you, I expect you will return to the USA in about eight days. I hope I will be able to see you when you get back, but there is a chance I won't be able to. You see, about six months ago, I was first diagnosed with pancreatic cancer. I was in stage three, but it was moving fast to stage four. I went to several specialists, but there is no cure.

Annie, in disbelief, continued to read as tears flowed.

I wish I could have stayed longer with you, but I wanted you to remember me while I was strong. I have always admired you and wanted to do something special with you. It made me happy to hear your laughter and to see you smile and enjoy yourself. You are such a strong and intelligent woman with a generous heart. I know you will do well in life. I have come to peace with my destiny and know that I will be okay. Don't worry about me. Saying, "I love you," has always been hard for me to say to anyone, but know that I do. Continue to laugh and let love find you.

Always, here and after, Sherman.

Annie could barely breathe, while tears rushed down her face. She clenched her hand to her heart, thinking it was going to break.

Anne thought, *Why does love abandon me?*

CHAPTER 23

Onward

After making a few phone calls, ironically, Annie discovered that Sherman was cremated and his memorial was held on the same day she had read his letter. It was still painful, but Annie knew she had to continue with the reality of living. Annie decided not to share Sherman's death with her daughter.

Whitney made it back from Memphis and seemed to have had a wonderful summer. Her father bought a pony and Whitney was totally in love with it.

Annie had a client in a small town near Sacramento that she needed to meet with. The client had a box company that manufactured boxes for shipping and storage. The owner was a forty-five-year-old Black man who was a very cautious businessman. He kept a close eye on his financial position. Annie and Mr. Scott got along very well. He was strictly professional.

After working with Mr. Scott for several months, he asked Annie a question that caught her off guard.

"Why are you so sad?"

"I didn't know I was," Annie responded.

"You are such an intelligent and beautiful woman, but I never hear you mention a special person or family."

"I didn't know I was supposed to," Annie said.

"Please, don't get me wrong, I am a very happily married man with children. I am not hitting on you. But if you are single, I have a friend and I think you and he would get along very well together. You're both professionals and have level heads."

"Maybe some other time, but not now. Thank you for thinking of me." Annie told him.

"Okay, but the next time I see you, I'm going to remind you of this conversation," he told Annie.

"That's fine." Annie smiled.

The following month was Annie's thirty-fourth birthday. Aaron had moved out into his apartment in Oakland. He invited Annie over to his apartment for dinner. Aaron and Whitney had been working hard to prepare the special meal.

Whitney made spaghetti with turkey and tomato sauce and Annie's favorite, carrot cake. Aaron made a salad. Both Aaron and Whitney were at the apartment when Annie arrived. They said "Surprise!" It was such a warm feeling for Annie to have her closest family with her on her birthday.

The three sat down to eat. Aaron blessed the food and everyone began to fill their plates. Whitney stuck the large fork into the spaghetti to serve. When she lifted the fork from the bowl, the entire bowl of spaghetti stuck to the fork. Everyone laughed, and tears ran down Aaron's eyes, followed by Annie.

The cake was delicious. Whitney shared that she made a few errors before she got the cake right. Aaron turned on some "Oldies but Goodies" R&B music. Annie did her freestyle dancing and she relished and appreciated her birthday with her brother and daughter.

****

A month later, Annie was back in her client's office when Mr. Scott once again presented her with the question.

81

"Ms. Hightower, may I give my friend your telephone number?"

"Tell me a little more about him."

"Well, his name is Richard White, he likes to be called, Rick. He's not handsome but looks decent. About six-feet-one. He's an attorney, single, and a nice person—so is it okay to give him your number?"

"I guess."

The next day, Annie was surprised by the phone call. It was Richard White. They talked for a few minutes on the phone. Mr. Scott failed to tell Annie that Rick lived in Sacramento, about a one-and-a-half hour away from Annie's house. Yet, this was fine with Annie because she wasn't quite ready for the dating thing. Phone conversations were enough at that time.

CHAPTER 24

Teenager

When Whitney returned home from Memphis, she became more involved in her dance group in Oakland. She was a really good dancer. Annie attended all her performances and always gave standing ovations after the performance and shouted, "That's my daughter."

Annie was so pleased with Whitney's progress in school and her social life. However, one evening on a Saturday around sunset, thirteen-year-old Whitney came home with a seventeen-year-old boy. Whitney was conservatively and nicely dressed and the young man was as well.

Whitney introduced the young man. "Hey, Mom, this is Walter. Walter, this is my mother, Mrs. Hightower."

Annie and Walter both said, "Hello."

"Where have you been Whitney?"

"We went to a movie."

"Oh?" Annie turned to Walter. "Walter, I'm sure you're a nice young man. But my daughter is only thirteen-years old and too young to be dating anyone. She will not be going out with you or anyone else for a few more years."

Walter looked surprised and Whitney looked embarrassed.

"Yes, ma'am. Well, I better go. It was nice meeting you, Mrs. Hightower." Walter replied.

"Nice meeting you, too, Walter."

Walter left the house.

"How can you do that to me? You embarrassed me!" Whitney shouted and ran into her bedroom.

Annie had always given Whitney the freedom to make sound choices and never wanted to control Whitney's every move. But Annie also realized that children, especially teens, didn't always make the right choices and they needed closer parental guidance. Annie knew Whitney was a good child. She didn't punish her that day but thought the embarrassment was enough to make a point.

Not too long after that, Whitney came home after school and told her mother that one of her classmates called her a Nigger. Very upset, Annie got up the next morning and went to the school to talk to the principal.

"I am here today because my daughter reported to me that her classmate called her the "N" word and I want to be sure that this does not happen again."

"Yes, ma'am. I truly understand. We have zero tolerance for such behavior. Perhaps your daughter didn't tell you everything."

"Everything, what else is there?"

"Well, the boy did call her that and Whitney seemed to handle the situation. She slapped him several times before she stopped."

"Oh, I see. Well, no she didn't tell me that part," Annie said, now embarrassed. "Well, thank you for your time and I hope we will never have to meet again on such matters."

"It was a pleasure to meet you, Mrs. Hightower." They shook hands. Annie exited.

When Whiney got home from school, Annie questioned her about the incident. Annie had been afraid to ask the principal, while she was in his office if the boy was okay for fear he may not have been. Annie asked Whitney to tell her everything. Whitney began to tell her story. When she got to the point where she started slapping the boy on his head, Annie stopped her.

"What was he doing and saying while you were hitting him on the head."

"He was trying to avoid me and said, 'Quit girl, stop hitting me,'" Whitney emulated the boy.

"What if he would have hit you back?" Annie asked.

"I don't know."

"It's something you should think about."

Although deep down inside, Annie thought the boy got what he deserved, still it was unsettling to Annie that her daughter was a hitter instead of using more nonviolent reactions.

On several occasions, Annie never could understand the need for Whitney to lie to her over very simple issues that had occurred.

"Whitney, why do you lie so much?" Annie asked her.

"I don't know why I lie."

This made it hard for Annie to know what matters to take seriously.

Whitney also made several attempts to call Annie by her first name instead of "Mom." Annie strongly disapproved each time and made it clear to Whitney that she preferred, "Mom." This went on for years.

While some parents have issues with their children drinking, smoking, and taking drugs, Annie never experienced that with Whitney. Instead, Whitney enjoyed going to church. She was active in a church located in Oakland.

Annie visited the church with Whitney a few times and tried to support Whitney's choice. Yet, Annie felt uneasy about this particular church. It was nondenominational and the people spoke in their tongue. Annie couldn't understand the words and it frightened her. Also, she was not impressed with the young minister.

Whitney began to cite Scriptures to Annie and questioned some of Annie's parenting and social activities. Annie tolerated it for a while because she truly believed that she would rather see her daughter in church than in a club or on drugs.

About a year later, Annie was preparing her income tax return when Whitney gave her a charitable donation statement from Whitney's church. Annie stood straight up and shouted.

"You gave them all this money. I gave you money to pay for your expenses such as gas, food, and school supplies. How could you possibly have given them all this money?"

Annie weighed the storm and prayed for a solution. Her prayers were soon answered when Whitney made her own decision to leave the church because she had learned some unsettling things about her minister.

Annie was blessed to have a well-rounded and smart daughter who was beyond her years in making sound decisions. Yet, she knew that there would be more hills to climb as a parent.

CHAPTER 25

Overwhelming Issues

The summer break came quickly and Whitney was off to Memphis again. Annie continued to work with her clients. She had stayed in touch with Kathy who was still teaching at Howard University. Annie had shared with Kathy that she was getting burnt out with the accounting and that the market wasn't doing well. Some of Annie's clients had lost contracts and some had closed their businesses. Annie was concerned about her long-term future. She had no insurance, no pension, and no type of sound security.

"What would you like to do for a career?" Kathy asked Annie.

"I would enjoy doing what you are doing, teaching."

"Well, go back to school and get your doctorate."

"Me, a doctorate?"

"Of course, you! You are much smarter than you give yourself credit for. I will guide you through it."

"Wow." I hadn't thought of that. But sounds like a plan," Annie said, now feeling confident.

Annie researched several universities' programs in the areas including San Francisco, East Bay Area, and Sacramento. She selected the university that had the best program and would accommodate her working schedule. With Kathy's guidance, Annie completed the entrance application for the program and waited for the upcoming oral and written exams. If she was accepted into the program, Annie would find reasonable financing that she could pay off over fifteen years.

Later that summer, Annie received a phone call from her mother.

"Annie, you should come home. Your father has been in the hospital for a few days."

Annie made the flight plans and was in Memphis within a few days. When one of her cousins met her at the airport, she felt so disappointed that it wasn't her father, Jessie.

When Annie entered the house, she could hear her mother's sweet angelic voice singing.

"Through the storm, through the night. Lead me on to the light. Take my hand precious, Lord, lead me home."

Margaret was tearful while she was singing. Annie gave her a tight hug and sat down at the kitchen table with her mother. She noticed that her brother, Junior, had moved into the garage apartment with his new wife and son. He had moved from Utah, where his son was born. His wife was from India.

Margaret began to tell Annie a lot of historical information that would bring her up to date on what was happening to Jessie, who was then seventy years old.

"Your father had prostate cancer when he was sixty-three years old. He never told me, and he hasn't been able to talk about it with me. I found out a couple of years later when I read some medical records he had hidden in his closet. I knew he had some type of surgery because he went into the hospital and told me that it was just a minor procedure. He stayed three days in the hospital and then he came home. When he went to sleep, I searched his body for the surgery and discovered bandages down in his private part. He has never touched me since then, and he refuses to talk about it. Sometimes my nature gets so high."

This was getting very uncomfortable for Annie, but she knew her mother needed a listening ear.

Margaret continued.

"He began to drink a lot and had car accidents. One time, he didn't have the money to pay his fine for driving drunk, so he had to spend the weekend in jail. He took his underwear and a pair of socks, that's all they let him take. That shook him up some and he slowed down on the drinking. But his mind started changing. He couldn't remember things and he started seeing things. One time, he woke up screaming. He thought I was the enemy. He kicked me so hard on my backside that I fell out of the bed."

"Momm, I'm so sorry you have been going through this," Annie said.

Margaret, now with more tears in her eyes said, "Your father gave twenty-seven years of his life to the military, and now they don't want to help him. They immediately claim that it is alcohol abuse and don't want to give him the care he needs. Even if it is alcohol abuse, your father didn't start drinking heavily like that until he came back from Korea and later, when he worked in that VA hospital. I don't know what to do. He's in the hospital now and he can stay there only for a certain period and then I don't know what to do. I promised Jessie that I would not put him in a VA place. I have an appeal for the government to help, but you know how slow they are."

"Wow, Mother, I'm here. I will do whatever I can to help. Is the car working?" Annie asked.

"Yeah!"

"Well, we will start by knocking on or knocking down doors." Annie smiled. Margaret smiled, too.

A cute young Indian girl came through the back door and into the kitchen. She had a lovely smile and her black hair was in a single long braid that reached below her waist. She had a very large stomach, but Annie didn't want to ask her if she was pregnant, because she had embarrassed herself once before when she asked someone that question and the person wasn't pregnant.

"Hello, my name is VanLila. How are you?" She asked with a deep Indian accent.

"Well, hello, VanLila. I am your sister-in-law, Annie."

They hugged.

"It is so good to meet you, my sister. Welcome to Memphis," Annie told her.

Junior walked into the kitchen carrying his son. Annie noticed that VanLila stopped smiling.

"Hi, Annie."

"Hi, Junior, how are you?"

"Good, you met my wife VanLila and this is my son, Mohamed."

"You have a beautiful family. Oh, my goodness! He is so cute. May I hold him?"

Junior placed Mohamed on the floor.

"He just turned a year-old and he can walk."

"Come on over here, Mohamed, to your Aunt Annie."

A little shy, Mohammed ran to Annie. She lifted him to hug him and kiss him.

Annie was amazed at such a massive contrast to see little VanLila at five-feet standing next to Junior at six-six feet tall. She visited a while longer with them and then took Jessie's car to drive to Samantha's house.

Annie had made arrangements to stay at Samantha's house during her visit. She had never met Samantha's husband, Richard. They had a wedding before many knew about it. He was a nice-looking man and a pleasant person. They bought a house in a very good area of the city. It was a one-story and had three bedrooms with two baths. Samantha loved to decorate. She had floral and earth tone décor. The three of them sat up awhile and talked. Annie got sleepy, wished them a good night, and prepared for bed.

The next morning, Samantha fixed breakfast. Annie ate a bite and headed to her mother's house. Margaret was up making breakfast. The vision was strange for Annie because she had never seen her mother in the house alone before. Margaret never liked being alone. Perhaps that was why she allowed Junior to move in. Jessie, in his right mind, would not have allowed it to happen. The two didn't agree on many things and Junior had changed his entire name to a Muslim name.

Annie heard Junior shouting at someone from the back of the house, but she didn't bother to look out. Curiously, Annie looked at Margaret, who just hung her head, and then she got up to get dressed for the visit to see Jessie.

When they arrived at the hospital, Margaret entered Jessie's room with Annie in tow. Annie watched the reaction Jessie had. He smiled, but it took him a moment to recognize Margaret. Then he said, "Hey, Margaret." He looked at Annie and smiled. Annie didn't wait for him to speak.

"Hey, Daddy. How are you doing?"

Annie went up to him and gave him a tight hug. It didn't feel like the last time he hugged her. She thought he didn't know

91

her. Annie felt so guilty for waiting so long to see her parents. She wished she lived closer instead of on the opposite side of the country.

Jessie wasn't talking much but made small talk to Margaret about things Annie didn't understand. Annie talked to her father about the times they went out into the country to pick greens and the time he brought twenty hens home to slaughter.

"Yeah… we ate good." Jessie smiled.

Annie was so glad to have her father talk to her. Although she was doing most of the talking, she reminisced with him about living in Europe and Missouri. She talked about the time they moved to Memphis and the iceman and ragman that came by the house. Jessie smiled and even laughed once. Annie wished she could stay there with him forever.

The nurse came into the room to give Jessie his meds. It wasn't long before he drifted off to sleep. Annie and Margaret left.

Annie drove Margaret to the VA Office to get more documents to fill out. Afterward, Margaret became hungry. Although she was battling diabetes and high blood pressure, her favorite spot was KFC. She ordered dark meat with biscuits, gravy, and coleslaw. Annie ordered a chicken breast and a biscuit. Then, they sat down to eat. Annie had questions but chose not to bother her mother. Instead, she let her mother enjoy her food since Margaret wasn't in any hurry to go home. When they finished eating, they stopped by a relative's house for a moment and by Margaret's closest friend's house. By the time they finished visiting, it was late and Margaret was getting tired, so Annie took her home. She sat with her mother for a while and later drove back to Samantha's house.

Annie only had one more day before she had to get back to California. She picked up Margaret and pretty much had a similar day as before. When Annie and Margaret returned to the house, Annie went inside to spend more time with Margaret because she was leaving the next morning.

Junior was in the kitchen with VanLila and his son, who was tearful. There were a couple of his friends standing in the backyard. He stepped outside with his friends for a moment and then came back screaming at VanLila.

"You are so stupid. Didn't I tell you how to do this? You don't know how to do anything. You aren't worth a damn, just so stupid."

VanLila was shaking and had total fear on her face. Little Mohamed was in tears clinging to his mother. No one was saying anything or coming to VanLila's rescue. Annie couldn't keep her silence any longer.

CHAPTER 26

VanLila

When Annie returned home, she had a few reports to get out for her clients. She also had to take a written exam for entry into the university program. Then, she had to meet with the university staff for an oral examination. Annie passed both written and oral exams and was officially a doctoral candidate.

About a month after Annie left Memphis, she received a phone call from Daisy. Daisy's voice left unpleasant thoughts for Annie.

"Annie, this is Daisy."

"Yeah."

"We need to forget all about the past 'cause we have a crisis here."

Annie, not hearing an apology from her sister, thought something was wrong with either of her parents.

"What's going on?"

"We have VanLila hiding out at a neighbor's house from Junior because he has roughed her up and she is seven months pregnant."

"How is she doing?"

"She is fine, she said she has some relatives in Los Angeles, but they may be traveling or something because they can't be reached now. So she thought she could come out there until they get back from where they are."

"VanLila is welcome to visit me. Where is Junior?"

"He's still at the house and asking everybody where she is. I pretended I didn't know a thing."

94

"Have you arranged for a flight?"

"No, we'll get back to you."

Not too long after the conversation with Daisy, Whitney called Annie. Annie was very upset that Daisy had gotten Whitney involved in the conspiracy. Whitney had suggested that one of her paternal aunts pay for the ticket and that she would be reimbursed. Annie didn't express the fury she felt towards Daisy, but she knew that when it was said and done, Daisy would come out of it clean and all the accusations would be against Annie.

Whitney's paternal aunt bought the airline tickets for VanLila and Mohamed. Then, Daisy drove them to the airport. After they boarded the airplane, Daisy went back to Margaret's house and told Junior that she heard that VanLila and Mohamed were on their way to the airport. Junior rushed to the airport to no avail.

Annie picked up VanLila and Mohamed at the San Francisco airport and drove them to her house. VanLila was very shy and frighten. Little Mohamed tightly held onto his mother. Annie showed VanLila her bedroom and walked her through the house.

VanLila continued to call her relatives in L.A. After about four days, she finally reached them. When she finished speaking to them, she handed the phone to Annie. The phone call wasn't what Annie had expected. VanLila's cousin told Annie that they were too afraid of Junior to allow VanLila to come to their home.

"Junior is a crazy man, we have children and he might cause us problems. We will send money to pay for the airline tickets. But they cannot come here."

Annie hung up the phone and, once again, got into crisis planning mode. There, standing before her, was a foreigner who was seven months pregnant with a one-year-old baby and nowhere to go. For Annie, the bottom line was, that they were kinfolks.

"Will you help me?" VanLila asked Annie.

Annie assured VanLila that everything would be all right. The first thing that needed to be done was to get her medical care. Annie was able to find government-assisted medical for VanLila and Mohamed.

VanLila had a little problem adjusting to the American cultural and social ways. But she soon caught on. One day, VanLila sat down at the dining room table where Annie was working.

"Your brother worked with my brother for an oil company in Saudi Arabia, where they became friends. Junior told my brother he was from Italy. My brother brought him home to meet my parents. They welcomed him and believed him. So they gave me to him for marriage. My family is not happy with Junior."

"My goodness, I'm sorry!" Annie was very surprised.

"Thank you for helping me and my son. Your brother treated me like dirt on the floor. I am afraid of him."

Annie knew a lot about fear and humiliation and she didn't want anyone to experience what she had gone through, not even her worst enemy.

Fifteen-year-old Whitney had decided to stay with her father for the entire school year. Annie was very disappointed with her choice but supported it. Annie felt tension between them since Daisy's interference.

Once again, Annie knew she was on her own and she had to find a way to make it all work out.

One day while Aaron was visiting Annie, her phone rang. VanLila answered the phone, it was Junior. She hung up the phone. Junior called back later that evening and Aaron answered the phone.

"She's on her way to L.A. to her cousin's house," he told Junior.

When Annie learned about the phone calls, she wondered if VanLila wanted Junior to know where she was.

Early one morning, in late October, VanLila's water broke and her labor pains were about five minutes apart. Annie drove her to the hospital. Little Mohamed sat in the back seat of the car and looked confused. Annie drove up to the emergency entrance and let the medical professionals assist VanLila, while she attended to Mohamed. Annie carried him in her arms and followed the medical assistant to a private room. She and Mohamed were allowed to stay until the delivery. Annie didn't have anyone to watch Mohamed, so she couldn't see the delivery. But soon after the beautiful baby girl was born, VanLila was moved to a private room on the first floor. Annie was disappointed that she didn't get a chance to see the baby right away, but she carried Mohamed outside of the building where they could look into the window and see VanLila lying in the bed. Annie called out, "VanLila" and Mohamed called out "Mommie."

VanLila looked towards the window. She smiled and waved at them. VanLila allowed Annie to name her baby girl Charu, which means beautiful. Little Charu had very thick, straight black hair and weighed nine pounds.

Annie had arranged for VanLila to get government assistance for food and baby needs. She was also on a waiting list for government-assisted housing. Her family in India had sent her some money, and Annie helped as much as she could.

Once they were at Annie's home, little Mohamed welcomed his baby sister, Charu. Their Uncle Aaron, who was still living in Oakland, drove up a couple of times to the house and snapped pictures of everyone. Aaron was very good with children and Annie could tell that someday he would be a great father and role model.

Shortly after the birth of Charu, Annie received a letter from Junior. He wanted to know where his wife and children were. Annie gave the letter to VanLila, who declined to respond to it.

"We will be fine without him," she insisted.

Annie did write her brother back to tell him about his new daughter and that all of them were doing fine. She also wrote that VanLila would contact him when she was ready.

As the Christmas holidays drew closer, it lost its zest to Annie because it was the second Christmas without her daughter. VanLila was Muslim and didn't usually celebrate the holiday, but she and Mohamed seemed to have gotten into it more than Annie. VanLila had befriended a few of the neighbors and babysat their children to earn some income.

Annie could see a huge change in VanLila. She became more fearless than when she first arrived. She got out and took walks in the neighborhood - something she had never done since she had been in the USA. She walked the children to the grocery store that was a block away from the house.

VanLila was doing well caring for her children. Annie could study and work without much distraction. However, she assisted VanLila with scheduling her medical appointments and with other errands.

After the holidays, Annie examined her financial status and became very concerned. Because of the revolving door of several people in and out of her home during the last few years, and the last-minute travel costs to Memphis, Annie had depleted her savings. She was making less money and now she was in school again. She earned enough to cover the mortgage payment but barely enough for the living expenses. She knew that she would have to make major changes.

CHAPTER 27

Sacramento Visit

Annie's newest gentleman friend, Richard White, from Sacramento, had been keeping in touch with her for several months. Rick was thirteen years older than Annie. He was divorced and had an adult son in college. He had been an attorney for the state for over twenty years. Rick had saved his earnings as a professional wrestler to pay for his law degree. He was also the president of the local College Board of Trustees and had other political ambitions at the state level. With both of them having a busy schedule, they managed to go out twice for dinner in the bay area. He also picked up Annie from her house and drove her to San Jose for his family outing, where Annie met his mother and siblings.

Not too long after the holidays, Rick invited Annie to his house in Sacramento. She agreed to go up during the next school break but on a weekday. Rick had already planned to take a few days off from work during that time.

About noon on a Monday, Annie drove the one-and-half-hour distance to Rick's house in Sacramento. When she drove up to the house, she was a bit surprised to see the small single-story house that needed some maintenance. She parked her car next to his old worn Porsche, got out, and knocked on the door. Rick answered the door wearing a beige sweater and brown trousers.

"Hi, Annie, come on in." He smiled at Annie and kissed her on her cheek.

"Hi, Rick." Annie smiled as she walked inside.

Although Annie and Rick had been dating for about a year, she had never been to his house. Annie quickly glanced through the house. It was decorated in earth tones of brown and beige with very used furniture and shagged carpet. It did not have a woman's touch.

"Are you hungry?" Rick asked.

"Yes, very much so."

"Well, let's go out to eat."

Rick took Annie to a local Marie Callender's Restaurant. He talked for a while about his job and his only son who was in college. Annie shared how she was doing in the doctoral program. They chitchatted on different topics and decided to leave the restaurant. Annie enjoyed the food and the conversation.

Rick drove Annie to his best friend, Bob's house. Bob also worked with the state and had taken off early from work that day. He was about the same age as Rick, friendly and nice looking. Bob had been in a relationship with a younger woman for several years. He was a fast talker and had a lot to talk about. Annie noticed that he had a very nice taste for decorating. The three talked and laughed awhile.

"Well, this has been very nice, but I have a long drive back to Pleasant Hill. I better get back to my car," Annie told them.

Bob extended his hand to Annie. She shook his hands.

"It's been a pleasure meeting you, Annie. I hope you will come back."

"I'm quite sure I will see you again, Bob."

"Okay, I guess we better go," Rick said.

Rick drove Annie back to his house in her car. Annie asked to use the restroom. Rick let her into the house and showed her the restroom.

Soon Annie exited the restroom and walked into the living area.

"Annie, sit down a minute. I would like to talk with you for just a moment." Rick said.

Annie sat down on the sofa that was near the glass sliding doors. Rick sat next to her.

"I was wondering how you felt about me and how far you and I can…."

"Bang." The sound of something hitting the door.

"Rick, I know you are home," said a woman outside the door.

Rick jumped up off the sofa.

Now surprised and concerned, Annie looked at Rick.

"Bang." Another rock against the door.

"You are no good," said the woman outside.

"What is going on? Is that your girlfriend?" Annie asked Rick.

"No, I broke up with her, and she is still mad about it," Rick said, standing there like an idiot.

"Does she have a gun or weapon?"

"No."

"Do you own a gun?"

"No."

"You need to handle your business. I am out of here." Annie said with disgust.

Annie grabbed her purse and went out the door. The woman had gotten into her parked car on the street. Annie backed her car down the driveway and into the street. The woman sat in her car and stared at Annie. Annie felt very uncomfortable and did not look directly at the woman and just drove away.

Rick called Annie the following day to apologize.

"I promise that will not happen again. I let her know that I would call the police if she came around." Rick pleaded.

"Rick, I don't have time for games. And I don't want to be in the middle of any mess. I have a lot going on in my life and I don't have room for any more problems," Annie told Rick.

"Let me make it up to you," he pleaded.

"Maybe, someday." Annie hung up.

CHAPTER 28

Drama

Annie continued her routines with school assignments and work. She was doing well in the doctoral program. She drove the forty-five-minute distance to San Francisco every weekend to the university. On some Fridays, she was able to spend a night with a girlfriend in San Francisco to arrive on time for her 8:00 a.m. Saturday class.

Rick called Annie almost every day to touch base. By springtime, housing was found for VanLila and the children. She would be able to move into the apartment within thirty days.

Shortly after the notification, Annie received a call from Memphis.

"Hey, Annie, this is your Cousin Bobbie."

"Hey, Cuz, how are you?"

"I am great. As you know, I am a guidance counselor at the high school where Whitney attends. So sorry to have to tell you this, but I thought you should know that Whitney has run away from her father's house because he beat her."

"Where is Whitney now?"

"I think she is still over at her aunt's house."

"Thank you, Bobbie, for calling me. I appreciate you keeping up with Whitney and all your help," Annie quickly responded and hung up the phone.

Annie dialed Floyd's twin sisters' house. One of the twins answered.

"Hello."

"Hi, Pamela, this is Annie. How are you?"

"Hi, sister, I am doing good, and you?"

"I'm calling to talk with Whitney. Is she there?"

"No, not right now, but she'll be back in a minute."

"What is going on?"

"Well, that crazy brother of mine whipped Whitney and she left his house."

"Have Whitney call me as soon as you hear from her."

"I will."

Rage grew so deeply within Annie as she thought about the years of abuse and the fear that Floyd had inflicted on her and how hard she tried to protect her child from his abuse. Annie had no verbal skills in confrontation – she had avoided discussions in upsetting matters by physically removing herself. But this time, her maternal instinct kicked in. She wanted to hurt Floyd. She dialed his number.

"Hello."

"Where is my daughter, Floyd?" Annie was pissed.

"What do you mean, your daughter?

"I told you many years ago not to touch my child."

"Your child?"

"You've spent your entire life hurting and destroying other's lives. If you ever come near me or my child again and try to harm us, you will regret it. I am not that same gullible bitch you treated like crap!" Annie shouted and hung up the phone.

Annie paced the floor, her heart raced, and she was angry. About a half-hour later, she received a call from Whitney.

"Hello."

"Hi, Mom, how are you?"

"I'm good, what is going on with you and your father?"

"He picked me up from school. When he drove up, he saw me talking to one of my classmates, who was a boy. He screamed at me and told me that I was going to get pregnant. Then, when we got home, he took his belt off and started beating me with it."

"Why didn't you call me?"

"I didn't think you wanted me to."

"I'm not angry with you. Do you want to come home?"

"Yes."

"Do you have someone there that can take you to the airport?"

"Yes."

"I will get you a ticket, be ready to fly out tomorrow."

Annie bought the airline ticket and arranged for Whitney to leave the following day. When she saw the date of the reservations, Annie realized it was Whitney's sixteenth birthday.

The next evening, Annie picked up Whitney from the airport and wished her a happy birthday. Whitney got settled in and interacted with her Aunt VanLila and her cousins. Whitney enjoyed the children.

Since school had not ended for the year, Bobbie arranged to transfer all of Whitney's records so that she could complete the year. Annie drove Whitney to school the following day and enrolled her.

Annie realized when she paid for the airline ticket, she barely had enough money to pay the next month's mortgage. She had to devise another plan.

A couple of months after Whitney returned home, Annie moved VanLila and the children into a two-bedroom apartment. Since VanLila still felt afraid to be totally on her own, Annie and Whitney moved into the second bedroom. The following month, Annie rented her house. Annie spent some weekdays at Rick's house in Sacramento, where she had new clients in that area.

Annie installed a second phone, with the same old number, in the apartment for Whitney's use. After getting the details from Whitney about where her father worked, Annie let her know that she filed for child support and that the funds would be deposited into an account that Whitney would have access to.

Once the child support complaint was filed, the old phone number rang.

"Hello," Whitney answered.

"This is, Rena, why are you letting your mother sue your father? You know he will take care of you. You need to stop her from doing it."

Rena was once again doing the bad deed for the coward, Floyd.

"I have no control over what my mother does. That is between her and Daddy."

In a couple of months, $150 was transferred into the account. Whitney had total control over it. Annie wanted no part of it. Floyd had less than two years of child support payments before Whitney turned eighteen years old. Annie could not understand his unwillingness to pay.

When the school term ended, Whitney found a summer job. VanLila befriended a Pakistani family and started working part-time in their restaurant. The children went to work with her. Annie took a couple of classes and worked with a few clients. She also worked with Rick on one of his political campaigns. There, she met several of the local people. Annie and Rick became closer.

By the end of the summer, Whitney had saved enough money for a nice down payment on a car. Annie thought of Whitney as a responsible and reliable person. However, Annie made it very clear to Whitney, that if she missed one payment, the car would be taken from her. Whitney accepted the terms. Therefore, Annie signed a loan for Whitney's brand new Nisan automobile. Annie felt so proud of her daughter who had worked so hard to make it happen.

CHAPTER 29

A Proposal?

The summer went by without any major events. Annie enrolled in classes and continued to work with her clients. Whitney enrolled in her senior year of high school. VanLila continued to work at the restaurant. Rick was re-elected as the president of the college Board of Trustees and re-appointed to a State board.

Annie decided to pick up the old flute she once played in high school. Not great, but she was surprised that she remembered how to play it. She practiced every chance she got and it became soothing to her. Since Annie loved to dance, she convinced Rick to take hand-dancing classes with her, and he graciously agreed. Annie was surprised to see how fast Rick learned the dances. They played similar music at the house and practiced the dance moves. Soon, they looked as though they had been dancing for some time. Annie would always try to find some type of entertainment to keep their relationship filled with excitement.

Rick invited Annie out to dinner. She was surprised when he selected a very nice seafood restaurant since he was usually very frugal. He told Annie to order what she wanted. So she ordered salmon, vegetables, and rice pilaf. Rick wasn't very good at expressing himself. He was a man of few words.

"I'm going to marry you," he blurted out.

"Excuse me?" Annie wasn't sure what he said.

"We should get married."

"We should?"

"Yeah."

"Why?"

"Because we are good together, and I love you."

"Well, if this is a proposal, did you bring the ring?"

"Yes, it is a proposal, but I thought we could go to San Francisco, and you can pick out a ring."

"That sounds nice. Let me think about it."

Even though it was sincere, Annie thought it wasn't the most romantic proposal, but she would consider it.

One of Rick's friends, Rosalyn, in Sacramento, invited him and Annie to a Presbyterian church. Annie truly enjoyed the services. The pastor, Thomas Clyde, his wife, Mary, and their three children, left a profound impression on Annie. The church was temporarily held in a storefront until the new building was completed. The congregation consisted of about one hundred people. Everyone was welcoming.

Annie became actively involved in the church. She acted as the treasurer and worked on the building construction committee. Annie also played the flute with the pianist in many of the Sunday services. Tom and Mary were very kind people and inspiring leaders.

Rick revisited the wedding proposal to Annie. She suggested that they have marriage counseling. Annie asked Pastor Tom if he would facilitate the counseling and he agreed. She thought it would be a good way to get to know some of each other's strengths and weaknesses and to determine if they had any well-suited qualities. The counseling was done over four weeks. What Annie got out of it was: Rick was much unorganized, both personally and professionally. He was financially irresponsible and although he had adequate funds to live better than he had, he did not like to pay his debts on time or in full.

109

Annie discovered that Rick's faults didn't bother her. Besides, he had suggested that she be in charge of the finances once they were married. She felt comfortable being around him. He was gentle and easygoing. She never felt that he was controlling or demanding. Rick had a kind heart and seemed loyal. She truly believed that she could love him and be with him forever.

Shortly after the Thanksgiving holidays, Annie and Rick drove to San Francisco to visit a jeweler in the China Town area. Before the trip, Annie had spoken to one of her current doctoral classmates, Lu Lee, who wore a stunning custom-made wedding ring set. Lu Lee said that she had it made in China Town and she paid the Chinese price, which was ten percent over the cost. Lu Lee gave Annie the location and phone number and told Annie to use her name. Annie was excited and shared the information with Rick.

When she and Rick entered the store, the owners were so kind. The jeweler brought out several types of diamonds and explained the qualities of each type. They offered alcohol and food, but Annie and Rick declined. Annie and Rick made their selection and the jeweler made the rings while they waited.

After a few hours, the jeweler brought out the finished rings. Rick's wedding band had a one-carat diamond on a fourteen-carat gold band. Annie's wedding band had five, .38-carat diamonds on a fourteen-carat gold band. But the engagement ring was brilliant. The fourteen-carat gold band had beveled designs with about two dozen small diamonds mounted along the architect of the designs, and in the center of the ring, a 2.3-carat diamond was mounted.

Rick placed the engagement ring on Annie's finger, and she didn't take it off. The jeweler boxed the wedding bands and Annie and Rick headed back across the bay bridge.

They stopped at VanLila apartment in Pleasant Hill, where she was in the kitchen cooking. Mohamed was playing with toys on the floor in the living room and baby Charu was asleep. Whitney was in her bedroom, but she came into the living area.

"Well, we are officially engaged," Annie announced to them all.

"Congratulations," VanLila said.

Whitney didn't say anything at the time. But later she told her mother, "You can do much better than that."

CHAPTER 30

Bringing in New Year

The wedding was held the day after Christmas, at another Presbyterian Church's wedding chapel. Whitney was the maiden of honor and Rick's son, Troy, was the best man. Aaron walked Annie down the aisle and VanLila and the children were in attendance. In addition, there were a few other church members and friends present.

The chapel was nicely and modestly decorated. Annie wore a silk peach color two-piece, long sleeve dress with cream accessories. Whitney wore a very nice cream-colored dress. Rick and Troy wore dark suits and ties. The ceremony was brief and lovely.

There was no reception because Annie and Rick made plans to fly to Memphis to see Annie's parents the following day. A few people did stop by Rick's house after the ceremony. There were cold cuts, cheeses, crackers, and fruit. Rick also served alcohol and sodas.

The next morning, bright and early, Annie and Rick placed their suitcases in the car and headed to the airport.

Once they arrived at the Memphis airport, they rented a car and drove to a downtown hotel. It was owned by Annie's previous coworker and mentor, Fred Cash. Fred was a CPA and had worked at the same nonprofit organization that Annie had worked for when she lived in Memphis. He was her supervisor and Annie never forgot how patient he was with her while he was training her bookkeeping procedures. He encouraged Annie to go back to school to get a degree in accounting. She kept in touch with Fred over the years to give him updates of her accomplishments. He was always excited for her. They developed a lifelong friendship.

Fred owned several business entities including a nightclub and hotel. On every visit to Memphis, Annie would patronize his restaurant or nightclub. Fred gave Annie and Rick a good deal on their New Year's holiday stay. The hotel was very nice.

After Annie and Rick got settled into their room, they drove to her parent's home. Since Annie rode in the passenger's seat, she could observe the community.

"Oh, my goodness, everything looks so small -the houses, the streets, the buildings."

Rick turned onto the main street in her parent's neighborhood.

"Look, that was a hot place one time—W.C. Handy Theatre. Wow, it's all boarded up. I wonder what happened to it…. There is my mother's church… I went there, too…" Annie pointed.

"There is my old high school… it is closed down now… part of it is now a nursing home… and senior center. They rebuilt the new high school down the street from my parents' house… there is the elementary school and the high school stadium… I use to march with the band on that field… and there is the community grocery store…. I loved to buy the two-for-a-penny cookies. Turn right at the light." She told Rick.

Annie saw more houses boarded up and some had vanished, instead, there were just vacant lots. What was once a thriving and beautiful community was then a dying neighborhood.

"Turn left here… my goodness, looks like people have abandoned their properties… okay, we are here—just park in front… right here."

Rick parked the car. They got out and started walking towards the house. Annie noticed trash on the driveway and in the yard. Automatically, Annie began to pick up the trash. She walked down the drive and placed the trash in a can. It was a reminder that her father, Jessie, no longer lived in the house.

"Come on, Rick, let's go to the back door. They are probably in the kitchen anyway."

Rick followed Annie to the back door. She knocked once and checked to see if the door was locked. She opened the door and called out.

"Hey, Mother, I'm home!"

She continued to walk through the kitchen looking for Margaret. Margaret came out of the front bedroom and smiled. Annie rushed to hug her.

"Hey, Mother, how are you?"

"I'm fair to mid'lin." She smiled again.

"This is my husband, Rick."

"Come on over here boy and hug your mother," Margaret told Rick. Rick hugged her.

"Can I get you guys something to eat or drink? You know I have some greens."

"No, thanks, I'm fine," Annie said.

"I would love some," said Rick.

"I will fix him a plate, Mother," Annie told her.

Samantha came out of the bathroom.

"Hey sistah, Annie, how's you doin'?" she hugged Annie.

"I'm pretty near good, my sistah." They laughed

"Is this my handsome new brother-in-law?" Samantha hugged Rick.

"I'm Annie's beautiful sister, Samantha, come on in the kitchen and I'll fix you a plate of greens and some hot water cornbread… got some turkey, too."

Rick's face lit up.

"That sounds great to me." He followed Samantha into the kitchen.

"Mother, how is Daddy?"

"Oh, he is in the hospital, they are running more tests, but we have found a center for him… I wish I could take care of him, but I'm not able to. He's too strong for me when he has his tantrums and I'm too weak to lift him when he needs to be." She said with sadness.

"You mean he can't walk."

"No, he can walk, but they have finally diagnosed him in an advanced stage of Alzheimer… and sometimes, he doesn't remember how to clean himself."

"Where is the place that he will be staying after he leaves the hospital?"

"It is quite a ways from here."

"How do you feel about it?" Annie asked.

"It is a clean place and they treat the patients well."

"We will come and get you tomorrow so that we can visit Daddy at the hospital," Annie said to her mother.

"That will be good."

Margaret and Annie joined Samantha and Rick in the kitchen. They all sat down at the table. Rick enjoyed his plate of greens with smoked turkey and cornbread. Everyone told stories and laughed.

The next morning, Annie and Rick rose early to eat and drove back to Margaret's house. She was dressed and ready to go. Annie took the wheel, Rick sat in the rear, and Margaret sat in the front passenger's seat.

Fortunately, Margaret was able to keep her promise to Jessie and not put him in the VA hospital. Jessie had worked there for about three years after he retired from the Army and made it clear to everyone that he never wanted to be a patient there. Instead, he was in one of the main hospitals. Annie parked in the hospital parking lot and they took an elevator up to the fifth floor. Jessie was awake and sitting up in his bed. Margaret walked into the room first. Annie and Rick followed.

"Hey, Serge," Margaret said to Jessie and kissed him.

"Hi," Jessie smiled.

"Hey, Daddy," Annie smiled at her father, then hugged and kissed him.

Annie noticed, as she did during her last visit, that Jessie was distant. He looked confused as if he was trying to figure out who Annie was.

"I'm your number six child, Annie," she told Jessie.

Jessie smiled.

"This is my husband, Rick."

Rick smiled at Jessie, but Jessie just stared at him.

"Did you eat today, Jessie?" Margaret asked.

Jessie looked at Margaret and nodded his head.

"Bathroom," Jessie mumbled.

"Okay. I'll get someone to help." Margaret pressed the button for assistance.

Jessie pushed the bed cover off of him and started climbing down from the bed. He moved gingerly, but he managed to get out of the bed and stand. Rick stood and observed. Annie grabbed Jessie's arm and placed it over her shoulder and walked him to the bathroom. Once Jessie was in the bathroom, he shut the door. A moment later, everyone heard Jessie's conversation.

"Man, I told you not to touch that…. didn't I tell you? I'm not going to keep telling you. Get out the way." Jessie shouted at the imaginary person.

The nurse stepped into the room.

"Please, check on my husband in the bathroom," Margaret told her.

The nurse stepped into the bathroom and spoke to Jessie. Shortly, she assisted him out of the bathroom and back into his bed.

Annie was tearful, she had never seen her father so helpless and confused. The Daddy she knew was gone, she grieved for him. She could barely watch him suffer. Jessie soon drifted off to sleep.

After leaving the hospital, Annie gave Rick a tour of the Memphis downtown area. She drove along Front Street to view the Mississippi River, the bridge, riverboats, and Mud Islands. They stopped at the National Civil Rights Museum, historically known as the Lorraine Hotel, for a tour. Margaret managed to get through the tour without a wheelchair, and they all enjoyed the tour.

Annie stopped at Margaret's favorite restaurant, Barnhill's. The three found a table and then walked around to fill their plates with food. Rick was enjoying the food. He piled his plate with various types of meat and vegetables. Margaret placed a pork chop, a chicken thigh, bread, and some green beans, on her plate. Annie piled on the hot vegetables - especially the rutabagas, greens, and cornbread. She also took a piece of the white fish.

After finishing the food, Margaret asked Rick to bring her a couple of chicken legs and a thigh. While Rick went for the chicken, Annie went to the dessert bar. She brought back three different selections. To her, they looked better than they tasted. She ate a couple of bites of each. Rick returned with the chicken and Annie looked away as her mother placed the chicken in her purse.

Annie drove back to her parent's house. She and Rick spent a little more time with Margaret and Samantha. Then, they drove back to the hotel. Rick turned on the sports, while Annie made some phone calls to former high school classmates and relatives.

The next day, on New Year's Eve, Annie invited Margaret and Samantha to see the movie, *Color Purple*. But Samantha had to work.

"That sounds good. I haven't seen a movie on a big screen in many years." Margaret shared.

During the movie, in the scene where Celie and Shug kissed, Margaret shouted,

"Oh! No - uh uh - You don't want to do that—No! No!"

Everyone in the movie laughed.

Overall, Margaret enjoyed the movie.

After the movie, Rick drove Margaret home. Then, he drove back to the hotel and parked the car. He and Annie walked down the Beale Street District. They stopped to have a drink and then headed back to the hotel.

Later, Annie and Rick got dressed in elegant attire to attend the New Year's Eve party at the hotel. There were about a hundred-and-fifty people in the banquet room. Annie saw Fred, who was busy talking to guests and observing the operations but soon, he made his way over to Annie and Rick.

"Hey, Fred, this is my husband, Rick."

The two shook hands and made small talk. Fred continued to move around the room.

The DJ played some of the latest songs: "Say That You Will" by Lionel Richie, "Freaks Come Out at Night" by Whodini, "Outta This World" by Ashford and Simpson, "Darling You Send Me" by the Manhattans, "Back in Stride Again" by Frankie Beverly.

But the party didn't get started until the DJ played the "oldies but goodies." The dancefloor was full. Everybody did their own thing... hand dancing, freestyle, and line dancing. Annie and Rick showed off their hand-dancing and cha-cha moves.

One minute before the New Year, everyone placed hats on their heads and grabbed party whistles, and other noise makers.

"Five-four-three-two-one... Happy New Year!!!" Everyone shouted. Rick pulled Annie close to him and gave her a passionate kiss.

The midnight breakfast buffet was opened and the people must have been really hungry that night. They acted like hungry heathens. They piled their plates up so high without thinking about other people. By the time Annie and Rick reached the food table, all the bacon and sausages were gone. It didn't bother Annie, but Rick wasn't pleased with it all. There were eggs, toast, cheese grits, and fruit left. Annie didn't like to eat that late, but she did put some eggs and fruit on her plate.

After eating, Annie and Rick danced a couple of times and called it a night.

****

On January 1, 1986, they drove over to Margaret's house. When they arrived, Annie remembered the old superstition about who first walked into a home on New Year's Day.

119

"You go on in, Rick, I'll come shortly," Annie told him.

Margaret was on the other side of the door when Rick entered the house.

"Happy New Year, Mrs. Fowler," Rick greeted.

"Happy New Year, and you can call me Mother… Well, I know you ain't poor and you probably have some money in your pocket." Margaret said to Rick.

"Ma'am?" Rick asked, confused.

Annie heard the conversation as she walked into the house.

"Happy New Year, Mother," she hugged and kissed Margaret.

"Hey, Annie, Happy New Year to you, too."

"Rick, there is a superstition that if the first man that walks into your house on New Year's Day is broke or penniless, it will bring the homeowner bad luck – back in the day, the man had to show the money in his pocket," Annie explained.

Rick laughed.

"Oh, okay. Well, I'm not rich, but I don't qualify as broke." Everyone laughed.

Annie and Rick spent the day with Margaret and Samantha. They went by to visit Jessie at the hospital, and later that day, other friends and relatives came by the house. When the R&B music played, Rick reached out for Annie's hand and they swing-danced on a few songs. They moved together in harmony as if they had been dancing together for years. Their dance lessons had paid off.

Everyone enjoyed the black-eyed peas, greens, cornbread, ham, chicken, and other trimmings and desserts that had been prepared by Margaret and Samantha. It was a wonderful way to start the New Year. The next day, Annie and Rick gave their goodbye hugs and kisses to everyone. Annie didn't know when the next time she would be back to visit, but she knew that she had to make it sooner.

"Happy New Year to All," Annie said, as she and Rick left to return to California.

CHAPTER 31

Pretty Smart Ass

When Annie and Rick returned to Sacramento from Memphis, they quickly resumed their work and school routine. Annie had set up an office in one of the spare bedrooms to work. By spring, Whitney was preparing for her high school graduation and college choices. She also elected to go into the Army Reserve boot camp in the summer and then start college in the fall.

Annie and Rick sold their houses and bought a newly built house not too far from where the old house was located. To maintain his elected position, Rick had to remain within that particular district. The house was a single-story with three bedrooms and two baths. It had a formal dining room, a living room, and a large open living area. The kitchen was also a nice size. They built a large deck with a hot tub in the backyard. Annie moved in some of the furniture she had stored and nicely decorated the house in light airy decor. They had agreed that when Rick's term ended, he would not run for another term and that they would purchase their dream home in a more desirable area.

Annie and Rick decided to get a dog. She had been bitten twice as a young girl, and those incidents caused enough pain to develop a severe fear of dogs. But, like most things in Annie's life that hindered her, she always tried to overcome them, by facing them. Annie thought if she started with a puppy, she would gradually overcome the fear. They went to a Rottweiler breeder who had four puppies that were about six-weeks old. One of the cute puppies came directly to Annie, and they decided that Nick was the right dog for them.

When fall came, Whitney moved in with Annie and Rick and enrolled at the local community college. It was the same college where Rick was the President of the Board of Trustees. Whitney had completed the Army Reserve boot camp. She traveled each month to serve a weekend in a town not too far from Sacramento.

Annie had completed all her coursework and had begun research for her dissertation. After completing the first three chapters of the dissertation, the chairman of her committee, chose to drive from San Francisco to Annie's house, to work with her. Her professor, Dr. Dorval, an Irish descendant, was about sixty-five-years old with all white hair. He was very thorough and explained clearly to Annie what was expected. Dorval traveled with her on the interviews at her targeted school and students for her research. Annie was so grateful to have a knowledgeable and consistent chairperson. When he arrived at Annie's home, she always had a snack and something to drink prepared for him. At that time, there was no spellcheck included in the computer software. Each page had to be carefully edited. As Dr. Dorval edited each page, he passed it to Annie and she made the corrections.

Annie worked hard to keep up with the demands of the research and the timelines. By the following spring 1987, she was in the position to defend her dissertation. Annie was so relieved when she received the letter of approval. It took a while for her to truly grasp the magnitude of her accomplishment. She was so thankful to God for the opportunity and the honor. Rick, Whitney, VanLila, and the children attended Annie's graduation ceremony.

As a gift to herself to celebrate her significant accomplishment, Annie elected to have breast implants. She didn't want large breasts—just enough to replace what nature had taken away. She went from a full "A" cup to a full "B" cup. No one noticed the difference except Annie and, of course, Rick.

Shortly after the surgery, Rick gave a party for Annie at their home. A newspaper journalist was present and prepared a story on the front page of the society section, with a large picture of Annie, standing with Whitney announcing the celebration of: "Dr. Annie Hightower-White."

Although Annie did not send out graduation notifications, she did let a few of her relatives know about it. She didn't receive any type of congratulatory acknowledgment except from her oldest sister, Elaine. The card was specifically selected but didn't have any personal comments. It simply said: "NO ONE LIKES A PRETTY SMART ASS!!"

Annie later learned how true that statement was as she struggled to succeed in her career and her interactions with her family and other professionals.

Sometime later, Annie was invited by her brother, Donny, to visit him and his new family. Donny had married a lovely woman from Malaysia and was then stationed in San Diego. His first child had been born a gorgeous baby girl. Shortly after the Thanksgiving holiday, Annie gladly accepted Donny's invitation and flew to San Diego.

Annie took gifts for the bundle of joy and snapped pictures of her. Donny's wife was very pleasant and liked Annie. Annie noticed that after she shared her recent accomplishment with Donny, he became distant toward Annie. Instead of being happy for her, he stopped inviting Annie to his home. Annie soon realized that sometimes a person may see others' success as their failure. But Annie continued to love her brother and made efforts to communicate with him.

CHAPTER 32

Problem Solved

Annie met a lovely woman, in Sacramento, named Tia. Despite her beauty, she was very friendly and down to earth, and she was about the same age as Annie. They met at one of Rick's campaign fundraisers, and both had similar backgrounds in accounting. Tia was divorced with two children about Whitney's age. She loved to dance and laugh, and she could curse like a sailor. Annie and Tia exchanged phone numbers. They stayed in touch regularly and visited each other's homes. At the time, Tia was in a relationship with a guy who also worked for the state. Annie and Tia became inseparable and very supportive of one another. If one got sick the other was by her side. Both were independent, earned their income, and took care of their responsibilities. They also experienced the same undermining and pettiness from the local women.

One day, Tia was visiting Annie when Annie's dog, Nick, became very ill. Tia helped Annie to place big ninety-pound Nick in the small rear area of the Porsche. Tia sat in the passenger's seat and Annie drove to the animal hospital.

The vet gave Nick some medicine that made him vomit. That's when it was discovered that Nick had eaten an entire chicken. Annie and Tia first thought Nick had eaten one of the neighbor's live chickens, but later learned that he had found a carcass that Annie had thrown in the trash. Annie and Tia laughed about that incident over the years.

Annie was devastated when Tia decided to leave Sacramento and move to Los Angeles to be near her mother and other relatives. Annie didn't have any other local close friends that she could trust or confide in. So she and Tia talked on the phone. A couple of times,

Annie drove to L.A. for a visit. The last time she drove there, Annie forgot to check the oil in the car. By the time she drove halfway back to Sacramento, a rod broke. The damages to the Toyota Cressida exceeded the value of the car, so Annie left the car with the mechanic and took a bus home.

Rick had traded the Porsche for the new BMW. On the days Annie had to meet a client, she drove Rick to work in his car and then to her client. However, on a few occasions, Rick loaned the BMW to his son, Troy, who already had his nice car. Troy just wanted to drive his father's BMW. This continued to happen regularly.

One day, Annie got ready to meet a client. When she went into the garage, the BMW was gone. But Troy's car was parked in the driveway and it was locked. Troy had keys to the BMW and drove off with it. Annie called Rick, who had given his son permission to take the car without informing Annie. She called Troy, but he would not return the car.

Annie called to reschedule her client's appointment. Then, she went into planning mode. The next day when Rick drove home in his BMW from work, he opened the garage door and saw Annie's new Jaguar. Problem solved.

CHAPTER 33

Family and Class Reunion

The following year, Annie flew to Memphis for her high school's twentieth class reunion and the McGwin Family Reunion. She was so excited about the visit because not only would she see her parents, but she would also have the opportunity to see many of her relatives and classmates that she hadn't seen for a long time.

Annie stayed with Margaret during her visit. She slept in the garage apartment, where her older brother, Junior, and his wife, VanLila had lived several years before.

All of Annie's siblings were in Memphis for the reunion. When Claudine came to Margaret's house, she barely spoke to Annie.

"Hey, Claudine, how you doing?" Annie asked.

"I'm good."

Nothing but silence. Claudine continued to talk to other family members. Annie joined in the conversation.

"Ain't nobody talking to you," Claudine told Annie with a very firm and condescending look.

"Claudine, I am not the same naive eighteen-year-old you knew."

"You need to get out of my face." Claudine picked up her purse and went outside to her car. When she returned, she opened it wide enough to show Annie that she had a gun.

Annie was shocked by Claudine's implication.

A few minutes later, Margaret's home phone rang.

"Annie, it's for you," Samantha said.

"Hello."

"I suggest you watch yourself, don't nobody mess with my family!!"

Annie immediately identified the voice as her brother, Junior.

"I don't understand—I am family."

Junior hung up the phone.

Annie became tearful at the thought of her siblings wanting to harm her. She couldn't understand their hatred.

****

Ever since Daisy's daughter, Ebony, was a baby, Margaret had kept Ebony for long periods. Ebony loved visiting her grandmother. When Annie arrived at the house, Ebony was visiting Margaret and she had planned to spend the night. She was such a sweet little girl, and she was very kind and respectful. Ebony asked if she could sleep out in the garage apartment with her Aunt Annie. But when her mother, Daisy, learned that Annie was staying with Margaret, she called Margaret and ordered Ebony to remain in the main house and not to speak to her Aunt Annie. Ebony was very disappointed, but she obeyed her mother.

Annie had never said anything negative to Ebony about her mother, Daisy. Two wrongs don't make a right, was Annie's belief. Annie could never do that to a child, especially when it related to a relationship with a mother. Daisy had no problem destroying relationships, including the one with her daughter.

Annie would never think about getting her daughter, Whitney, involved in any sibling rivalry. She had taught her daughter to respect her aunts and uncles. Annie didn't have to tell her daughter anything negative about her siblings, because they showed their true colors. Whitney didn't like visiting the Fowler family, due to their wicked deeds, and not because of anything Annie said about them to Whitney. Furthermore, the conflicts were usually initiated by Daisy.

Margaret was aware of Daisy's deeds. She shared with Annie her thoughts on it.

"I know my daughter, Daisy, has done some evil things, but at the same time, she has the power to bring the family together for happy times and can do some nice things. I wish she would use those powers more. When I was pregnant with her in Germany, and your father got upset with me, he kicked me sometimes in my shinbone. It would hurt. Maybe Daisy felt that pain too and caused her to be so evil."

Annie didn't dismiss her mother's analysis and sympathized with her mother, but she believed that Daisy's issues were much deeper.

Annie took Margaret to visit Jessie. He was in a convalescent home that was quite a distance from Margaret's house. Margaret had told Annie it was the only decent place that would accept Jessie based on their income.

When they entered the home, Annie was relieved to see that it was clean and didn't have the usual urine odor like some nursing homes did. As they walked down the hall to Jessie's room, Annie watched the elderly patients. Some were sitting and watching television, another was alone in a corner talking to themselves, and some were pacing the floor. There were a few other visitors present.

They arrived at Jessie's room where he was sitting in his chair. Annie immediately noticed that Jessie was restrained with his wrists tied to the wheelchair arms. Annie was upset.

"Hey, Serge," Margaret said as she kissed Jessie.

"Hey, Daddy," Annie said and kissed him.

Jessie's expression was emotionless. Annie was so overcome with feelings of helplessness for her father that she left the room. In moments, she brought an assistant in and demanded that they take the restraints off of Jessie.

"Well, he got a bit violent and started to hit a person," the assistant explained.

"We will watch him and be responsible, just take them off or I will!" Annie shouted.

When the restraints were removed, Jessie began to show movement. He began to focus on Margaret.

"Hi," he finally said.

It was the only word he said that day, but Annie still saw a glimpse of her strong and loving father.

The McGwin Family Reunion banquet was on the following day. It was held at a community center that was located on the old campus of Annie's high school. The school had been demolished and rebuilt a few blocks away.

The banquet was well-attended. Annie greeted and hugged her relatives and met many new members for the first time. She was especially happy to see her mother's younger brother, Uncle Shooey. He had retired from his pastoral position at the church in St. Louis and returned to Memphis. He bought a house only a block from Margaret's house. Uncle Shooey and Margaret had remained very close.

Annie could never forget how her Uncle Shooey and her Grandma McGwin opened their home to her and baby Whitney when they fled from Memphis to escape a violent marriage.

Uncle Shooey facilitated the banquet. During the event, he acknowledged Annie's recent accomplishment of earning a Ph.D. There were a few applauses and congratulatory comments. Annie was grateful and thanked them. The event was very nice and everyone seemed to enjoy one another. Annie did not know that night would be the last time she would see her Uncle Shooey alive.

****

Several days later, Annie attended her high school class's twentieth reunion which was also held on the old high school campus but in the gym. Although there were about three hundred graduating class members, only about one-hundred members attended. Everyone was so pleasant. Annie remembered some of the faces but was so thankful for the name tags.

Annie saw her close friends in high school, Leola, Rhonda, and Marie, who all had played the flute in the band with her. Marie still lived in Memphis with her husband and only daughter. She was Annie's main connection to what was happening in Memphis. Annie spent the night at Marie's home a few times during her visits to Memphis. Marie's husband was well-known in Memphis. Annie attended a few fun parties at their home. There was always plenty of good food and music.

Marie was a very petite woman and the oldest child of a large family. She had a strong personality, was very bossy, and could curse like a sailor. But she was one of the most generous and kind persons Annie ever knew.

131

During the reunion event, someone touched Annie on her shoulder. She quickly turned and there stood, Thomas, her "First Kiss." Thomas had kept in touch with Annie throughout the years. He sent her postcards whenever he traveled and when he made transitions in his career. Despite the extra pounds, Thomas had the same wonderful spirit. Annie was surprised and happy to see him.

A moment later, she heard a voice say, "Hello, Dr. Fowler."

Annie was surprised by the formal greeting. It had been over a year since she earned the degree, and none of her classmates had acknowledged her accomplishment. But it had not bothered Annie. She turned to the voice.

"Hello, Mr. Wilcox."   She wondered how he knew.

"Congratulations on your outstanding achievement."

"Thank you. You are very kind."

Mr. Wilcox was a popular teacher and coach at the high school. He had been invited to the reunion as a special guest.

The class reunion was memorable and everyone was pleasant. Annie experienced some anxiety when it was time to bid her farewells, she promised to keep in touch with many of them.

****

Annie spent the next day with her mother and drove to visit Jessie again. It was excruciating for Annie to see her father in his poor health condition that he was in.

Oh, how I wish I lived closer, I could at least take him for walks, Annie thought.

After they left the convalescent home, Margaret asked Annie to drive to a location where she and Jessie had bought a lot several years before. The lot was in a recreational community and right off a beautiful golf course. They had planned to sell their house and

132

build a small house on the lot then retire there someday. Annie was surprised to hear about their plans. Margaret believed that the lot was worth at least twice what they had paid for it. Annie still didn't understand where the conversation was going.

"I am having a difficult time trying to pay the bills. I need to get some money soon or we might lose the house." Margaret explained.

"What do you need to get straightened out?" Annie asked.

"About two-hundred-and-fifty dollars a month. I will sell you the land. I don't want you to just give me the money. This is a beautiful lot and I'm sure the value will increase over the years. Someday, you might consider using it. My attorney is handling the sale."

"Why don't I call and talk with your attorney tomorrow and see what I can do?"

"Thank you so much."

Margaret knew that when she asked Annie for anything, Annie would find a way to make it happen.

Annie contacted the attorney and managed to send Margaret the $250 a month plus ten-percent interest until the total amount was paid off. Annie also knew that she paid much more than the property was valued, but the purpose was to help her mother.

About a day before Annie left Memphis, her younger brother, Donny, visited Margaret's house while Annie was there. Donny was divorced and had full custody of his two small children. He was a skilled carpenter and painter. He converted the girl's old bedroom into a den and remodeled the garage apartment into a very nice unit with a kitchen and living room. Donny and his children lived in it for a while.

During this particular visit, Donny approached Annie while she was sitting in the den.

"Hi, Annie."

"Hi, Donny, how you doing?"

"I'm okay, I just want to run something by you ... Uuughhh, I know you are trying to help Mother, but I'm the one that needs the money. She already has some income. I don't know why you are giving her money."

"Donny, I don't have to explain to you what I do for our mother." Annie rebutted.

"I knew you were going to act like that." Donny stood up. "You can go to hell!" He yelled at Annie and walked out of the room.

Annie was very surprised by his peculiar behavior, but she had already had a few negative experiences with Donny and his financial needs and issues. Yet, years after his vocal outburst, Annie sent money for Donny and his children upon Margaret's request. Regardless, if Donny knew the actual source of the gifts, he never showed gratitude for them. Annie was surprised by how relieved she felt when Donny chose to disconnect from her.

This time, Annie left Memphis with a bit more anxiety and concerns. She couldn't understand the disregard and hatred her siblings displayed toward her—even after her mother's reassuring comments to her, "Annie you are a lot like your father. You take care of your business, and your health and body. I don't know why your sisters and brothers act the way they do towards you. Some have had the same opportunities as you and some had more. And you all made your own choices in life. Annie, you've done nothing wrong."

CHAPTER 34

Teaching

Annie accepted a faculty position in business at a college about twenty miles outside of Sacramento, where she taught accounting and other business classes. She was the only black person in the business division and she was also the only one that had a doctorate. That didn't bother her and she believed everyone was comfortable around her.

The student population consisted of mostly Native American and White harvest workers. Annie's students liked and respected her and she enjoyed teaching and working with them immensely. One of the most memorable gifts Annie received from one of her students was a small piece of brick. The student had visited East Germany and participated in the demolition of the Berlin Wall.

Annie felt very welcomed by her students and faculty, but she gradually became aware, through subtle insults and undermining, that one of her coworkers, Bob, had issues with her working there. Bob was a very short, White man who also taught accounting. As a peer review process, Bob came to Annie's class to observe her teaching style. Bob's review had nothing kind to say. On a few occasions, Bob waited until there were other faculty members present when he would "kiddingly" say something insulting to or about Annie.

Finally, Annie got fed up with Bob's meanness. She didn't need an audience to let him know that she wanted him to stop his bad behavior. She knocked on his office door and entered.

"Bob, it appears that you have major issues with me. Get over it. I am not going anywhere until I'm ready to go. You and I are very different people, and we have very different teaching

135

styles. I don't want to be like you, so stop trying to make that happen. We should work together and get along. Have a nice day."

Just before Annie closed his office door to return to her office, she saw Bob's face turn red. However, from that day forward, he acted much kinder toward Annie throughout her tenure.

CHAPTER 35

Come This Far by Faith

The following year, during the summer, Margaret graciously accepted an air ticket from Annie to come to Sacramento for a visit. Annie wanted to spend quality time with her mother and had planned as many outings as Margaret could handle.

At sixty-nine-years old, Margaret was a bit fragile. Several of her sisters and a brother's children were in California and she looked forward to seeing them. Annie gave a party at her house and invited all the relatives, even those that lived in L.A. attended. Margaret hadn't seen most of her nieces and nephews since her father's funeral, in 1971. She enjoyed the wonderful activities that Annie had planned.

Margaret's youngest sister, Aunt Olivia, still lived in the same house that Annie lived in when she first moved to California. She and Uncle Larry had divorced and one of her sons lived with her. Annie drove Margaret down to the Bay Area to see her sister and other relatives.

Aunt Olivia and Margaret embraced one another and tears began to flow from all eyes. It had been years since Margaret had seen her baby sister. Aunt Olivia had informed some of the other relatives in the Bay Area of Margaret's visit and the gathering was a wonderful turnout. Margaret cried with joy throughout her stay. She and Olivia belted out a couple of gospel hymnals that melted the hearts of all.

Annie and Margaret slept overnight at her Aunt Olivia's house. The next day, Annie drove Margaret across the bay bridge to San Francisco. They visited the Fisherman Wharf and walked in several of the stores. One store they entered was a candy shop.

Margaret's eyes lit up like a child's. Every candy you could think of was there. Margaret began to sample some of the candies in the barrels. Then, she began to put some in her purse.

"Mother, you can't do that, it's not free." Margaret emptied her purse and then, Annie gently led her mother out the door. They laughed about it over the years.

They took a ferry to tour Alcatraz Island. Margaret wasn't too impressed with the prison but was thrilled to be there and to share the history. After the tour, she mentioned to Annie that she usually didn't care for boats but was amazed that she enjoyed the ride.

They stopped in China Town to have something to eat. Margaret had gotten chilly from the cool breezes, so she ordered some Wonton soup before her main meal. Then, she had pork fried rice and mixed vegetables. Annie ordered a chicken dish and vegetables.

After eating, Annie drove to an area that gave Margaret a close view of the Golden Gate Bridge.

"It is beautiful and very red—why didn't they paint it gold?" Margaret asked.

Annie just laughed and drove back to Aunt Olivia's house.

They stayed up a little late that night and shared stories and laughter. Margaret and Olivia belted out a beautiful hymnal, "Amazing Grace." Annie was amazed at how strong her mother's voice had remained. The duet was astounding, chills filled Annie's body.

Annie got up early the next morning and she and Margaret drove to Sacramento. Margaret had agreed to sing a solo at Annie's church. The choir rehearsal was the following day. When they arrived at Annie's house, Margaret laid down for a nap and Annie started to cook.

The next morning, Margaret got up early and made breakfast. Rick enjoyed the breakfast and left for work. Annie graded student assignments, while Margaret watched her soap operas.

Later that afternoon, Annie took Margaret to the pharmacy to refill a prescription, and then they drove to a newly built church for the choir rehearsal. Annie had worked closely with the church committee to oversee the construction of the new church. It was a long process, but the church turned out beautifully.

Everyone present welcomed Margaret and accommodated her with her song selection. Annie played her flute along with the pianist, who was much more skilled than her. They repeated the song a few times until everyone was comfortable with it.

On Sunday morning, Margaret wore a choir robe and sat with the choir. Annie had brought a camcorder and tripod to capture the moment. The pastor sat in the pulpit and the church was almost full.

The pianist, and Annie on the flute, played the introduction and on cue, Margaret and the choir stood up. Her voice resonated with a beautiful and heart-wrenching melody of the gospel "We Come This Far by Faith."

Annie would never forget the memory of her mother and her angelic voice that reached the hearts of those who were present.

Margaret stayed a few more days before she returned to Memphis. Annie knew she had to make plans to see her mother and father again soon.

CHAPTER 36

Jamaica

Rick introduced Annie to his friends, Carlos, and his wife, Sue. Both worked in state law enforcement. Carlos was Black and Mexican and his wife, Sue, was White. He was several years older than she, and they were an attractive couple. Shortly after they met, everyone decided to take a seven-day vacation to Jamaica.

The trip started exciting, but no one had prepared for the significant cultural difference when it came to time and patience. Once they flew into Montego Bay, they had to catch a shuttle to the hotel. They gathered their entire luggage and placed them on the back of the shuttle. Each of them mounted the shuttle and found seats. Everyone talked and laughed while waiting on the driver. After an hour, still no driver. By this time, Carlos was upset. About twenty minutes later, the driver finally showed up and sat behind the wheel. The driver didn't drive, he just sat there. Carlos had had enough.

"Let's go—now!! We have been sitting here for over an hour!" Carlos shouted at the driver.

Annie, Rick, Sue, and the other passengers looked on. The driver showed no expression and just sat there. About ten minutes later, he cranked up the shuttle and drove to the hotel. Carlos soon learned that shouting was not effective in Jamaica.

The two couples spent a day in Montego Bay and toured some of the sights. The next day they headed to Ocho Rios, where they stayed for four days. Annie loved the outdoors, but she wasn't a strong swimmer and didn't like to swim. The three others stayed either in the ocean or in the hotel's pool, which had a view of the beautiful ocean. However, during the tour of Dunn's River Falls,

Annie took a dip into the falls with a "fyne" young Jamaican man, who worked at the falls. It was a fun experience, but it took Annie hours to get her hair back in order.

Carlos and Sue went on a scuba diving adventure. Rick jogged on the beaches. Annie made up for the lack of daytime activity when they all got together and met for dinner and dancing. She stayed on the dancefloor. Some local people taught her a few of the latest dances.

On the way back to Montego Bay, was a one-night stop at St. Ann's Bay. The next day, Annie had fun watching the dolphins at Dolphin Cove. The weather throughout the trip was perfect. After a tasty lunch, everyone packed up for the trip back to Montego Bay and then to the US.

Carlos had his camcorder rolling most of the time during the vacation and captured some special moments of the trip. The couples got along wonderfully and they remained close friends.

CHAPTER 37

Less Secure

Life was good for Annie and Rick. They got along pretty well. Rick was a calm person. He had never hit Annie, nor had he cursed or shouted at her or called her ugly names. Rick never questioned any of her decisions and seemed always encouraging. Annie thought of him as someone she would spend the rest of her life with. Yet, she recalled a few disturbing incidents between them that made her feel less secure.

The first incident was when she was selling her house in the Bay Area. There was a problem with the buyer and Annie needed some legal advice. She asked Rick about it. Rick simply dismissed Annie.

"I don't want to get involved," Rick told Annie.

"I'm just asking you for advice, not for you to represent me." Annie pleaded.

"I'd rather not." Rich insisted.

Annie hired an attorney to handle the matter. As the result, the attorney took all the proceeds from the sale of the property as his payment for services. Annie pleaded with the attorney to give her some of the money, but in the end, Annie didn't get a penny from the sale.

About a month after that incident, Annie discovered four legal letters on the kitchen counter, ready to be mailed out. It was addressed to Rick's ex-wife and he was representing her in a legal matter. Annie screamed for Rick to come to the kitchen. He rushed out because he had never heard Annie yell.

"Yeah, what's up?"

"What is this? You represent your ex-wife and you can't advise me." Annie shouted, waving the letters.

142

"What are you doing with those?"

"I'll show you what I'm doing!"

Annie started ripping the letters. Just as Rick rushed over to her to take them from her, Whitney ran into the room.

"You better not touch my mother," Whitney told Rick.

"I'm okay, Whitney," Annie assured her and continued to tear up the letters.

Rick grabbed what was left of the letters and walked away.

The second incident occurred when Annie was away in Memphis. She had called Rick for a couple of days and was not able to reach him. Annie caught an earlier flight back to Sacramento and took a cab to their house. It was a Sunday evening and Rick wasn't home. Annie decided to sleep in the guestroom and wait for Rick. She took the cordless phone from her business line with her.

When Rick finally arrived home, Annie heard him go into the bathroom. She called the house phone.

"Hello."

"Hi, Honey, I've been trying to reach you."

"Hi, I've been busy working."

"How was your day today?" Annie asked.

"Oh, I haven't left the house. I've been outside working in the yard… That's probably where I was when you called."

Annie left the bedroom and rushed into the bathroom. Rick was taken off guard. Annie raised her hand and slapped him across the face so hard, that it scared her. She had never hit anyone before. She stepped out of the bathroom and went into the den.

"I'm sorry, I went to Lake Tahoe. I've been gambling all weekend." Rick confessed.

Annie remained silent, she was still in shock from what she had done.

There was a third incident that made Annie question what her husband would do to protect her.

While working on Rick's campaign, Annie met with people who were a part of a nonprofit organization that helped the homeless. They invited Annie to sit on the board as their Treasurer. Annie accepted the nonpaid position. One of the policies was that each board member paid membership dues to help the cause.

One of the board meetings was held at a center. The president asked Annie to report on the membership dues. Annie stood up and made the report on who paid and who didn't. There was only one person who had not paid anything. Annie attempted to walk back to her seat, when a man about six-feet-two, brown skin, and medium built, rushed over to Annie and pushed her against the wall. It happened so fast and unexpectedly, Annie screamed.

"Are you trying to embarrass me?" The man shouted at Annie.

He had both of Annie's arms pinned against the wall. A few men jumped up and tried to pull the man off of Annie.

"Let her go, man. Are you crazy?" They finally pulled him off.

Two of the guys walked the man outside.

"Do you want to call the police?" The president of the board asked.

"I want to talk with my husband first," Annie replied, tearful.

Annie rushed home and called Rick who was out of town for his job. He was expected to return the following day.

"I was at the meeting and this man attacked me. They had to pull him off of me. I have bruises on my arm." She told Rick.

"He doesn't know who he is messing with," Rick responded.

The next day when Rick came home, it was as if he and Annie had not had the discussion. Annie showed him the bruises on her arm. Rick had very little to say and went by his business. He did not want to get involved in the matter. Annie believed that Rick was more concerned about his political career than her well-being. She did not make a police report and the matter was never discussed again.

These incidents made Annie feel less secure in her marriage.

CHAPTER 38

Dream Home

The following year, Annie and Rick decided to build their dream house outside of Sacramento. They placed their current house on the market and found the right location and design. It was located in a small town, about twelve miles north of where they had lived. Annie decided to work closely with the contractors. She selected light and airy colors, hardwood floors, cabinetry, tiles, and carpets.   The house was located at the end of a cul-de-sac with only about nine houses in the area. It sat on a fenced one-and-a-half-acre lot, 4,500 square feet, two-story dwelling, two master bedrooms, and three additional bedrooms. Also, it had four full baths, a living area, four car garage, a very large kitchen, 2 large dens, a large living room, and a formal dining room. In addition, it had a fully regulated tennis court, three balconies held by large pillars, two wooden decks, one with a spa, a concrete patio, and a clay roof.

The new house was completed by the following spring 1990. The neighbors were very friendly and helpful in getting them settled into the area. Annie and Rick were the only people of color in the area, but it didn't seem to bother anyone.

During that time, Whitney graduated from the Community College. It was so gratifying for Annie to see her daughter walk across the stage and be presented with an associate degree by her husband, Rick, who was still the President of the Board of Trustees.

Whitney started to work at a full-time job that provided credit for her bachelor's degree program. She moved into an apartment near the university.

CHAPTER 39

Concerns

$\mathbf{N}$**ow** that Annie and Rick had made a major investment together, Annie became concerned about a few incidents.

Before they moved into the new house, Annie had been getting several hang-up phone calls late at night and early in the morning.

A couple of times, while at work, Annie removed notes from her car. Each time they were maps with her home address circled. Frighten by it, she shared the information with Rick.

"It's probably an ex-convict who is upset because he didn't get parole when he wanted to." He told Annie.

"How do they know where I work? Shouldn't we call the police?"

"No, I'll take care of it."

Annie felt confident that Rick would take care of the problem.

About a week later, the ringing of the phone woke Annie at about one a.m. and the person hung up. Annie looked across the bed and Rick was gone. She got up and searched the house. Rick was nowhere in the house. Annie sat in the chair and waited. Soon Rick came in the front door carrying a pillow and her thirty-two caliber gun.

"Where have you been? What have you done?" She asked.

Rick was very surprised to see Annie up and waiting.

"Augh. I wanted to test out the gun, just in case we have any problems."

"Are you expecting to have problems?" Annie asked.

"No, just wanted to be prepared."

He walked past Annie, laid the pillow on the couch, and placed the gun in the closet. Annie noticed gunpowder on the pillow. She regretted buying the gun.

Strangely, the hang-up phone calls stopped. The matter caused Annie some concerns, but she didn't dwell on it. She had rather thought that her marriage was going in a positive direction.

CHAPTER 40

Good Life

Despite that Annie and Rick had made a major investment together, Annie became concerned about a few incidents.

Before they moved into the new house, Annie had been getting several hang-up phone calls late at night and early in the morning.

A couple of times, while at work, Annie removed notes from her car. Each time they were maps with her home address circled. Frighten by it, she shared the information with Rick.

"It's probably an ex-convict who is upset because he didn't get parole when he wanted to." He told Annie.

"How do they know where I work? Shouldn't we call the police?"

"No, I'll take care of it."

Annie felt confident that Rick would take care of the problem.

About a week later, the ringing of the phone woke Annie at about one a.m. and the person hung up. Annie looked across the bed and Rick was gone. She got up and searched the house. Rick was nowhere in the house. Annie sat in the chair and waited. Soon Rick came in the front door carrying a pillow and her thirty-two caliber gun.

"Where have you been? What have you done?" She asked.

Rick was very surprised to see Annie up and waiting.

"Augh. I wanted to test out the gun, just in case we have any problems."

"Are you expecting to have problems?" Annie asked.

"No, just wanted to be prepared."

He walked past Annie, laid the pillow on the couch, and placed the gun in the closet. Annie noticed gunpowder on the pillow. She regretted buying the gun.

Strangely, the hang-up phone calls stopped. The matter caused Annie some concerns, but she didn't dwell on it. She had rather thought that her marriage was going in a positive direction.

Chapter 41

Darkness Surfaces

Early one cold morning in March 1992, Annie received a phone call.

"Hello."

"Hello, Ms. White, this is Detective Anthony Ritz."

"Yes."

"I'm calling you about a matter you might not be aware of."

"What matter?"

"Do you own a handgun?"

"Yes. It's registered."

"We believe it has been involved in an incident with Ms. Marie Walker, who your husband has been involved with."

"I don't understand."

"Well, we have been investigating her complaint for quite a while. Mr. White has been harassing and stalking her."

"This is the first I've heard of this."

"We are going to get him. Mr. White shot your gun at her. He thinks we aren't watching and listening. But it's a matter of time before we get him."

"I'll talk with my husband."

"I understand, I will call you in a couple of days." The detective concluded.

Annie was paralyzed with confusion, disappointment, and anger. She didn't understand anything that was going on, but she did remember the night Rick used her gun.

She had some final preparations to complete for her eleven o'clock class that morning. But she didn't know how she was going to teach when she couldn't focus. Yet, Annie managed to get through her class without any problems.

Annie was home when Rick arrived that evening. She allowed him to get settled in and eat. When Rick finished, he turned on the TV and sat on the sofa with a glass of brandy.

"I received a phone call from a Detective Ritz early this morning. Do you know him?" Annie asked Rick.

"I don't think so."

"Well, he said that you have been stalking and harassing Marie."

Rick got nervous and took a sip of his brandy.

"I'm not stalking her. She was the one that was calling and hanging up on you."

"You told me it was an ex-convict."

"I know, but she made me mad. She wanted me to endorse her for a state election and I refused. So she started with the hang-up phone calls."

"You shot my gun at her. Who are you?"

"She made me mad," Rick said in defense.

"Is she the same woman that was throwing bricks at your door when we begin dating?"

"Yeah."

"If you don't quit what you are doing, two things will happen. One, you will be going to jail, because they want you there, and said that they are going to get you. And number two, most importantly, I will leave you and divorce you. So whatever you are doing, you need to stop."

Annie didn't like the darkness she discovered but felt hopeful that Rick would change and work on securing their marriage.

CHAPTER 42

1993

Whitney graduated from the university in the spring of 1992 and received a bachelor's degree. She decided to invite her father to the graduation ceremonies. They had not spoken to one another for over four years. She moved out of her apartment into Annie's home. Rick, VanLila, and the children also attended the ceremonies. Annie hosted a graduation party for Whitney. It was a nice turnout, however, her father did not attend.

Shortly after her graduation, twenty-three-year-old Whitney walked into her mother's bedroom. Annie was alone while Rick was at work.

"Hey, Mom, I need to talk." They both sat on the bed.

"Thank you for everything you have done for me. Things have always come easy for me. I have not had it hard at all. I have decided to move to Memphis to spend some time with Daddy and other relatives."

Annie was surprised and confused by Whitney's decision and felt that there was much more to what she had said. Why would anyone want a harder life? But Annie respected Whitney's decision.

Shortly afterward, Whitney informed Annie that she would be a grandmother by early February of the next year, 1993. Annie was stunned, but she knew that Whitney was a strong independent woman and wanted a child. Annie was happy for her daughter.

When Whitney was seven months pregnant, she flew back to California for a baby shower hosted by Annie. The shower was very nice. There were games and a lot of food and drinks. Whitney knew she was having a boy and took her Great Aunt Olivia's suggestion and named him Fowler McGwin Hightower-Dalton. A long name for a little guy, but it represented three generations of his maternal family. Annie had met his father only on two occasions.

Annie had planned to fly to Memphis in time for his birth. But little Fowler came ten days before Annie reached Memphis. He was a handsome baby with a full head of kinky reddish hair, like his grandmother Annie. Whitney took pictures of Annie holding Fowler. Annie felt so blessed to have a healthy grandson.

Floyd also visited Whitney's home while Annie was there. He was cordial and respectful.

"Hi, Annie, I see you have let your hair grow long."

"Yes, I have. How are you, Floyd?"

Annie caught Floyd staring at her as if he was searching to find fault in her.

Annie was in excellent physical condition, slim, and tight. However, sometime later, Whitney had something to tell her mother:

"Daddy said that you have changed and that something was wrong with your eyes. I told him that you are over forty. What did he expect?"

Annie wondered why Whitney told her only the negative things her father or others said about her.

****

Annie visited her mother while she was in Memphis and they visited Jessie. He was bedridden and unable to sit up. Annie checked him closely and saw that Jessie was soiled. She pushed the button and demanded that someone come and clean her father. When the aide came in, Annie took one of the face cloths and washed her father's face. The cloth was dirty.

155

"Why is my father's face so dirty? This is not acceptable. He needs to be cleaned properly and regularly. This is just nasty," Annie told the aide.

Annie put some more soap on the cloth and started to wash her father's armpit. Jessie couldn't talk, but he squealed. Annie flinched—she could see that Jessie's skin was so thin and it hurt him to be touched.

Margaret had been sitting in the chair next to the wall with tears in her eyes. Annie continued to watch and assist the aide until Jessie was cleaned and properly dressed.

After visiting Jessie, Annie and Margaret stopped at Barnhill's. Margaret wasn't very hungry that day, but it gave them a chance to talk.

"Have you ever thought about moving back here?" Margaret asked Annie.

"No, I haven't. Besides, I haven't gotten over the fear of some of these southern folks and their mean behavior."

"The south is really a beautiful place and it isn't nearly as bad as it used to be. You should try to visit some of it and check it out."

"I will think about it."

"I have a friend in Mississippi, her name is Ramona. We met when Jessie and I first got married. She married Jessie's best friend who was also in the Army. We used to go out together and dance. She never had children and now she is a foster mom. She keeps a few children at a time. We can start there and then, we can drive to other states like Alabama, Georgia, and the Carolinas— maybe Florida, too. We can use Jessie's car, it's still in good shape"

"Wow, that sounds good. I will give it some serious thought."

****

While Annie was still in Memphis, Floyd's sister, Ruby, invited Annie to a family gathering at one of their twin sister's homes. Annie accepted the invitation and stopped by. Several of Floyd's relatives were present, all of whom were very happy to see Annie. Although she was divorced from Floyd, Annie always felt close to his kinfolks.

Some time during that visit, Annie stepped outside for some fresh air. She noticed a well-dressed businessman walking in the neighborhood and stopping to talk to people. His face seemed familiar to her. He soon approached the house where Annie stood. A few of her in-laws approached the man with smiles and greeted him. They invited him in for some food. But he declined. He was campaigning for a reelection position in the city.

"Hi, Mark Rooks," Annie said. She remembered who the man was. The memories filled her mind.

Mark Rooks, was the nephew of a well-known judge in Memphis. The judge was nationally known during the civil rights movement. Mark was the same age as Annie. Although they did not attend the same high school, Mark spent a lot of time in her neighborhood and at her school activities. She would see him with some of her classmates. Annie thought of him as a nice person but felt no romantic interest. They would always say hello.

At the end of Annie's junior year, a few classmates talked about getting together for a snack and maybe music and dancing.

157

Annie was still on the campus talking with her close friend, Leola when Mark Rooks drove up in his car, and his friend, Ben, sat in the passenger's seat.

"Hey, Annie. You want a lift to go get something to eat?"

"Hey, Mark, let me check with Leola first." Annie turned to talk with Leola.

"It will have to be quick, Annie. I have other plans." Leola said.

Annie and Leola got in the backseat of the car and Mark drove away.

Mark stopped at Ben's house about four miles from the school.

"We need to pick up a couple of items before we eat," Mark said. He and Ben stepped out of the car. Mark looked through the rearview window.

"Can I get you anything?" He asked the girls.

"No, thank you," Leola said.

"I could use a glass of water." Annie requested.

"Come on in and get it on ice," Mark replied.

"Are you coming, Leola?" Annie asked.

"No."

Annie hopped out of the car and went into the house. She soon realized that Ben's parents were not at home. Ben showed her to the kitchen and poured a glass of water. Annie drank the water and walked to the door.

Ben went behind Annie and grabbed her arms and held them tightly with Annie's back against him.

"What are you doing, Ben? Let me go!" She pleaded.

Mark walked up to Annie without a word and began to feel her breast. Annie immediately saw the reality of the situation and went into her "combat mode." She kicked and screamed. She was able to free herself for a moment when Mark grabbed her. She pushed him and fought back, hitting him on the arms and face.

"Nobody hits me!" Mark shouted at Annie.

He raised his hand and slapped Annie across her face with great force. Annie screamed louder. Ben grabbed her again.

"Let me go! Let me go!" Annie screamed.

Annie was not going to let this be easy for them. She continued to kick and scream.

"Let that crazy girl go, Ben!" Mark shouted.

Ben freed her arms. Annie ran out the door and to the car where Leola was still waiting.

"Let's go, Leola. Let's go now!"

"Why—what happened?" Leola got out of the car.

They walked four miles back to their neighborhood.

Twenty-five years later, in 1993, Mark Rooks stood before Annie as a politician.

"Do you know who I am, Mark?"

"Hi, you look very familiar, did you go to Melrose? I use to hang out there with my buddies."

"Do you have a moment? I would like a few words in private with you," Annie asked nicely.

"Sure." Mark agreed.

They walked from the house onto the sidewalk.

"I am Annie Fowler. Many years ago when I was seventeen, you and your "buddy" Ben, roughed me up and attempted to ra..."

"Say no more, Annie, I was a terrible and spoiled teenager. I felt entitled to everything. I have worked hard to become a better person. I am very sorry for the pain I caused you. I wish there was something that I could do to erase those bad memories from your mind. You did not deserve what I did. I'm very sorry and I ask you to please forgive me." Mark looked at Annie with sincere empathy and regret.

Annie wasn't sure if Mark's words were from his heart or from a skilled politician with the ability to sway. But she was certain that Mark was the second person that ever apologized to her for any evil deeds against her. Frankie had been the first.

"I forgive you, Mark, and maybe one day, if I ever see you again, I will look at you without pain."

****

Annie returned to California and continued her routine of teaching her classes, doing church activities, playing tennis, and playing the flute.

Not too long after Annie returned home, she was awakened early in the morning by a phone call. Rick had just left for work.

"Hello."

"Hello, this is Detective Ritz. Did you just call Marie Walker?"

"Who? No. Why would I?"

"Someone from your number called her not too long ago and hung up. We have a wiretap on her phone and it showed the number came from your phone."

"I just woke up," Annie said.

"Is your husband there?"

"I'm sure he's left for work."

"Well, we will get to the bottom of this."

Annie realized that Rick had made the call before he left for work. What bothered her was Rick's disregard for implicating her in the mess he created. First, using her gun to shoot at his ex-girlfriend and now made more harassing phone calls from the house. Annie had enough. She picked up the phone and called her mother.

"Hello, Mother. How are you doing?"

"I'm fine and you?" Margaret asked.

"Let's take that trip we talked about this summer. Plan to take at least two weeks or more."

"That sounds great to me," Margaret said.

****

Meanwhile, Annie thought a lot about what Floyd and Whitney had said about her eyes, earlier that year. At forty-three-years old, she had never thought about her eyes as unpleasant to look at. But their statements really bothered her and made her feel a bit insecure when talking with people. She constantly, critically examined the details of her eyes. Immediately after the spring semester ended and before her trip through the Deep South, Annie schedule surgery to have her lower lids repaired.

Annie didn't ever see a noticeable difference after the surgery. She later had regrets because instead of the fine lines, she now had permanent scars.

****

When Annie made her airline reservations to Memphis, she discovered that she had a three-hour layover in St. Louis. She thought it would be a perfect time to see her dear friend, Valencia, who she hadn't seen in twenty years. Valencia was still living in St. Louis and they had periodically talked on the phone and via emails. Annie contacted Valencia, and they agreed to meet at the airport.

Annie made her way to the gate to meet Valencia. Annie sat down and waited anxiously to see her friend.

"Girrrl, you are still looking good." Annie was very familiar with the voice. She turned around and shouted.

"Valencia!!!"

Annie ran toward Valencia and gave her a tight long embrace. Tears flowed from Annie's eyes.

"It is so good to see you, Valencia. It's been too long!"

"Yes, it has. It is wonderful to see you, too!"

Except for a few added pounds, Valencia had not changed. She was cute and still talked fast, had the same unique laugh and a big beautiful smile.

They sat down to reminisce and gave a few updates on their lives. They promised to keep in touch more often. Annie was relieved that they never spoke about Dmitri and the status of his case. She did not want to relive the traumatic events of his death.

Time seemed to pass quickly for Annie, she wished she had more time. But she had to walk several gates for her connection. She and Valencia hugged and gave farewells. Annie could never forget her friend's compassion when she and her daughter became homeless in St. Louis.

It was only June of 1993 and several unexpected events had occurred in Annie's life. But that year had many more marvels to come.

CHAPTER 43

Deep South Tour

It was Annie's second visit to Memphis in 1993. She arrived in time to get Jessie's old Chevrolet tuned up and the oil changed. She and Margaret packed up the car with the anticipation of being away for a while. Annie was somewhat nervous about the trip because she had never been south of Memphis. With faith that God would keep them safe, Annie put her foot on the paddle and they began the Deep South tour. She had several road maps of every southern state they had planned to travel to, which were Mississippi, Alabama, Georgia, South Carolina, and Florida. Annie had planned to drive only during daylight, sleep only at Comfort Inn Hotels, and eat only at Margaret's favorite Shoney's Restaurant.

Their first stop was a six-hour drive to Meridian, Mississippi. Annie drove south on Highway 55 to Highway 20 East.

"Look out for Smoky," Margaret told Annie.

She was referring to the highway patrol. Annie didn't want to be stopped in the south. She thought that would be the worst that could happen to her and her mother.

They arrived at Margaret's lifelong friend, Ramona's house. The large building was old but well maintained. Ramona came out to the car to greet Margaret and Annie. Margaret cried as she and Ramona hugged. They had not seen each other for more than thirty years. Although Ramona was a few years older than Margaret, she looked much younger and moved much faster. Ramona was about five-feet-nine with long salt and pepper hair, a beautifully smooth, creamy brown complexion, and a very nice smile. Ramona hugged Annie and told her that she remembered when Annie was first born.

Ramona showed Margaret and Annie where they would be sleeping. She gave them a little tour as they walked to their rooms.

163

There were eight bedrooms. The inside of the building needed work, but it was livable and clean. Annie relaxed while Ramona and Margaret caught up.

Annie and Margaret spent two nights with Ramona. They rose early to drive five hours to Birmingham, Alabama. Annie drove by some of the historical locations and continued to drive to Montgomery. They stopped to eat at Shoney's before they drove by the State Capitol building. They also toured the Civil Rights Memorial.

It was a long and very active day, but Annie continued to drive to Atlanta, Georgia, where they rented a hotel room. They got up early for breakfast and then drove by the State Capitol. They spent most of the day at the Underground Atlanta. The mall was booming then. There were many minority business owners and various types of entities. Annie and Margaret ate lunch and cruised around the mall. Margaret bought a couple of items and sat on a bench to rest. She became tearful when she learned that the bench she sat on was where African slaves stood to be auctioned off to a slave owner, not too long ago.

After a wonderful day, Annie and Margaret went back to the hotel for a good night's sleep. They rose early to drive six hours to Charleston, South Carolina.

Annie drove from Memphis to Augusta, Georgia, before they stopped to eat at Shoney's. At almost seventy-three-years old, Margaret was a trooper. She took her meds and she did well during the travel.

When they arrived in Charleston, South Carolina, they were both a little worn out and relaxed in the hotel. Later, Annie went out a moment to survey the hotel and inquire about interesting tours.

They decided to drive by some of the local places including the "Old Slave Mart" and the "Magnolia Plantation and Gardens."

She also drove down "Rainbow Row" to view the large and colorful houses. Annie continued to drive, and about three hours later, she reached Savannah, Georgia.

The first thing Annie thought about when she arrived in Savannah was the movie, "Gone with the Wind." She had watched the movie at least a dozen times and read the six-hundred-page novel. In the story, Scarlett O'Hara made it appear that Savannah was the only place to be. It was a very nice city.

Annie stopped by KFC for Margaret to get a meal and something to drink. She then drove to Forsyth Park and parked the car. She helped Margaret out of the car and found a bench near the large flowing fountain. They sat down and enjoyed watching the children playing, tennis players, joggers, and people strolling along. The weather was perfect—not too hot and with a gentle breeze. Annie walked awhile and Margaret walked as much as she could.

After the visit to the park, Annie drove through a couple of historic districts and found a hotel. The next trip was to Annie's youngest sister, Janis, who lived in Jacksonville, Florida. She and her husband were in the Navy and had two adorable children, a ten-year-old boy, and an eight-year-old girl.

When Annie and Margaret arrived, Janis ran to Margaret to give her a tight hug and kiss. Janis was happy to see both her mother and her sister. She got Annie and Margaret settled in and later, they ate lunch. Everyone talked and laughed about the past and enjoyed each other.

The next day, Janis took Margaret and Annie for a tour of the city. Most memorable were the River Walk and the Landing which were very nice places. They had a wonderful lunch while updating each other on their lives. Margaret was again in tears. She thought about their plan to drive the next morning to Tallahassee.

Before the trip, Annie had shared her Deep South travel plans with her dear friend, Kathy. Kathy had suggested to Annie that she travel to Tallahassee to visit one of the universities there. She told Annie to specifically visit the economics and business divisions and to say hello to one of her professional acquaintances.

Annie agreed to make the visits, besides, she had never been in the state of Florida.

When Annie arrived in Tallahassee, she found a hotel off of I-10 and got her mother settled in. She drove to the university to first talk with Kathy's friend, Dr. Cobs, who was in the economics department. He warmly welcomed Annie and shared some information about the university and the city. He walked Annie over to the business division where Annie waited to see the dean. Annie had no idea what to expect, what she was going to say to the dean, or why she was even there.

The Dean's assistant showed Annie to Dr. Norton's office. When Annie entered, a woman, about five-feet-two, with a short reddish afro, and a beautiful smile, extended her hand to Annie.

"Hi, Dr. Hightower, I'm Sylvia Norton, come on in."

"Hello, Dr. Norton. Thank you so much for seeing me on such short notice. It is a pleasure meeting you."

"What brings you here today?"

"I am touring the south with my mother, and a friend asked me to drop by the university to say hello and to tour the campus."

"That is so nice of you to spend some quality time with your mother, where do you live?"

"I leave in northern California, my mother lives in Memphis."

Dr. Norton asked Annie about her education and work experience. She and Annie hit it off immediately. They talked about family and where they grew up.

"I would be happy to have one of our graduate students show you around the business school and the campus."

"That would be so kind," Annie replied.

"If you could come back tomorrow, I would also love to invite you as a guest of our "Close Up" where our graduate students would interview you. I'm sure they would learn a lot from you. Do you have a resume?"

"No, but I could probably get one by tomorrow."

After the discussion with the dean, Annie called her mother to check on her. Based on the steep hills and steps on the campus, Annie thought it might have been too challenging for her mother. So Annie suggested that her mother order room service for food.

A student escorted Annie to a campus shuttle. The student, who was professionally dressed and articulate, described each building and gave a little history of the university. After an hour, the tour was completed and Annie headed back to the hotel.

Margaret had gotten a lot of rest and looked refreshed. So, Annie gave her mother an update on her unexpected day. She had not brought any interviewing clothes, and the only suit she had with her was bright yellow. The "Close Up" was at ten o'clock the next morning. Annie called Rick to also update him and to ask him to fax a copy of her resume to the hotel.

After dropping off her resume at the dean's office, Annie walked into the room where tables were set up in a U-shape. Annie immediately felt intimidated by the students who were all dressed in navy-blue and dark gray suits. Her bright yellow suit was the focus point.

Annie stood at the podium located in the center. The students raised their hands and Annie randomly selected one of them. The student asked Annie a question, and as soon as Annie answered the question, all the students raised their hands again. This went on for about a dozen questions. When the interview was over, the students thanked Annie for coming. Annie was very impressed with the graduate students and the business program. Another student escorted Annie back to the dean's office.

Annie was greeted again by Dr. Norton's big smile.

"What did you think of the Close Up?"

"The students were outstanding! I hope I did just as well?"

"I'm certain you did."

"I've had a chance to look at your resume. It's very impressive. Have you ever thought about moving here?"

"Thank you. No, I haven't, what did you have in mind?"

"Come and go with me, I want you to meet a couple of people."

Dr. Norton led Annie to another office. She introduced Annie to the Chair of the Department, Dr. Bornes. They talked for a moment and went to another office. Dr. Norton introduced Annie to another faculty member. They talked for a few minutes. Annie and the dean walked back to her office.

"I think you would fit in very well in this program. We have a position available that you should consider."

Dr. Norton offered Annie a salary that was a few dollars more than she was earning. With the cost of living difference between California and Florida, it was a significant increase.

"After such a generous offer and consideration, I greatly appreciate everything. This has been unexpected. May I have a little time to give your offer more consideration and to get back to you?" Annie said.

"Certainly, but keep in mind that the contract date begins August 6th, that's not too far away."

"I understand. Thank you so much for this opportunity. I will get back to you as soon as I return to California."

"You are quite welcome. I hope you decide to join us. Continue to enjoy your travels with your mother. I wish you a safe trip back." Dr. Norton said.

Annie rushed back to the hotel where Margaret was packed and waiting for her to drive to Mobile, Alabama. Annie hopped on I-10 and drove for about four hours when they found another hotel in Mobile. Annie didn't want to do anything but rest, but first, she found a Shoney's for Margaret. They sat and talked for a while.

"They offered me a faculty position with the university," Annie told her mother.

"Oh, my goodness. That is wonderful. What are you going to do?" Margaret asked.

"I'm not sure. It sounds exciting. I love what they are doing in school. Some of my best experiences have been with minority organizations such as my high school, a nonprofit entity, and a CPA firm."

"I guess you have a lot to think about."

"Yeah, I will also have to talk it over with Rick."

They went back to the hotel and watched a movie together. Annie checked to see what places they could visit before they headed north, back to Ramona's house in Meridian.

Annie and Margaret took their time getting up and packed. Margaret decided to eat a piece of chicken and a biscuit that she saved from the night before. She also drank a cup of instant coffee. Annie took the bags to the car and checked out of the hotel.

Annie drove downtown and then through the Oakleigh Historic District. The houses were huge and eye-catching. She also drove by the Immaculate Conception Cathedral. But Annie parked the car to walk into the National African American Archives and Museum. The artifacts and furniture were amazing.

After the tour of the museum, Annie drove the two-and-a-half-hour drive back to Meridian. Ramona was waiting for Margaret and Annie and had lunch prepared for them. Margaret shared the travel stories with Ramona while Annie relaxed.

The next morning, Annie and Margaret had a quick breakfast with Ramona before they drove back to Memphis. It was a very hot day, but surprisingly, when they arrived at the house, the inside of the house was cool without air conditioning. Margaret explained that the neighbor's tall trees that hung over the house and the property helped to keep the house cool. Samantha had moved back home with Margaret. The three of them had dinner together and went down memory lane. There was a lot of laughter.

While in Memphis, Annie took Margaret to visit Jessie. She also visited Whitney and baby Fowler.

One amazing outcome of Annie's incredible tour of the south was her overwhelming fear of the Deep South had disappeared.

As Annie contemplated her life, she thought about what had happened in Tallahassee and wondered if it was fate. Annie had a lot to think about and a major decision to make about her future. It seemed to her, that at every major turning point of her life, God placed her mother as the initiator. Unknown to Annie, the year 1993 would indeed include more crucial episodes in her life.

CHAPTER 44

Return to the South

Rick picked up Annie from the Airport in mid-July 1993. He hugged her and kissed her.

"How was your trip?" He asked Annie.

"It was very good. How have you been?"

"Good. How are your parents doing?"

"Mother is fine. Daddy is barely holding on."

"Sorry to hear that."

"I was offered a job at the university, it was a total surprise."

"Oh, yeah, what type of job?"

"Assistant Professor in the business division."

"What are you going to do?"

"I thought we could talk about it. Especially, since you've been having a problem."

"What did you have in mind?" He asked Annie.

"Maybe we could move to Florida together. You are eligible to retire from the state and you could practice or teach law at the university."

"That's something to think about?"

"Okay, but I have to give the dean a response pretty soon."

They were silent throughout the remaining drive home.

The next day, Annie made several phone calls. One call was to check out if Tallahassee had a Jaguar dealership. Since there was no dealership, she decided to trade in her Jaguar for another car.

Two days later, Annie received a priority letter from Dr. Norton. It was a letter of offer for the position. She shared the information with Rick.

"What do you think I should do?" She asked Rick.

"Accept it," Rick replied.

Annie was a bit surprised at his unwavering response. She wondered if that was truly an affirmative that he would join her.

Annie exchanged her Jaguar for a Nissan. Rick was surprised, but he understood. She also submitted a letter of resignation to her employer.

****

During the first week of August, Annie and Rick packed the Nissan with only things that Annie would need immediately. She had planned to fly back during the Christmas break for additional items. Rick took a one-week leave from work.

They drove away in the fully packed Nissan on a three-day trip to Tallahassee. Annie was able to find a two-room town apartment near the campus. She thought it would be fine until Rick relocated there and then, they would buy a house.

It was raining when Annie and Rick reached Tallahassee, but it stopped within minutes. They found the apartment and the manager provided Annie with the keys. The small front room was a combination of a living area and a kitchen. The back room was the bedroom with a bathroom. It had a stove and refrigerator but was unfurnished. So Annie and Rick decided to spend the night in a hotel and look for furniture on the following day. Before they left, they unloaded the car and hung up Annie's clothes.

The next day, Annie and Rick found a discount furniture store. They selected a full mattress, box spring, a card table with two folding chairs, and a small two-drawer nightstand. Rick placed the table and chairs in the car. The store delivered the remaining items later the same day. They went to the grocery store and to Sears to purchase a set of eating utensils, a pot, and a skillet.

By the time the food was cooked and eaten, the furniture arrived. It was set up and Annie and Rick settled in. Rick managed to bring along a small TV. The cable was working, so he hooked up the TV and watched sports.

Annie drove Rick to the campus for a tour of her department and the university. The summer term had ended and there weren't any students and faculty in her department. There was staff available to answer some questions. Annie drove Rick to another university's law school to tour the facility and its programs. Rick collected information and seemed to be interested.

The following day, Annie drove Rick to the airport to return to Sacramento. Annie felt something wasn't right between them. During the ride, Annie thought that Rick didn't ask enough questions, especially for someone who was considering relocating to the other side of the country.

CHAPTER 45

Jailed

Before the fall classes began, Annie met with the department chair, Dr. Bornes, who was a nice guy and had worked there for several years. He provided Annie with her teaching assignments, textbooks, and course syllabi. Annie's office was between two other faculty members' offices. She was assigned three classes and some committee work. Annie had taught for over five years, therefore, she felt comfortable with the assignments.

The faculty conference and college meetings provided Annie the opportunity to meet faculty and staff. There were seven new faculty members in Annie's department, which made her feel better about being a newcomer. She befriended several faculty members and staff.

The semester was challenging, but Annie felt very good about the results. She accomplished her expected goals and the students seemed to enjoy her teaching. The dean had briefly observed her teaching style.

"Dr. Hightower, I liked and enjoyed what I saw," she told Annie.

"Thank you so much, I enjoy teaching."

"I see."

****

Annie had talked with Rick about putting their house on the market so that he could move to Florida. She had contacted the same realtor that had sold them the property to make the arrangements.

174

Rick called Annie before the Christmas break and told her that he had moved his son and daughter-in-law into the house and had given them their master bedroom. Annie was furious that he made such a decision without talking with her and because they had agreed to sell the house. In addition, he only charged them less than a third of the mortgage payment.

"I will not be a guest in my own home. And I will not be coming there for the holidays." Annie told Rick.

For the third time in 1993, Annie drove ten hours to Memphis to spend the holidays with her parents, her daughter, and her new grandson. A few of the siblings were also in Memphis during that time. Samantha, Donny, and his son and daughter, Daisy and her daughter, Martha and her son, and Robert Lee were there. Everyone seemed to enjoy each other. Margaret and Samantha cooked a lot of food. As usual, there was a lot of storytelling, jokes, and laughter.

Everyone went to visit Jessie who was awake but very fragile. Annie held his frail hands and each person spoke to him. Jessie could not speak, but he smiled at times.

After the visit with Jessie, Daisy suggested that everyone go downtown for some entertainment. Several of the siblings went to one of the nightclubs located in downtown Memphis. There was live music and singing and dancing. One outstanding group emulated The Temptations.

Despite the dysfunctional behaviors of her children, Margaret was pleased to see her children getting along and having fun together as they ended the year 1993 and began a new year.

So many overwhelming and life-turning events happened to Annie in the year 1993. She was relieved that it was all behind her and she looked forward to a peaceful New Year.

175

****

Annie was happy to return to work in the 1994 spring term. She taught over two-hundred students without an assistant. In addition, she was responsible for a new learning concept method in accounting and was on a few college and university committees. Needless to say, it was a stressful semester.

One evening after work in February, Annie received a call from Rick, who was in tears.

"I was arrested, they handcuffed me, fingerprinted me, and threw me in jail."

"Where are you now?" Annie asked.

"I'm at home. I can't talk anymore. I'll call you tomorrow." Rick hung up the phone.

Annie had never heard Rick in such distress. She felt helpless.

Rick had been arrested for stalking his ex-girlfriend, Marie Walker. Since he was a political figure, the news was on television and in the Sacramento newspaper. Annie and the police had warned Rick, and she tried to protect him by getting him to move with her.

Did he think that he was untouchable? Annie thought.

Annie believed, once again, that "Angel Claudine" had intervened and guided her away from the humiliation that she would have faced if she had remained in Sacramento when her husband was jailed.

CHAPTER 46

Prozac

Annie completed her first year at the university. She felt satisfied with the work that she had accomplished. Annie decided to accept a summer assignment. But, before she could start, she had to make a brief trip to Sacramento to meet with Rick and his attorney.

Fortunately, despite the seriousness of his alleged crime, Rick was able to retire from his state position and keep all of his retirement benefits. When Annie arrived at her house, it didn't feel like home to her. She and Rick were sleeping in one of the other guest rooms while Rick's son and daughter-in-law slept in their master bedroom.

The next day, Annie and Rick met with his attorney. The attorney explained to Annie that his goal was not to go to court. The attorney also told them how much it would cost to proceed with the case.

"I don't have any money so Rick will have to find the funds," Annie told them.

"Can't you use your credit card to pay for some of the cost?" Rick pleaded with Annie.

"No. I suggest you put the house up for sale" Annie said.

Annie had no intentions of providing any financial support to help Rick. He had deceived her and now he wanted her to stand by him.

He made the mess— let him deal with it, Annie thought.

She knew there was much more behind Rick's story that she didn't know and she didn't have the desire to know.

Annie returned to the university, where she loved her work, and took special efforts toward perfection. Dealing with the pressures of work and her marriage had begun to take a toll on her.

177

She wasn't sleeping much and was forgetting to eat. She only slept about three or four hours a night, sometimes not at all. Many mornings she could barely get out of bed and her head ached. She felt extremely tired and experienced severe body aches, tense muscles, and soreness. Annie decided to see a doctor.

After an examination and blood test, Annie's doctor diagnosed her with Anxiety-Depression. Annie's understanding was that her overly stressed condition caused her anxiety which could also lead to depression. Her physical and emotional states were no longer in balance. The doctor prescribed her Prozac.

In a few months, Annie began to feel better. But the side effects included loss of natural emotions and she required more sleep.

During the early stage of taking the Prozac, Annie received a phone call from her dear and close friend, Kathy, who was at a hotel in the area and wanted to see Annie. They hadn't seen one another for years. It was late evening and Annie was already in bed. Annie was in no physical or emotional condition to make the drive. Annie didn't tell Kathy about the meds but told Kathy that she wasn't able to make the drive. Annie felt no empathy for Kathy's disappointment. Kathy became upset with Annie. But soon forgave her.

Not too long after that, a former coworker asked Annie for a letter of recommendation, but she needed it immediately. Annie liked the person and had intended to write the letter. But, somehow under the pressures of her job, it slipped Annie's mind. The coworker moved out of the area and never spoke to Annie again. Normally, Annie would have lost a lot of sleep about her actions. But not with Prozac.

CHAPTER 47

New Roots

It was apparent to Annie that Rick was not ready or had no intentions of leaving Sacramento. He pleaded guilty to the charge of stalking and was placed on probation. He found work in an attorney's office.

After two years in Tallahassee, living in a two-room apartment, Annie decided to purchase a house. She found a newly constructed community about six miles from the campus. Only the concrete foundation had been poured. She signed the purchase contract to complete the house to her specifications.

When summer arrived, Annie went to Sacramento to get furniture. Rick's son and daughter-in-law were still in the house sleeping in Annie's bed. Annie stayed in the guest room.

The day after she arrived, Annie, with Rick's help, packed boxes. The following day, the mover arrived to load the furniture for shipment. There were plenty of furniture items in the house. However, Annie took about half of the furniture including her bed and the baby grand piano. The furniture was shipped to Tallahassee and stored until the construction of her new house was completed.

Annie returned to Tallahassee to oversee the construction of her new house. It was a two-story and 2100 square feet duplex townhome. The community consisted of nineteen association homeowners. Annie's home would be the last house completed. Her new house was less than half the size of the Sacramento house. But it was adequate for Annie. For some reason, she felt it would be her last home.

The house was completed just days before the fall semester began. Annie moved all of the furniture into the house and purchased a few antique items to accent her décor. After completing the decorations, Annie could relax and feel at home.

As soon as Annie got settled into the house, Whitney called.

"I came to Memphis to rekindle with my father, I've done that and now it's time for me to move on. I would like to move to Tallahassee." Whitney told Annie.

Whitney and two-year-old Fowler arrived in Tallahassee before the fall semester classes started. Despite the late notice to the university, Annie was able to get Whitney a fellowship into a master's program. Annie was happy to have her daughter and grandson in her life.

Annie had a fun time with little Fowler. He was a talker and wasn't shy at all. He enjoyed the daycare center near the campus where he was enrolled. He sang solos during certain activities. Annie liked taking Fowler to some of her dance class rehearsals. Sometimes, Fowler would join in with his awkward moves. Annie thought he imitated her moves because his mother, Whitney, was a much better dancer.

Annie and Whitney also shared some fun times. Whitney joined Annie during a few dance classes. Annie's home was located near several restaurants. Sometimes, she and Whitney would go out for margaritas and chips. Both were very light drinkers and could have done fine without any drinking. After a few outings, Whitney told her mother:

"Mom, drinking doesn't do anything for me and I rather not drink anymore."

Annie had an epiphany and felt relieved. She realized that she only drank to be sociable with others. Besides, she didn't like alcohol and its effects of it. Annie also decided then to never drink alcohol again.

****

That same summer in August 1995, Margaret turned seventy-five years old. The family planned a family banquet to celebrate the special occasion.

Annie drove ten hours to Memphis to participate in the festivities. Margaret was dressed as a royal queen, robed in purples, gold, and ivory. When her entrance was announced, Margaret held her baby boy, Aaron's, arm as she strutted down the aisle to her special chair at the head table. The majority of siblings attended the affair, along with many cousins, aunts, and guests. The banquet was emceed by a close family friend, Bonnie, who lived on the next street south of Margaret's house. Annie made a special presentation to her sister, Samantha, who gave a heartfelt response. The Mayor of Memphis attended and presented a resolution to Margaret. Tearful Margaret was speechless. It was one of Annie's most memorable events.

The family visited Jessie on the following day. He was wheeled out into a visiting area. Jessie was very frail and wasn't able to sit up. He did not recognize his children, but his eyes lit up when he saw his wife, Margaret. The family gathered around Jessie to take pictures. Annie waited until they wheeled Jessie back into his room for a closer observation of his living condition. She checked to see if he was soiled, and he was. Annie called for assistance. Jessie squealed as he was being cleaned. Her heart ached to see her father suffering and in so much pain. Annie wished she could be more help to him. During her farewells to Jessie, she pondered if she would ever see her father again.

Sometime during that trip, Annie had a little alone time with her younger sister, Janis. Annie was eleven years older than Janis.

"I want to share something with you, Annie," Janis said.

"Okay – What's going on?"

"I was only seven, almost eight, but I remember something very clearly. When you were having problems with Floyd and you came home. Floyd came to the house to see you, but you wouldn't see him. I heard him talking to Daisy. She told Floyd, 'You need to beat Annie, she is just too spoiled.'"

"She said what?"

"Yeah, Daisy, is so evil. She told him to beat you. She might be the one who told him where you were staying in St. Louis."

Annie wasn't surprised based on her experiences with Daisy. But she now had a full picture of Daisy conspiring with Floyd—and his comment about "an enemy among you." Now that she had this information, she didn't know what to do with it. But Annie never confronted Daisy.

****

After returning to Tallahassee, Annie had a good fall semester. She continued her responsibilities without any problems. Annie had joined the dance organization on campus, a year prior. It was directed by a professor named, Dr. Brenda Baines, who was from Detroit. She had been at the university since the sixties. Annie wasn't as skilled as the students and some of the other dancers, but she did her best and enjoyed every moment. Annie had to work extremely hard to remember the routines. She performed in a few concerts and tours and was told she did well.

Rick flew to Tallahassee to spend the Christmas holiday with Annie. She gave a small open house party over the Christmas break. She asked each person to bring a small ornament to hang on the tree, and the attire was dressy. She hired a pianist and a server for the food that she had prepared.

Annie felt good when a few of the guests arrived. They were dressed nicely and each brought an ornament. But sadly, there were a few who acted like heathens. They wore jogging outfits and didn't bring an ornament. They stood over the food table and devoured the food. Annie didn't serve any alcohol, but a couple of people brought a bottle of wine and opened it. It was her first party with her coworkers and she decided it would be the last time certain coworkers would get an invite to her future parties.

Rick seemed to enjoy his stay, but he did not discuss with Annie their future together. Annie wasn't sure why he came, but she was certain he had no intentions of moving to Tallahassee. She felt then that she would be on her own. This meant planting new roots and beginning a new journey alone.

CHAPTER 48

Jessie

Although Annie had had a wonderful Christmas break, she was ready to return to work. Just as she had gotten into the groove of things, there was always something new to do. Her students were marvelous. They had the motivation and were ready to explore new adventures.

Annie had decided to give herself a birthday party on her upcoming forty-sixth birthday. She looked much younger than her age and had the body of a thirty-year-old, slim and curvy, with a tiny waist and flat tummy. Although she dressed conservatively, her tailored fitted suits accented her qualities. Annie felt blessed to be fit and healthy. It had been almost two years since she started the Prozac, but her anxiety was still an issue. She believed that in time, the matter would be resolved.

Annie's birthday party held on March 1, 1996, was simple. She invited about twenty people. Annie cooked fish, chicken, veggies, rice, salad, and desserts, and made a bowl of ginger-pineapple punch. The music was playing and everyone was mingling and having a good time. The phone rang. Whitney answered it. "Mom, the phone," she called to Annie.

Annie took the phone and went into another room where she could hear.

"Hello."

"Daddy, died today," Samantha told Annie.

Annie was very surprised at her reaction. There was a calmness she felt within as if that day was meant to be Jessie's celebration and not hers. He suffered for over ten years. Now, he had crossed over and was no longer suffering or in pain. It was time to celebrate for him. Annie thanked God for liberating her father and allowing her to celebrate his transition on her birthday.

****

Annie's sister, Janis, had taken the lead to help their mother with the funeral arrangements. The funeral was a week later. The beautiful services were held at a funeral home in Memphis. Margaret held on to her oldest son, Junior's, arm and looked magnificent and strong. All eleven of Jessie's children attended his service. Janis had done a wonderful job decorating the "Serge" in his uniform and his medals. Sgt. Jessie Jacob Fowler looked handsome. But most importantly, he was at peace.

Jessie received military honors at his gravesite. Annie believed that Jessie got the last laugh when the seven honor guards shot off the first round of the twenty-one-gun salute and several people hit the ground.

The Fowler family always found laughter in everything.

CHAPTER 49

Floyd

During the same year of Jessie's death, Whitney became engaged to a man she met in graduate school. She and her fiancé', Andy, had planned an August wedding on Margaret's birthday in Memphis. Annie helped Whitney with the wedding plans. Her paternal aunts also played a supportive role in the preparations and her Aunt Samantha offered to prepare the food.

Two days before the wedding, Floyd's twin sisters prepared a dinner. Annie and several of Whitney's paternal cousins, aunts, and uncles attended the dinner. As usual, there was a lot of delicious food.

Floyd arrived late. He had lost a lot of weight and looked frail. He was only fifty-two years old but looked older. Annie wondered if he was ill but didn't say anything to anyone. His wife, Rena, was not with him. He had been married to Rena for many years but did not have any children with her. Instead, he had sired a nine-year-old boy and a one-year-old girl, from two different women while married to Rena.

"Hi, Annie, how have you been?" Floyd asked.

"I'm great, Floyd, and you?

"I'm okay."

"Are you ready for this?" He asked

"Yes, I am. How about you?" Annie asked.

"I think it is wonderful."

Floyd had renovated another house separate from the marriage home that he used for his entertainment. He invited Annie, Samantha, and several other people to his house. Annie noticed that

186

it was a large nice house, but it was only a shell. The electrical and plumbing were practically none existent. For example, there was a toilet in one of the bathrooms, but no plumbing was attached.

Annie saw Floyd again at the rehearsal. The wedding wasn't quite a traditional one. Instead, Whitney elected to have both of her parents walk her down the aisle. When the facilitator asked, "Who gives her away?" Both Annie and Floyd, simultaneously said, "We Do."

After the rehearsal, Floyd complained to Whitney that Annie spoke too loudly when she said, "We Do." Whitney confronted her mother and asked her not to speak too loudly. Annie wondered why Whitney did not ask her father to speak up or to even dismiss Floyd's petty comment about Annie. Although it hurt Annie's feelings, she didn't complain and soon shook it off.

The wedding was small and elegant. Whitney was a lovely bride and her dress was gorgeous. It was truly a family affair when Margaret sang a solo, Annie's first cousin facilitated the wedding, and Samantha prepared tasty food for the reception.

A few relatives gathered at Margaret's house after Whitney's wedding reception to wish Margaret a happy birthday.

Annie kept little Fowler while Whitney and Andy went on their honeymoon. After the honeymoon, they returned to Tallahassee and lived in Andy's house. Annie, Whitney, and Andy had planned to return to Memphis for the Christmas holidays.

When the fall semester started, everybody was back to school and work. Annie had a full teaching load and committee work. Whitney was in her last year of grad school.

The day before the trip, Whitney received a phone call from Memphis and she immediately called Annie to give her the news.

"Daddy is dead!" Whitney told her mother.

Annie was totally surprised. It was the second time that year, that the same message was given.

"What? I'm so sorry. What happened?"

"I don't have the details yet, but he died from a heart attack."

"How can I help?"

"I don't know yet, I will have to contact Rena and get more information. I will let you know when I know more."

Whitney took the lead in the funeral arrangements. Annie assisted as much as she could. Whitney asked Annie to travel back to Memphis to help her clear out Floyd's second home that he had left to Whitney. She also asked Annie to view Floyd's body because she couldn't.

The funeral director allowed Annie to view Floyd. They had not dressed him or placed make-up on him. He looked like he was just taking a peaceful nap. Annie leaned close to him.

"I forgave you a long time ago," she whispered.

The funeral was held at a Baptist church. It was a very nice service. There was a good turnout of friends and family.

It was revealed that Floyd had a wife, a fiancée' and a girlfriend. His fiancée' was the mother of his one-year-old daughter, and the girlfriend was the person he was having sex with when he died. His death was determined as 'Died in the Act of sexual intercourse.' Annie felt a little pity for the girlfriend, who did not attend the funeral, but the fiancée and the baby did.

After the funeral, Annie met with Whitney at Floyd's house where he died. The goal was to get rid of his personal items, have an estate sale, and put the house on the market. Annie never would have believed that twenty-five years later, she would be cleaning her ex-husband's house and picking up his dirty underwear. But Annie would do almost anything to help her daughter. It was a laborious process and it was done in a few days.

Annie was pleased that Floyd left Whitney a little nest egg for her family. It was ironic to Annie that her daughter and she lost their fathers in the very same year.

CHAPTER 50

Grandma Again

Life's tragedies and losses cause a person to see the world differently and prompt one to readdress or revisit their current life status or situations. Annie had come to peace with her decision to file for a divorce. She had determined that marriage wasn't intended for her and believed that God had another plan for her. If Rick wanted to be with her, Annie surmised that he would have made the effort. Along with the deceit and disrespect, another factor in deciding to file for divorce was Rick's no-show at her father's funeral. She didn't receive a simple expression of condolences.

Annie found a California attorney and initiated the divorce. It was a costly process but within a year, Annie was divorced. Yet, the marriage house had not been sold because there was a dip in the market for real estate during the time of the divorce. They decided to sell the house later when the market improved. Rick wanted to continue to live in it and agreed to pay the full mortgage note. They agreed to revisit their agreement when the market was better.

That same year, Whitney gave birth to a very cute baby girl, Jada. It was Annie's second grandchild, and it was a very unique experience. Annie witnessed little Jada's entrance into the world. To Annie, it was a wondrous experience, and to immediately hold Jada in her arms felt surreal.

Annie had never seen a big brother as proud of his little sister as was five-year-old Fowler. He loved his sister and even as they grew older, he was her protector.

Jada was always very attached to her mother and she usually experienced separation anxiety every time she and her mother were apart.

Several years later, when Annie scheduled a visit to Memphis, she invited Fowler and seven-year-old Jada to go. Jada reluctantly went, only because she felt comfortable with her grandmother Annie.

Once in Memphis, Jada called her mother in tears.

"Hi, Mommie, I want to come home. I miss you. Didn't I tell you I was going to miss you!!! Didn't I?"

Annie enjoyed the time spent with her grandchildren. Despite her anxiety, Jada managed to enjoy the visits with her relatives as well.

CHAPTER 51

Tenure

Soon after Annie became a new granny and was divorced, she was summoned to meet with her dean, Dr. Norton. Annie had detected earlier that there had been a change in the dean's behavior towards her. Annie entered the dean's office.

"Dr. Hightower, you have been talking to some of my enemies and I don't want you to associate with them?"

Annie was taken off guard by the accusation and didn't understand what she was being accused of.

"I don't understand, Dr. Norton."

"There are faculty members here, that are always undermining me and they are up to no good."

"Dr. Norton, I'm not aware of these people and I don't know of any conspiracies against you. I thought I was on good terms with everyone."

"It exists, and I don't want you associating with them."

"Who are they?"

The dean gave Annie a couple of names. One of the faculty members, that she named, was a nice lady and hard worker, who had helped Annie during her tenure, and neither of the faculty members named had said an unkind word to Annie about the dean or anyone. Annie realized that she was in a no-win situation. She knew it was time to make a move.

After several months of scrutiny and through the initiation of Dr. Norton, Annie and the dean of education completed negotiations and Annie was able to transfer to the secondary education department. The downside was that Annie had to postpone her application for tenure for another two years. The dean of the education division was Dr. Edward Evans. He was five-feet-five, with thinning hair, large protruding eyes, and married with children. Annie was not aware that Dr. Evans was also known as a womanizer.

Annie was assigned a full-teaching schedule with four classes, committee work, and community service. Again, Annie had no class assistants for over two hundred students. It was a stressful assignment. In addition, Annie needed to publish at least three research articles for tenure requirements.

On several occasions, Annie had to meet with her new dean in his office. The dean had made subtle moves on her such as brushing against her or giving her the "I want you" look. One incident, in particular, that was unnerving to Annie was when the dean called her into his office.

"Hello, Dr. Hightower, have a seat." Annie sat down.

"You always look wonderful. How do you stay so fit?"

"Thank you. I work at it."

"What are you doing this weekend?"

"I'm not sure, why do you ask?"

"I have been invited to an event in New York and thought you might want to join me."

"Is this business?" Now curious, Annie asked.

"Well, in a way."

"How does it relate to my job here?"

"It doesn't, I'm asking you to go with me."

"I can't go. It is inappropriate. Is there anything else we need to talk about?" Annie stood up.

"Not at this time, but I hope you will give it some thought."

Annie left his office and thought, *When does this crap stop?*

The song, "Build a fence all around me," began to play in her head.

The dean didn't stop. He became more persistent over the next two years. Sometimes, he called Annie at her home, and once, he went to her house. Finally, Annie had to come up with a plan to stop it. She became aware that the dean was married to a smart woman who controlled their domestic finances. So, for the next "rendezvous" that the dean proposed to Annie, she had a prepared script for her response.

"Dr. Evans, a trip to Chicago sounds wonderful. But I have a better idea. If we are going to become an item, let's do it in a big way. There would be no chance of us getting caught. Let's plan a trip to Paris, France, or even Spain, and we can consummate our new relationship." Annie told the dean.

Needless to say, Annie never got another invitation from the dean—and when she did see him at work, he barely looked at her.

****

Annie had completed more than the requirements for tenure. So she was ready to apply. Her application had to be approved on three levels: the department; college; and university. She had a great rapport with her department chair, but the faculty, mostly women, had been less warm towards her.

Annie's department chair met with her on the results of the department members' vote on her tenure application. He reported that the vote for her tenure was three "for," who were male faculty

194

members, and six "against," who were all female faculty members. She was shocked by the results.

"Did they review my files?" Annie asked.

"No, they didn't touch your files. They were concerned about your entrance process into the department."

"I don't understand."

"Well, you're probably aware of the dean's reputation"

Annie was very disappointed. Subsequently, her supervisor forwarded her files to the college committee. As a result, the college and university committees approved her application. Annie was officially tenured.

About three days after she received her notice of approval for her tenure, a female faculty member came to her office. After small talk, she asked Annie a question.

"How did you transfer over to this department?"

Annie was very annoyed by the question.

"I certainly didn't get over here by fucking the dean." Annie didn't bat an eye.

CHAPTER 52
2000

On New Year's Eve of 2000, Annie did not panic about the cyber problems that were predicted to happen throughout the world. When the clock struck midnight, Annie was relieved that she hadn't gone out to buy the expensive anti-software, anti-virus, or other technology that was suggested to protect the computer. Nothing happened and the year 2000 was a special year for Annie. She turned fifty-years old and had planned various activities and trips.

For the first trip, Annie flew back to San Francisco to party with some of her old acquaintances and relatives. She had a great time with all of them. While she was in the area, Annie contacted Rick to let him know that she wanted to check on the house. She knew Rick was not a very good caretaker, and she hoped that he had not caused any major damage to the house. The house had not been placed on the market and Annie had not felt the rush to do so, until then.

When Annie arrived at the house, the community looked different to her, but it was still well maintained. Rick opened the door for Annie to enter. He had gained a fair amount of weight and didn't look very healthy. When Annie walked through to the living area, another woman was sitting in a chair. She was full-figured with a pretty face and long black hair. She didn't stand but she said, "Hi, Annie, I'm Becky."

"Hi, Becky." Annie walked towards her but, Rick rushed Annie upstairs to the upper den area.

"What is going on Rick, who is Becky?"

"She and I were involved."

"Were?"

"Yeah, it's complicated. She won't leave."

"What do you mean?"

"Well, I asked her to leave, but she told me that she wasn't going to leave until she was ready. She's not working and won't help out. She told me that if I made an issue of it that she would call the police on me. She knows that with the legal problem I had, the police would believe anything that she told them."

"So, what you are saying is that Becky is living in our house without paying a penny and is blackmailing you?"

"I guess you can put it that way."

Annie kept her cool and went into her crisis planning mode again and decided to stay at the house. She slept in the same king bed as Rick but dared him to touch her and he didn't.

The next morning, Annie went downstairs to the kitchen to check the refrigerator for something to eat and drink. Becky immediately came out of the downstairs master bedroom and into the kitchen.

"Good morning, Annie."

"Good morning, Becky."

"Are you finding everything you need?"

"Yes, I guess I need to go to the store."

"Can we talk?" Becky asked Annie.

Annie was relieved that Becky opened the communication.

"Oh, sure let's sit down."

They sat at the table.

"I don't know what Rick has said about me, but I thought we should talk."

"He didn't say much at all, except that you are looking for a place to live."

"Well, I can't move anytime soon. Did he tell you that his son got my niece pregnant and I've been keeping the child here? His son will be coming in a little while to bring the baby."

"I didn't know that."

"We were lovers for a while, but things changed between us. What are your plans with Rick?"

"He asked me to come back to him." Annie lied.

"I knew he was never over you. He still holds on to some of your pictures."

"How can I help you find another place to live?" Annie asked to change the subject.

"I have a place, but it will take a couple of months before I can move into it."

Annie got a chance to see Rick's first grandchild who was a very handsome baby boy. She stayed a couple of more nights and talked to Rick about putting the house on the market.

After Annie returned to Tallahassee, she and Becky remained cordial and they exchanged contact numbers. Becky called Annie a few times with updates. Yet, two months later, Becky moved out of the house and they never spoke again.

****

The next trip Annie had planned to celebrate her fiftieth birthday was a great adventure drive from the east coast to the west coast. She invited her friend and coworker, Brenda, to travel to San Francisco with her. Brenda loved to travel, so she didn't hesitate to accept Annie's offer. Annie had bought a 1995 Corvette and had driven it to Memphis a few times. But she wanted to do something different and special for her life's turning point.

198

They packed the Vette with everything they thought they would need. Then, early one morning in June, the two of them, like in the movie, "Thelma and Louise," headed west. Annie did most of the driving. They decided to drive only during daylight. They took the northern route to California and planned to take the southern route on the way back to Florida.

The ladies headed west on I-10 and stopped in Mobile, Alabama, for lunch. Then, they continued until they reached Shreveport, Louisiana, before sunset. It had been about two years since their last visit to Shreveport when Brenda's mother had passed away. Annie and a few other friends rented a van and drove there for her mother's funeral. On this trip, Annie and Brenda stayed overnight with a friend.

The next morning, they drove to Dallas and spent one night with Annie's brother, Robert Lee. Then off to Wichita Falls and Amarillo, Texas, Albuquerque, New Mexico, Grand Canyon, Arizona, Las Vegas and Reno, Nevada, and San Francisco, California.

The ladies did not rush to get to the west coast. Instead, they enjoyed many attractions, sites, food, and entertainment along the way. It took about ten days for them to reach San Francisco. After Annie gave Brenda a tour of the bay area, Brenda flew back to Tallahassee for a week to attend to personal matters. Annie visited her friends and relatives who lived in the San Francisco Bay Area and Sacramento.

When Brenda flew back to San Francisco, she and Annie drove to Los Angeles, where they stayed with Annie's lifelong friend, Tia. They had not seen much of each other since they both moved from Sacramento. Tia gave her master bedroom to her guest. She lived in a luxurious apartment with an ocean view in the Marina.

Annie and Tia always enjoyed seeing one another. They had so much in common--both had an accounting background. They were only about eight months apart in age and were very youthful for their age. They loved to dance, and together, they would start a party and be the last one on the floor. Annie and Tia shared the same hard work ethic and were still very humble and generous to others. They were vain about keeping a fit body. There were times when they would walk about twelve miles in one day and Tia could do more. Both were certified fitness instructors.

During the two-day visit, they did plenty of walking, while Brenda mostly enjoyed the sights and restaurants. Annie and Tia said their tearful farewells. Overall, the visit was a lot of fun.

Annie and Brenda drove to Phoenix where they spent another two days with Brenda's lifelong friend, Curtis, who was a kind person. He introduced the ladies to some of his friends and took Annie and Brenda to a cultural event and other fun activities. Annie noticed that there wasn't much greenery in Phoenix, mostly rocks and cactus. She couldn't imagine living there.

Once on the road again, the ladies cruised along and visited places in Tucson, Arizona, El Paso, San Antonio, and Houston, Texas. When they reached New Orleans, they decided to stay a few days. The ladies enjoyed the entertainment and food, and they went on a couple of organized tours.

On the final day of travel, they stopped again in Mobile for a meal and arrived in Tallahassee before dark. Although Annie and Brenda had truly enjoyed their adventure, they felt blessed and blissful to be back home in Tallahassee.

****

Annie planned the next activity with her high school classmates in 1968. Annie had arranged a potluck at her mother's house during July. She drove the ten-hour trip there a couple of days early to make sure that things were organized. Of course, it gave her some quality time with her mother.

Shortly after Annie's arrival, Daisy came to the house for a visit. Despite Daisy's evil ways, she always had a way of making people smile with her jovial greetings and playful actions. Annie and Daisy sat outside on the porch and had a cordial talk. Annie was not expecting the conversation that followed:

"When I was a little girl, Junior would come to my bed and hump my butt with his penis. I heard that he had done something similar but worse to you." Daisy told Annie.

Annie was silent as Daisy continued.

"I told Claudine about it, but she made excuses for Junior. She said he was just a boy. But I was nine years old and he was twenty-one-years old. I heard we weren't the only ones he did that to," Daisy said.

Annie could no longer hold her silence. She then told Daisy, "What you described happened to you is exactly what happened to me at the same age of nine. Although Junior did not have sexual intercourse with us, it does not make it any better. It is still sexual molestation. It is wrong by law and by God and for anyone to condone what he did, whether he was fifteen years old or twenty-one, is heartless."

The following day was lovely. Samantha helped Annie set out long tables under the tree. They placed the tablecloths and chairs. They also made a green salad and a fruit salad.

Annie had flown to Indiana the year before to celebrate her sister Claudine's fiftieth birthday. Annie was surprised but happy that Claudine came for her birthday celebration.

There weren't many classmates that showed up for the celebration, but Annie was so happy to see all who did come. Everyone laughed and talked about ole' times. Annie felt blessed to share the moments.

Annie left Memphis but, returned in August to celebrate a major turning point for her mother—her eightieth birthday.

Margaret, her children, grandchildren, other relatives, and friends set sail on a dinner riverboat cruise down the Mississippi River. There was plenty of food, music, and great conversations. The sunset was divine. Margaret looked elegant and radiant as she walked along the boat. She told the family, "I feel like a Queen."

Annie invited her high school friend, Thomas, on the cruise. He was a gentleman and very kind to everyone. The next day, Thomas and his father came over to Margaret's house and barbequed for her. Several people attended and everyone had a delightful time. Annie would never forget the thoughtfulness of Thomas and his father.

****

The next grand adventure Annie had planned in September was a fourteen-day trip to Egypt, but it was canceled when Annie landed in the hospital to have an emergency hysterectomy. She had been aware of the fibroids that were growing inside of her. Annie's last examination revealed that the fibroids had grown about half the size of a newborn infant. But, she had postponed the surgery, thinking she had more time to plan for it. However, things didn't go as she planned.

Annie fully recovered in about six weeks after the surgery and returned to work. She felt blessed and grateful that she had the opportunity to travel and celebrate her half-century mark with her family and friends throughout that year.

CHAPTER 53

Mohamed and Charu

During the spring of 2001, Annie's nephew, Mohamed, graduated from high school. Annie flew out to San Francisco to attend his ceremony. Afterward, she, Mohamed, and Charu flew back to Florida. Mohamed was seventeen years old and Charu was sixteen years old. They were the children of Annie's brother, Junior. Although Charu was the youngest, she was the most outgoing and outspoken. She and Annie had developed a close bond and always kept in touch. Many had described Charu's personality as being similar to Annie's.

The flight landed in Jacksonville, where Annie's younger sister, Janis, lived. They spent a couple of nights with Janis before Annie drove to Tallahassee. Janis gave the kids a tour of the area and took them to the beach. Both kids were amazing swimmers.

In Tallahassee, Annie gave them a tour of two university campuses and the local area. Mohamed was excited about the campus tours and wanted to stay.

After a few days, Annie drove them to Memphis. This would be their first visit. They first stopped overnight in northern Alabama to visit Annie's sister, Elaine, who had moved there to work for the government.

Once in Memphis, Mohamed and Charu were disappointed that they were not able to meet with their father, Junior, who was not available. Mohamed was only a year-old when he last saw his father and Charu had never met her father. However, they were elated to meet their cousins, aunts, uncles, and grandmother. They toured Memphis and stayed overnight at different cousins' homes.

203

A few days later, Annie drove back to Florida. During the trip, Annie became seriously ill. She wasn't aware, at the time, how seriously ill she was until it became difficult for her to breathe. Annie managed to reach Panama City Beach, but she was unable to drive any further. Both kids could drive but neither had a permanent driver's license. Annie waited in the car while the kids went swimming. She didn't want to spoil their vacation so, she didn't complain, but she felt something was very wrong. Her breathing became more difficult. She finally gave the car key to Charu and they headed to Tallahassee.

After traveling a while east on I-10 and through a few beautiful canopy roads in Tallahassee, Mohamed complained. "There is nothing but trees everywhere."

Annie visually understood his comment. The two highways (I-580 & I-80) where Mohamed grew up in the Bay Area, California, didn't compare to east I-10 in Tallahassee. Ali observed that the Bay Area's highway scenic routes were not as beautiful. Lack of rainfall caused many droughts, so many of California's rolling hills would become extremely dry with mostly amber-colored weeds. In addition, occasional mudslides didn't allow too much foliage to grow. Therefore, a lot of trees were very unusual to see for Ali.

Annie got the kids settled into her house and fought her illness until early the next morning. The doctor fussed at Annie for waiting so long to come to the hospital.

"You developed a rare pulmonary infection that was causing your esophagus to rapidly close. Not much research has been done on this, and we don't know the cause. But it is curable. After we give you this injection and some meds, you should begin to feel a difference right away. This may never happen again, but if it does, come to the hospital immediately. This is life-threatening... you could have died."

The next day, Annie began to feel stronger. The kids stayed with her for two more days, and then they flew back to California.

Later that year, on September eleventh, the USA was faced with the most devastating and worst terrorist attack in its history. It was then, that Annie saw for the first time all Americans' alliance. Everyone set aside their race, religion, and creed to survive the threat. Less than two years before the attack, Annie had visited New York City and toured the Twin Towers. She could feel the loss.

****

The next year, Annie traveled to San Francisco for Charu's graduation ceremony. After the ceremony, only Charu returned with Annie to Florida.

Charu was eager to get to Memphis because she heard her father, Junior, was there. She could hardly wait to meet her father for the first time. Annie drove from Florida to Memphis for the reunion. Yet, Charu's excitement quickly died, when her father refused to see her. Annie's heart ached for Charu as she watched Charu cry from disappointment. It would be about three years later before Charu would have a brief encounter with her father.

When they left Memphis, Annie decided to drive Charu to Atlanta for a tour and a little excitement to boost her spirit. Once Annie checked into the hotel, she and Charu toured the city. They had dinner at a restaurant located in the Underground Mall.

Since they both loved to dance, Annie inquired about a nearby place to dance. One of the hotel workers suggested a club that was only about two blocks from the hotel and told Annie that the music would be great.

Charu and Annie got dressed up and walked to the club. Annie paid the cover charge and they went inside and found a table. Annie noticed that there were mostly women present. But it didn't bother her because she had no problem dancing freestyle.

When the music began to play, two men came out onto the dancefloor. They were dressed in tuxedos and began to dance. They moved their bodies provocatively and sexually. A moment later, they removed their tops. Annie was surprised and she looked at Charu who was laughing. A moment later, the men took off their pants and wore only G-strings.

"My goodness, where are we?" Annie asked Charu.

"Oh my! We are in a strip club." Annie looked at Charu, who was still laughing.

Suddenly, Annie felt a couple of taps against the back of her head and quickly turned her head.

"Did he slap my head with his penis—I know he didn't." Annie looked at Charu who continued to laugh but had her hands over her eyes.

Lord, have mercy. I could go to jail... here I am in a strip club with a juvenile. Annie thought.

Annie stood up gracefully and led Charu out of the club. Charu was still laughing.

Annie didn't laugh that night but over the years, she and Charu reminisced about the incident with laughter.

CHAPTER 54

Grand Ole Opry

Margaret had loved Country music for as long as Annie could remember. One of Margaret's dreams was to see a performance at the Grand Ole Opry. Annie knew Margaret had lost two of her sisters within the last six months, and she was feeling depressed. To lift her spirit, Annie returned to Memphis to pick up Margaret for a trip to Nashville.

They packed up the Chevy Blazer and drove the three-and-a-half-hour trip to Nashville. Annie had reserved a room at a hotel near the Grand Ole Opry House.

They arrived early enough to take a lunch cruise on the General Jackson Riverboat. At the entrance of the boat, they posed for a photo. Margaret usually didn't like getting on boats, but she was relaxed and enjoyed the entertainment. It was a very nice day for a cruise and the food was good.

On the night of the show, Annie and Margaret had dinner at a local restaurant before show time. They didn't care about the casual attire that would probably be worn at the show. Instead, they dressed up. Margaret wore a beautiful pink dress with shiny jewelry, silver flat shoes with a matching purse, and she carried a beautiful floral shawl. Annie wore a black semi-formal beaded dress with low-heel pumps and gold accessories.

The parking lot was very large at the Opry House. Margaret had a disabled parking permit. However, the closest parking available was about three hundred yards from the entrance. To Margaret, that was miles. Annie held her mother's arm and walked slowly with her down the walkway for short distances at a time. When Margaret tired, Annie showed her a bench to rest. They continued in this manner until they reached the entrance. Fortunately, it wasn't crowded and there was no reserved seating. Annie walked Margaret to the front row of the hall.

Annie and Margaret were amazed and looked at one another in disbelief. They were sitting in the Grand Ole Opry House. That night, the main guest was Trace Akin's Induction, with Jimmy Dickens. Others sang and the singing was fantastic. Margaret sang along with many of the songs.

When the comedian performed, Margaret was in stitches. Her tears of laughter ran down her face as she held her belly.

It was another great experience for Annie and to have her mother experience it with her, made it even better.

CHAPTER 55

BVI- *Better Than Good*

After ten years of service at the university, Annie was granted a full semester sabbatical in the spring of 2003. She elected to complete her research with the British Virgin Islands (BVI) Education Department located on the island of Tortola. It was the largest island of the four BVI Islands and was populated with about eighty-five percent Afro-Caribbean.

The BVI provided an apartment for Annie. She was warmly welcomed by the department's staff and administrators. If it had not been for the steep hills and the local accent, Annie felt as if she had never left the southern region of the USA. Everyone was friendly and had similar cultural values. Annie observed that many of the ladies wore lovely natural hairstyles. It was then, that Annie decided that she would never perm her hair again.

Annie befriended a few staff members and was invited to their homes. Just like the southern cultural Annie grew up in the USA, and her Island friends loved to cook and eat. There were plenty of local dishes such as callaloo and fish soups, kingfish, conch, salt fish, fungi, Johnnycakes, pates, and much more. Since Annie was a sugarholic, she loved one particular dessert called the "black cake." It wasn't too sweet, and it was very moist and tasty.

One of the staff members, Lilly, was the key person that helped Annie with her work, housing needs, tours, and introductions. Lilly was very thorough in her duties and always made herself available to Annie. Lilly also took Annie to her home and introduced Annie to her lovely mother.

Tortola had steep hills throughout. The Education Department was located across from a cruise harbor. Annie's apartment was located on a steep hill looking over the department and the harbor. It had a wonderful ocean view. On most mornings, Annie enjoyed the walk from her apartment to the department and back.

When the department had a conference for the educators, Annie was asked to choreograph a dance routine. She truly enjoyed the interaction with the staff and the results of their performance. She also attended a few workshops and activities that allowed her to meet various levels of educators and make presentations.

Annie visited several schools of different grade levels. The children were so well-behaved and respectful. One student in mid-school approached Annie after one of her presentations.

"Dr. Hightower, are you related to Michael Jackson?"

Another asked her.

"Are you from Alabama?"

Annie had to restrain herself from laughing.

Each morning when she arrived at work, she was always greeted with a smile.

"How are you?"

"Pretty near good, and you?" Annie replied

"Better than good," said Tommy, a staff member in the department.

The workers always smiled or laughed at Annie's response, but Annie loved Tommy's response even more—so much that when she returned to the USA, she immediately adopted it.

Another worker, Cindy, was a US citizen and was born in St. Thomas, Virgin Islands. She had two beautiful children, a boy, and a girl. Cindy invited Annie to take a ferry from Tortola to St. Thomas to meet her mother, Sally. Annie spent the weekend at Sally's house. She was a very kind person and also worked full-time. Sally invited Annie to participate in the annual festival parade. Annie gladly accepted. The theme for the parade was, "Mermaids of the Sea." Sally took Annie to the seamstress to measure her for her beautiful costume. The bra was silver, green and blue, with decorative beads attached. The skirt was cut into the shape of a mermaid and matched the bra, and the headpiece was a large blue, green and silver glittered shell with large paper pearls.

The weather was perfect for the parade. The sea of colorful costumes, music, and performers was so invigorating. Many floats and vehicles were decorated. As the music played, Annie danced down the road with about twenty women in her group while people waved and danced along the road. There was excitement everywhere and Annie enjoyed every moment.

After the weekend, Annie went back to Tortola where she stayed for another week before returning to the USA. The department hosted a farewell luncheon for Annie. Several people brought homemade cultural dishes. Annie enjoyed the unique black cake, various vegetables, and fish. Importantly, she enjoyed the laughter and interaction with her newfound friends.

By the end of Annie's stay in BVI, she had collected enough research data to write four articles. But, most importantly, she gained an experience that would remain dear to her heart, and she acquired lifelong international acquaintances. She knew that someday she would return to Tortola. Annie went back to the USA with a greater appreciation for life.

****

Later that same year, Annie drove to Memphis for the Thanksgiving holiday. Several siblings and grandchildren came to dinner. Margaret baked a ham, made dressing, and cooked greens and other vegetables. Junior cooked several turkey legs and beef links. Samantha baked many of her special desserts. Martha made potato salad. Annie mostly watched as her family members devoured the food. Annie got full just looking at all the food. But she did enjoy the food and especially the desserts.

After dinner, there was more storytelling at the table. Music was playing in the background. Margaret was using a walker during that time, but it didn't stop her from getting on the floor and making a few moves to the beat of the music. Everyone left the table and spread out into the adjoining dining and living rooms. Margaret set on the sofa.

Donny's son Russell, and daughter, Robin, were present. She brought her karaoke machine and sang a nice R&B song.

The microphone was passed to Margaret who sang a lovely hymnal, "Oh, It is Jesus." Daisy continued the gospel singing with a great song, "I Go to the Rock."

Once again, Margaret took the microphone to tell her joke, "Thank you, Lord, for my…" Everyone looked forward to hearing her tell the joke, and they laughed as if hearing it for the first time.

As usual, Donny recited the MLK speech, "I Have a Dream," and to end the evening, he sang Carol Burnett's sign-off song:

"I'm so glad we had this time together. Just to have a laugh or sing a song. Seem we just got started—and before you know it—come the time we have to say so long."

Annie was caught up in the moment and videotaped everything. She felt good being home and appreciated the positive interaction with her family. Annie also believed that Margaret was very pleased with her children. To Annie, the year 2003 had been "Better than good."

CHAPTER 56

The Devil is a Liar

For a few years, Annie continued her challenges in teaching, committee work, and research. She had been promoted to associate professor and was preparing for a promotion to a fully honored professor. She had been friendly with her fellow faculty members and always offered them a helping hand.

During the spring of 2004, while working in her office, Annie received a phone call from a former education faculty member named Donna Howard. She had left the department to work in the university president's office and was now ready to return to the department. She and Annie had worked in different divisions, and she had never worked with Donna on any projects, but she had had a few brief conversations with her. Donna called to ask Annie for a letter of recommendation. Annie remembered her as a nice person so she wrote a letter of recommendation for Donna. A few days later, Donna invited Annie to her office. Annie walked across the campus during her break to visit Donna.

"Hey, Annie, come on in." Annie walked in and sat down in a chair in front of Donna's desk.

"Thank you for the letter."

"Not a problem. When do you plan to transfer over?" Annie asked.

"I'll start at the beginning of spring term," Donna told Annie.

"That's less than two months away."

"Yeah. Augh—I would like for you to meet the president."

"Sure, I would love to."

213

Donna escorted Annie into the president's conference room. A few minutes later, the president walked into the conference room. He had a frown on his face and looked straight at Donna.

"What do you want now?" He asked in an irritated voice.

"This is Dr. Hightower who wrote the letter of recommendation for me."

"I am a busy man, what do you want, Dr. Howard?" He asked, still irritated with her.

"I just wanted Dr. Hightower to meet you," she said, now looking foolish.

"Hello, Dr. Hightower," he said and quickly left the room before Annie could respond.

Given the dialogue between the two of them, Annie felt very uncomfortable and realized that perhaps Donna's transfer back to the college wasn't by choice.

Little did Annie know that her small act of kindness would cause her a few years of hell.

Donna transferred over to the college at the start of the spring semester as she had mentioned. At the end of the semester, Donna asked Annie to meet with her and the education interim dean. The interim dean was an education faculty member named Ronald Lime. He was acting dean until the position was filled.

Annie didn't get a straight answer from Donna when she asked her what the meeting was about. But out of curiosity, Annie agreed to meet with them.

"The Business Education Department is having a lot of difficulties," Ronald said.

"But I am in secondary education," Annie responded.

"We know, but your credentials also qualify you to work in that division also." Donna pushed.

"How can I help?"

"We think that you should run the department," Ronald said.

"We? There is already a chairperson." Annie said, confused.

"She will be leaving the position," Ronald responded.

"I need to think about it, but I will do what I can to help," Annie told them.

"If you accept the position, you'll probably need to get started by the first of July to prepare for the fall semester," Ronald said.

For the next few weeks before the summer break, Donna and Ronald continued to encourage Annie to take the position. Finally, Annie said she would.

Once Annie became chair of the department, Donna began to make subtle suggestions to Annie about how she should run the department, who she should and should not trust, and even who she should have removed. Donna's personality switched from day to day. Sometimes Donna agreed and the next day, she acted as though there had been no discussion. She was easily irritated and acted offensively. When Annie dismissed most of Donna's suggestions, Donna flipped the switch and devised a plan that antagonized a couple of faculty members who fought against Annie. She went as far as to incite negative confrontations between graduate students and Annie.

The preceding chair of the department, who had gone back to teaching, became so angry with Annie. Especially, after her application for tenure was denied by the university. She cursed

Annie and made false accusations that Annie was responsible for her denial.

It was obvious to Annie that Donna was a master at manipulating and deceiving people. Although a bit late, it was clear to Annie that Donna's goal all along was to become the chair of the department. First, Donna had to get rid of the previous chair, and she used Annie to do that. Unbeknownst to Annie, Donna's initial friendliness and deceitful personality, made it easy for Donna to sway Annie to reach her goals.

This was confirmed when Annie had to leave unexpectedly to go to Memphis on a family emergency. When she returned from the trip, Donna and another faculty member, Mona Smiles, had set up a coup d'état. Donna had called an emergency department meeting and asked the faculty to vote to overthrow Annie's chair position. As a result, it backfired and the two didn't get the desired votes. Donna was outraged that her plan didn't work.

During Annie's absence, Mona Smiles removed office furniture and equipment from the department without Annie's approval. The dean would not support Annie in getting the items returned to the department.

"Pick your battles," he told Annie.

Smiles told lies to the dean and faculty to discredit and undermine Annie. Annie confronted Smiles about the lies and the horrific acts she made against her. Smiles expressed no remorse for her deeds. She didn't deny her acts and mocked Annie.

The acts of hostility and undermining by these pompous women increased over the years. Finally, after three years as chair, Annie decided to submit her resignation and return as a faculty member.

Annie went on a summer break before she had a chance to remove her files from her office. Donna's computer skills enabled her to remove all of Annie's working and personal files from her computer. Then, Donna moved into the office as a Chair. She did this with the support, again, of the interim dean, Ronald Lime.

When Annie returned, she received no support to retrieve her files. Donna, the "Evil Lena" finally got her to wish to become the chair of the department. But her reign was short-lived because the department was soon closed due to a lack of student interest.

Annie transferred to another education division, where she taught in the Ph.D. program until she retired from the university. What was so ironic to Annie was that both Donna and Mona were members of the same church and where Annie performed periodically as a guest liturgical dancer. Annie often observed how freely they used God's name and cited Scriptures amid their evil deeds. Annie quickly learned firsthand that the "Devil is a liar."

CHAPTER 57

Feel Homeless

Margaret's bout with high blood pressure and diabetes had taken a toll on her. To make it worst, her oldest son, Junior, had moved back into her house. The family first thought since she was alone, it was a good thing to have someone responsible for Margaret. But Junior was everything, but responsible. He wouldn't give Margaret any money while he was living there. Instead, he would borrow money from Margaret and refuse to pay it back. Junior had never respected women, including his mother.

Margaret always knew that if she needed something she could always call on Annie. But when Annie learned that Margaret was mismanaging her money and not paying her bills, Annie stopped sending her money. Instead, Annie would pay the bills directly. Annie never understood the relationship her mother had with her sons and why Margaret would take from her daughters to give to her sons.

One day, while Annie was at work, Margaret called.

"Hey, Annie, how are you?"

"I'm better than good, and you?"

"I have a bad cold and am out of cold medicine. I use an over-the-counter medicine that cost about $8 but I don't have any money. Junior said he didn't have any money and I asked Donny to buy it for me, but he hurt my feelings when he said to me, 'I can't give you any money. I have my own children to take care of.' I don't know what to do." Margaret told Annie.

"I will take care of it, Mother," Annie said. She hung up and immediately called a friend who lived in Memphis.

"Annie, don't worry. I will buy the medicine and take it to your mother." Her friend Hamilton assured.

Annie's friend, Hamilton, was a medical doctor and had his practice. She was introduced to him many years before by a close childhood friend, Carmela. Hamilton was one of the gentlest and kindhearted people she had ever met. Annie felt so blessed to have him as a dear friend in her life.

Annie lost more respect for her brothers. She couldn't comprehend how they could let their mother suffer. Margaret had always provided generous support to them when they were in need. After all, they did live rent-free in her home for long periods.

****

During the summer of 2005, Annie visited her mother. Margaret looked very frail and sad. Annie remembered when her mother was full of life and talking on the phone every day with at least one of her sisters. But, early that year, Margaret's last living sister passed away.

"I feel so lonely. I have no sisters. I lost four of them within the past five years. And now my best friend has passed away. There is no one I can talk to. Junior has wired up my house with cameras and alarms like a detention center, and he speaks to me with no respect. No one wants to visit me because of him. I feel like a prisoner in my own house." Margaret cried.

"How can I help, Mother?"

"Take me back to Tallahassee with you until Junior moves out of my house."

Annie drove to Memphis, helped Margaret pack her bags, and drove her back to Tallahassee. She immediately scheduled a few medical appointments for her mother. Daisy and Claudine called to check on Margaret, and Annie reported to them whatever the doctors told her. Daisy called several times a day. Sometimes, Margaret would tell Annie that she didn't want to talk to Daisy. Margaret shared with Annie a few details.

"Daisy has opened credit cards in my name."

"Did you give her permission?"

"No, she said she was going to pay them off. But I keep getting bills and phone calls from the creditors, and Junior won't give me any money for the bills around the house."

"You have been getting money from the rental of my properties each month. Hasn't that helped?"

"I'm not sure where the money is going. Daisy collected the rent for me. I needed help."

"Do you want me to manage your expenses for you?"

"What do you mean?" Margaret asked.

"Find out what you owe, how much income sources you have, and pay your bills for you."

"That sounds great."

"Well, you will have to make it legal and when you are ready, let me know."

One day, when Annie came home from a work, she felt extremely tired and Margaret was agitated.

"All I do is sit around in this house, I need something to do. I don't have anyone to talk to!" Margaret shouted at Annie.

"Mother, I understand how you must feel, but please don't attack me like that."

Annie got on the phone and invited several friends over to the house. People were coming at different times to meet Annie's mother. It kept Margaret entertained for a while. On a couple of weekends, Annie drove Margaret to visit her younger sister, Janis, and her family in Jacksonville.

After five months, Margaret became very ill and had to be hospitalized. The specialist diagnosed Margaret with kidney failure and because of her age, eighty-five, the doctor highly recommended no kidney dialysis. He told Annie that her mother had a life expectancy of six to twelve months, less if she underwent dialysis. This was such a shock to Annie. She shared this information with Claudine and Daisy. Having to cope with the daily hostile work environment and now being told that her mother may die soon had become physically and emotionally hard on Annie.

Daisy had left a message on Annie's phone to have the doctor tune up Margaret's heart pacer. Annie immediately called Margaret's doctor in Memphis and the office referred Annie to another physician. Annie called that physician, who stated that he would call the hospital in Tallahassee to give them the details on the pacer. Annie also told the attending doctor at the hospital and reminded one of the nurses to remind the doctor about the pacer.

Margaret had decided that she wanted to return to her home. She wrote a letter to Junior to tell him that she wanted him gone before she returned. He refused to leave. On New Year's Eve, Margaret flew back to Memphis, but instead of going to her home, she went to Daisy's condo in downtown Memphis. Daisy was unemployed during that time and had the time to help take care of Margaret.

About a month after Margaret returned to Memphis, she passed out on the floor in Daisy's condo. Margaret was rushed to the hospital where the hospital gave her kidney dialysis and tuned up her heart pacer. Daisy made the assessment that Annie had been negligent in Margaret's care and told the other siblings that Annie had tried to kill their mother. It was easy for a couple of the siblings to believe such allegations and they chose to stop speaking to Annie.

Annie didn't care what lies Daisy was telling. It was a blessing to hear that her mother would live longer than the physician had predicted. However, Annie wanted to sue the damn hospital for their incompetence. But she didn't have the strength to do so.

Meanwhile, Annie's youngest brother, Aaron, flew to Memphis to help Margaret evict Junior. But the courts wouldn't evict him and Junior stayed in the house. Soon after the utilities were turned off, Junior moved into the garage apartment for a few months and later he moved out. He took with him, Margaret's stove, refrigerator, washer and dryer, dishes, some furniture, family pictures, Samantha's clothes, jewelry, and shoes. Furthermore, the house was in foreclosure. The property insurance had lapsed and the interior of the house was in shambles. By that time, Daisy was still unemployed and had used Margaret's money to pay her rent and expenses. In the process, she abused Margaret's credit.

Around the same time Junior left the property, Daisy dropped Margaret off at Martha's house which lived a block from Margaret's home. Daisy claimed it was temporary until she returned from a cruise. But everyone knew that wasn't true. Martha was Samantha's daughter but was raised by Margaret and Jessie as their own. Martha was then married with three children, two of them were still living at home. Their house was small with limited space for Margaret.

So Who Do You Call? Margaret called Annie.

"Hi, Annie, I'm ready to go home, Junior has left my house. Daisy took good care of me when I was at her place. But now, I'm here and I am so miserable. I feel like I'm in everybody's way. Can you help me? I don't know what to do. I feel homeless." Margaret cried.

"I will get someone to cover my summer classes. I will be on my way as soon as I can. Hang in there." Annie told her mother.

Annie had a close friend who lived in Maryland. Craig was an attorney, real estate agent, and he had great carpentry skills. They met and became partners on a theatrical project. They soon became close friends. Annie and Craig talked a lot on the phone and visited each other a few times. Craig was divorced with five adult children. He was about thirteen years older than Annie but was very fit and agile. Craig was a spiritual and kindhearted person who always offered a helping hand. He had been semi-retired for a few years.

After Annie told Craig about her dire situation, he immediately volunteered to help.

Craig flew to Tallahassee to drive with Annie to Memphis. They loaded up the car with all types of tools and equipment. As a previous landlord of several rental properties, Annie had collected hand tools over the years that any skilled handyman would envy.

Once Annie and Craig arrived at the vacant and trashed house in Memphis, Craig assessed what needed to be done. All eight rooms needed some work but five were in bad condition and the back door needed a wheelchair access ramp.

After a list of supplies that were needed had been outlined, the total cost was about eight thousand dollars. Annie did not waiver, she bought the supplies and between her and Craig, they would do the labor. It was a pleasant surprise when Donny offered to help with floors, walls, and ceiling repairs. Martha's oldest daughter, Vonnie, did a beautiful job painting the dining and living rooms.

On several occasions, Martha came by the house only to ask when the work would be finished. She never offered to help or offered Annie or her out-of-town guest anything to drink or a snack. Annie soon understood why her mother felt unwelcome in Martha's house. Yet, Annie knew Martha was a kind person, and perhaps, she was feeling overwhelmed at the time.

Annie and Craig worked about twelve hours a day for about five days to get enough work done to get Margaret into her home. Annie's fingers and hands were cut and swollen from the tight grip on the hand tools she used to scrape away the padding that had been glued to the hardwood floors. The same dirty and infested brown shagged carpet had covered the beautiful hardwood for over twenty-five years.

In addition, Annie had injured her back. She didn't know how it happened, but she was in much pain. As usual, Annie did not complain. The floors had to be sanded, buffed, and varnished.

As soon as Donny and Annie had completed varnishing the hardwood floors, Martha was at the door, insisting that Margaret move back into the house.

"Martha, I believe the fumes from the varnish could be harmful to Mother," Annie explained.

"She'll be okay," Martha insisted.

About an hour later, Annie received a call from Margaret.

"I want to come home now." Margaret pleaded to Annie.

Apparently, Martha had said something to Margaret that upset her.

The front bedroom had always been where Jessie and Margaret slept. Craig cut a doorway to allow more direct access to the bathroom. Meanwhile, Annie and Craig shut off all the doors to the dining and living area and opened all the windows, so that the fumes would not escape throughout the rest of the house. Margaret's bed was set up in the center bedroom that was closest to the bathroom. Then, they sprayed down the entire house with disinfectant. Margaret was back in her house and her bed before sunset.

Once Margaret was settled into her home, she asked Annie to handle her financial and medical affairs. Annie became Margaret's Power of Attorney and began to organize Margaret's life. When Annie researched Margaret's financial affairs, she discovered some disconcerting matters.

As a result of Annie's actions, the house was saved from foreclosure when Margaret refinanced the mortgage and her outstanding debt. Annie was also able to reinstate the home insurance.

"We will reinstate this policy only if you can assure us that your sister, Daisy, will not be involved. We have had a very bad experience with her, and we refuse to deal with her," the insurance agent told Annie.

In addition, Annie discovered past due bills from credit card accounts that were fraudulently opened by Daisy and cell phone bills that were never paid. Annie filed a police report and contacted all the related companies to inform them of the matter. But the police did not want to get involved in family matters and companies continued to call to harass Margaret for several months.

"I don't know why Daisy would do that to me. I didn't open those accounts." Margaret told Annie.

Annie drove Margaret down to Sears to open an account for a washer and stove. Martha gave Margaret a nice used refrigerator that worked fine.

Annie closed Margaret's bank accounts and opened a new account with online banking so that Annie could handle business matters from a long distance.

Gossip soon flowed among the siblings that Annie was stealing Margaret's property.

Margaret asked Annie to contact an attorney so that she could prepare a will. In it, Annie was the executor, and Margaret left everything to Samantha. Annie felt relieved.

"Annie, after I die, please see that Samantha is okay. She's been here for me. I left everything I have, that ain't much, to her because the rest of y'all are doing fine." Margaret pleaded.

"I will do my best, Mother," Annie said.

****

Shortly after returning home from Memphis, Annie saw a referred neurosurgeon about her back and neck pain. After various tests, the doctor diagnosed Annie with the deterioration of two cervical discs located on the upper spine. He highly recommended surgery to fuse the discs.

"How did this happen to me, doctor?"

"It can happen several ways, but the most common is working on a computer for a long time in an improper position, and other occupations including construction, driving long periods or any job that causes stress on your neck and spine." The doctor explained.

Annie suddenly realized that she had done some work in all of the mentioned jobs over a short time. After Annie learned how invasive and the long recovery period was, she decided to delay the surgery and work with pain management for a while.

For over a year, Annie met with the pain management doctor for quarterly injections. About one week before her planned trip to Costa Rica, Annie was scheduled for her fourth injection. She arrived early that morning. The doctor told her that her pressure was too low to give her a "Cocktail" shot. This particular shot relaxed a patient before the pain injection.

"Doctor, I am too tense, I need the cocktail."

"You will be okay." The doctor assured Annie.

The doctor proceeded with the injection.

As he injected the needle into her neck, Annie screamed. The doctor completed the injection. The pain she felt almost caused her to faint. It radiated down her left shoulder, arm, and to her fingertips. The hand and fingers became so painful and it felt like fire throughout. Tears ran down her face. Annie had to be helped from the table into a chair.

"This is the second time in my entire career that this has ever happened," the doctor stated.

"On a scale of one to ten, how much pain are you in?" The nurse asked Annie.

"Fifteen." Annie could barely speak.

The nurse rushed to give Annie another pain injection into the upper arm.

Over the years the pain eased, but Annie never totally recovered from the damage.

Annie continued all her regular activities and assisted her mother through her financial and medical needs.

CHAPTER 58

Costa Rica

After a long and difficult year and a much-needed break, Annie decided to visit one of her closest friends, Athea, and her husband, Jack, for two weeks in Costa Rica.

Athea had left Oakland and moved to Costa Rica several years before. Annie and Athea had been communicating regularly by email and letters. Early November 2007, Annie traveled to Santo Domingo, Heredia, Costa Rica, in the Central Valley Region, where Athea and Jack lived. They picked up Annie at the Juan Santamaria International Airport, in the Capital City of San Jose. Annie was filled with wonder at how youthful Athea remained. She was about six years older than Annie. What was more amazing, Athea's husband was about ten years younger, but she looked even younger than he.

Annie was always happy to see Athea and could always expect a wonderful adventure. Athea was very active and she enjoyed jogging, cooking, writing, and exploring new things. Annie had always considered herself well-organized but nothing even close to Athea's organization. Athea documented everything and she loved snapping pictures. Anyone could ask Athea about any event or situation that occurred many years before. Within moments after she had gone through her journals, Athea announced the date, time, and all details about the event.

The next day after Annie arrived, Athea and Jack took her shopping to find her a foam mattress. Athea drove that day and she had pretty much mastered the local language, whereas, Jack had not. The ride in the city was a very new experience for Annie. The traffic on the roads was intense. There were lots of fast drivers, bumper-to-bumper drivers, and horns blew constantly. Athea was calm and managed to hand out money through the window as beggars approached the car.

After returning with the mattress, Athea prepared one of Annie's favorite salads. Athea's salads were always great creations. They included various vegetables, nuts, fruits, and homemade dressing.

The next day, Annie was surprised when Athea asked Annie to join her on the large trampoline that was located in the backyard. Although both were far into their fifties, they jumped as if they were kids. There was so much laughter and a special moment for Annie.

Athea had planned out a schedule of sights and tours in Curridabat, the Capital, San Jose, Santa Ana, Grecia, and Escazu. The sights were interesting and fun. They included a lot of history and the architecture was unique.

A few days later, Athea drove to the South Central Region until she reached Manual Antonio National Park and its beach. Annie thought the view was heavenly. Although she didn't swim, Annie enjoyed the walks in the park and along the beach.

Athea provided Annie with a guest pass to a health gym. After the first visit, Annie was invited to teach a Zumba class. As usual, Annie was prepared to give a challenging workout. Everyone enjoyed her class and invited her to come back.

Athea also drove Annie to the Pacific Coast Region and toured the Guanacaste Province to Playa Santa Rosa, Playa Conchal, and Playa Flamingo. The views were awesome and Annie enjoyed every moment.

Annie had thought about retiring to Costa Rica. The healthcare and living costs were very appealing. But Annie began to have second thoughts about becoming a resident after observing some of the local communities on every economical level. Most of the houses she saw had iron bars on the windows and there was severe traffic gridlock almost everywhere she went. This was a turnoff for Annie.

Costa Rica was a life learning experience for Annie. She met so many humble and thoughtful people who were generous in sharing whatever they had. It was a tearful day of departure. Annie and Athea maintained their sisterhood and kept in touch regularly.

CHAPTER 59

Know When to Fold

The long drives to Memphis and the stressful job had taken a toll on Annie. For two years, Annie made the ten-hour drive to Memphis on every break and holiday that she could.

Annie had been taking pain management injections to avoid the inevitable surgery on her spine. She knew that if she had the surgery that she would have to take at least two months to leave to recover. But she had too much to do at work and Margaret needed her.

During the Christmas break of 2007, Annie drove to Memphis and stayed with her mother. She drove Margaret to and from her kidney dialysis session three times a week. Annie also ran general errands, cooked, and cleaned. Samantha was living with Margaret and had a job at a grocery store. Sometimes, Annie drove Samantha to and from work. Margaret's therapist came to the house twice a week.

On New Year's Eve, in the late afternoon, Margaret was lying down in her bedroom, while Samantha and Annie were talking in the den. Suddenly, Annie felt a sharp pain from her upper spine and through her left shoulder and arm, with such force that it knocked Annie to her knees. Annie screamed so loud, that Samantha came to her side. Annie managed gingerly to get up and sit in a chair. She continued to scream with tears running down her face. Samantha didn't know what to do. Annie knew it was time to go home. She asked Samantha to call her daughter, Whitney, and ask her to reserve a flight for Annie to return to Tallahassee.

Within an hour, Annie's younger brother, Donny, who still lived in Memphis, drove her to the airport. She could barely stand alone and was unable to walk. Annie had to be in a wheelchair from the car to the airplane.

Whitney met Annie at the airport in Tallahassee and took her straight to the hospital emergency. Her surgeon was on holiday leave, but three days later, Annie had the surgery.

It was a difficult recovery for Annie, both physically and emotionally. She didn't want to be a burden to anyone, especially to her daughter, who was divorced with two children and working full-time. Annie was alone most of the time and assured Whitney that she was okay.

Late one afternoon, Annie's pain increased so badly that she had to call her doctor's office. The nurse recommended to Annie that she increase her dose of pain meds. Annie doubled the dose as the nurse told her, but within minutes, she began to have disturbing illusions. The walls and furniture in her bedroom began to move in slow motion. The chairs began to dance and the fireplace mantel made bizarre and aggressive faces. Annie closed her eyes, thinking that the situation would change to normal after she opened them. But, even when she closed her eyes, strange and disfigured faces appeared. Annie opened her eyes and spoke to the moving objects.

"I am not afraid of you!" Annie shouted. "I know you are not real. This is my house and I'm not going anywhere. I know it is the drugs, so back off!"

To Annie's relief, her illusions finally disappeared. She had experienced firsthand how drugs could affect a person's mental stability. She felt blessed that she was able to ride the waves without any drastic outcomes. She did not use any more of the prescribed drugs. Instead, she decided to stick with extra strength Tylenol.

A day later, Annie became hungry and there was nothing prepared that she could eat. She was too unstable to stand at a stove.

So Annie thought she would call her dear friend, Brenda, who was retired.

"Hey, Brenda. How are you doing?"

"Hi, Annie, I'm good. How are you?"

"Better than good. I'm just a bit hungry. Would you please pick up a sandwich for me and drop it by the house? I will have the money here when you come." Annie asked.

"I can't. I'm expecting a repairman in about an hour, but you order it and I will pay for it."

"That's okay. Sorry to bother you. Thank you."

Disappointed, Annie hung up.

Annie was hurt by the lack of concern her friend had shown. She recalled the times she would stop whatever she was doing to respond to Brenda's needs. From that point, Annie viewed the friendship quite differently. Annie managed to cut some fruit and make toast, which satisfied her until Whitney arrived.

Annie thought that it might be some truth to what Whitney had said to her when Annie was in the emergency. "Mom, you are too proud, stop holding your pain inside and let people know how you are really feeling."

After a two-month recovery, Annie returned to work. Her temporary disability made her reevaluate her life. It was humiliating to her to feel like a burden to anyone. Just in case something similar would happen again to her, Annie purchased long-term care insurance and made other arrangements that would make her feel less of a burden to anyone. Her experience taught her to "Know when to fold."

Annie had been a certified aerobics and fitness instructor for several years. She had volunteered at the YMCA and other centers to teach dance fitness classes. Annie was feeling good, but since the surgery was on her spine, she had lost confidence in the way she moved her body for fear of causing injury. She continued to work out and danced, but it took her about a year to regain her confidence.

****

Annie continued to volunteer as an instructor in Zumba and dance fitness at various gyms, schools, and centers. One day, a friend asked her if she would teach a class at her house and Annie gladly accepted. Her friend invited several women.

The class went well. However, one participant complained throughout the routine.

"I can't… do that. That's too hard. Oh, my…," said Ashni.

Ashni was born in Jamaica but had been in the USA since she was a preteen and became a medical doctor. She continued to attend every class and learned every step. Although the rhythm and beat were challenging for her, Ashni became so confident that sometimes, Annie had to calm her down during the routines.

Another medical doctor attended the class that night named, Joanna. She struggled to catch on to the moves but got through it without any complaints. Surprisingly, Joanna invited Annie to have weekly aerobic classes in her medical office. Annie delightedly accepted. Joanna also became Annie's primary physician.

The weekly classes were later moved to Ashni's church. She also called Annie to exercise at each other's house. Annie met Ashni's family. She had a sister, Donna, and a brother, Alex. Her mother, Mary Sue, was a firm outspoken woman but generous and kindhearted. They all made Annie feel like part of their family. Annie soon joined them for weekly prayer meetings. Ashni's family showed concern for Annie in every aspect of her life, including through her sickness and accomplishments. They became Annie's closest extended family.

CHAPTER 60

Mother Knows

During the same year of Annie's spinal surgery, her high school's fortieth class reunion was planned for the summer, in Memphis. As usual, Annie was excited about seeing her classmates again.

The reunion was a three-day event. Annie prepared to attend all activities. Again, Annie had a hard time remembering many of her classmates' names but thankfully, some were wearing name tags. In some cases, Annie just didn't remember the person but laughed and talked with them as if she did.

One evening, when there was dancing, a classmate came up to her. Annie had no idea who he was.

"Hi, Annie. I'm Stanly Jones. You haven't changed at all. Would you like to dance?" He reached out for Annie's hand.

"Hi, Stanly." Annie stood up and followed him onto the dancefloor.

Stanly made moves like he was still in the sixties. It was cute to Annie and she laughed.

Stanly was about a five-foot-ten, thin, creamy light brown complexion. He wore a black pullover, short sleeve shirt with beige trousers. Annie thought he looked nice, but he didn't spark her interest.

Music to a cha-cha beat began to play. Annie waited on Stanly to make the move. When he didn't make a move, she grabbed both of his hands and showed him the cha-cha. He caught on pretty fast. After the dance, he walked her to her table.

The event soon ended and everyone headed to the exit. As Annie approached her car, Stanly rushed to her.

"Aren't you going to give me your number?" He asked.

"Well, I hadn't thought about it."

"Well, give it to me." He smiled.

"I'm staying at my parent's house, it's listed," Annie said.

"Are they still on International Avenue?"

"My mother and sister are, Daddy passed away."

"I'm sorry to hear that, I lost my mother not too long ago," Stanly said.

"I'm sorry, too, for your loss."

"You probably don't remember me. I had the biggest crush on you." Stanly smiled.

"Why didn't you say anything?"

"I thought someone as pretty and fine as you already had someone."

"That's amazing. I've heard that a few times. That is probably why I didn't have a date for the prom. I went with my cousin."

Stanley gasped. "You're kidding me?"

After a few more minutes down memory lane, Stanly wrote his name and number on a piece of paper and handed it to Annie. She noticed that he spelled his name without an "e." Annie wished Stanly a good night and drove home.

The next day, Stanly drove up to Annie's parent's house in a truck. He was wearing dark short pants. When Stanly walked into the house, Annie wondered to herself, *How are those skinny little pencils for legs holding him up?*

Stanly lived only a few blocks from her parent's house. He had moved back into his "home house" before his mother passed to help take care of her. He was a government employee, but that day, he was on his way to doing some handy work.

Stanly visited Annie a few times during her stay with Margaret. One time when he came by, he took off his shoes and laid across the sofa in the rear den that used to be Annie's and her sister's bedroom. Margaret was also in the den, sitting in a chair and watching TV.

"You got something to drink?" Stanly asked Annie.

"Would you like some water?"

"Here," he handed Annie a six-pack of beer.

"Open one and put the rest in the fridge." He stretched back with his legs on the sofa.

Margaret was observing him. When he left, Margaret, disgusted, told Annie, "I don't like how he talks to you. Who does he think he is?" Margaret wanted him to leave but didn't say so.

One day, Stanly took Annie by his house. He had two dogs, a puppy (CiCi), a schnauzer, and an adult dog (Moe) a shepherd. Both were large dogs. The adult dog was intended to be an outdoor guard dog and the puppy stayed inside the house. Annie immediately fell in love with the puppy. But she felt uncomfortable about being around the unfriendly guard dog.

Stanly invited Annie out to dinner with his sister and her husband who were visiting him from Atlanta. Annie enjoyed the dinner and Stanly's relatives. Stanly's brother-in-law snapped a nice picture of Annie and Stanly. The event soon ended.

Annie soon left Memphis and returned to work. She and Stanly talked on the phone almost every day. Talking with Stanly was so easy for Annie. They could talk for a long time on the phone about things that no other new relationship could discuss, because of their similar past. It felt nostalgic for Annie to talk with someone who shared some of the same histories.

During the Thanksgiving break, Annie returned to Memphis. When Stanly came over to Margaret's house to take Annie out, Margaret had her say.

"I hope you two don't ever plan to marry because you are too different." She told them.

They both laughed, but, Annie clearly understood what her mother had said and why. She believed that "Mother Knows." Annie didn't think any more about it because she already believed that she would never marry again. Her ideal relationship with a man would be to have a best friend who would also be a companion to travel with and enjoy living.

Annie had been on a few dates, but she had not been in a serious relationship in several years. She hadn't thought about the length of time because it wasn't a priority. Staying busy with her job responsibilities and her mother's needs made the time pass quicker than she was aware.

Annie spent Christmas with Whitney and her grandkids. Two days later, she drove to Memphis to spend the New Year with Margaret and Samantha.

While in Memphis, Annie visited Stanly. She noticed that she and Stanly had a lot in common as far as housekeeping. They both loved a clean house and didn't wear their street shoes in the house. She thought Stanly was a bit more excessive when he bleached everything. It was evident by his faded appliances and furniture. Annie also noticed that he had a lot of clothes that filled all of his closet space. But he was not as organized as Annie. Stacks of paper, mail, and documents were visible throughout the house.

Annie was determined to be friendly with Stanly's guard dog, Moe. She did not like being afraid of anything or anybody. Periodically, without Stanly's knowledge, Annie would sneak a piece of baked chicken to Moe, until finally, she could pet him. Annie and Moe became close and he would follow her commands. Annie laughed when Stanly called Moe a traitor. Both of the dogs were always happy to see Annie.

Annie and Stanly became an item over the holiday and enjoyed their time together.

A few months later and days before Annie's fifty-ninth birthday, Stanly had a surgical procedure. Not too long afterward, he had two more surgeries. These incidents caused a major turn that limited intimacy. Annie was by Stanly's side during each procedure and surgery while still taking care of her mother. She cooked, cleaned, and ran errands for both of them. She also took care of Stanly's dogs. Yet, still physically attractive and sexually desirable, Annie decided that the sex didn't matter. As time passed, she believed that Stanly was her best friend and that he would do anything for her unconditionally.

CHAPTER 61

China

In March of 2009, Annie took leave off work to join her oldest sister, Elaine, on a twenty-one-day trip to China. The trip was organized by Elaine's friend, Rodger, a director at another college in Texas. Since it was an educational adventure, Annie's leave was approved by her university.

Elaine had moved from Washington to Alabama. Annie had made several visits to her sister's house. Sometimes on her way to Memphis, Annie would stop over to visit her. Not too long before the planned trip, Elaine had a bout with cancer and had to have chemotherapy. Annie visited Elaine to give her support. She did a little cooking and cleaning and went to medical appointments with her. Elaine was the second sibling with breast cancer. A few years before, Claudine had a mastectomy and Annie flew to Indiana to be with her sister. She arrived in time to go with Claudine to remove the stitches from the surgery on her breast and stomach. Annie stayed a few days to cook and clean and to give Claudine support.

Annie had also traveled to Indiana for Claudine's fiftieth birthday party several years before. Samantha and her youngest sister, Janis, also were present. The celebration was amazing.

Annie had a fear of losing her sisters during their battles with cancer and was so relieved when they both survived it. She loved them so much. These were the same sisters that helped Annie many years earlier during a difficult time after leaving Memphis. Then, Annie was desperate, uneducated, and homeless, and needed help to care for her child. But since Annie became independent, educated, and prosperous, she felt more distance from them than before. Yet, she was determined to show them love. However, Annie learned that her sisters did not feel the same about her. She resented Annie tremendously.

It was a known fact that Elaine didn't like to give or help Annie in any way. When Annie visited her, Elaine would immediately say, "You're on your own."

Annie was financially secure, which she had accomplished through hard work. She had never asked anyone in the family for anything, instead, she only gave to them. There were times Annie would have paid the dining bill, if Elaine wasn't too quick to say, "This is a Dutch treat."

During one of Annie's visits, Elaine shared a few of her historical family experiences.

"Mother treated her fair complexion children better than she treated the darker complexion ones."

Annie looked at Elaine and thought to herself, *Wow! She has a smooth creamy caramel complexion that anyone would pay thousands of dollars in a tanning salon to obtain. What is she talking about? People called me 'dirty red' and I have large pores and freckles.*

"Mother didn't support me when I was nominated for the queen at the high school. She told me, 'They must be desperate to select you.'" Elaine complained to Annie.

"Wow! Sorry to hear that. Mother is known to say some rough stuff."

Annie, now pondered within, *What is the point of this— Mother is dying and Elaine is sixty-six years old. When do you let go and grow up?*

There was another occasion when Elaine showed determination to make sure she didn't give Annie anything. Annie had started a traveling business that was similar to a pyramid. In other words, for her to profit, the owner had to recruit other investors. Annie discussed the business details with Elaine without pressure. Elaine didn't say anything at the time, but a few weeks later, Elaine called Annie.

"Annie, I decided to go with my white friend, who is local, since you are in Florida. Besides you didn't ask me."

Annie noticed that whenever Elaine talked about her friends and acquaintances, she always gave a title or description of them such as, "My doctor friend. My friend, who is an educator. My Asian friend…"

Elaine's resentment towards Annie was also apparent during their visit to China.

Elaine drove to Annie's house to fly from Tallahassee to Miami to catch a direct flight to China. The time between the connecting flights was close. Still recovering from her illness, Elaine didn't have the endurance to walk fast. So Annie trotted along to the gate to see if they would hold the flight for Elaine. They would not. It was a blessing, instead, Annie and Elaine were booked on a Korean flight to Seoul Korea to catch a flight to China. The flight services were wonderful and they gave the passengers a lot of good quality frills.

There was a four-hour delay in Seoul for the connection to Beijing, but it was worth the wait. The airport had so much culture and activities that kept Annie busy. She dressed in Korean ethnic attire and took professional pictures and visited several shops.

Once they arrived in Beijing, Rodger was waiting at the airport with a shuttle to the hotel. It was a nice hotel and the environment was clean. Twenty travelers in the group included educational administrators, faculty, students, and guests.

The next morning, the group had breakfast together and introduced one another. Later, they went to the Beijing University of International Business and Economics to meet with faculty and administrators. After introductions and lunch, the group returned to the hotel. While in Beijing, the group attended dialogue sessions with the university educators. They visited several tourist areas including, The Great Wall of China, Tiananmen Square, and Forbidden City.

During one tour, Annie was wearing low-cut jeans and a sweater. She reached up to look at an item at a vendor's booth when the tattoo on her lower back was revealed. One of the travelers commented on it.

"Nice tattoo. Is that an Egyptian Queen?"

"Yes, it is."

"Why did you select her?"

"Oh, because… I'm her reincarnation." Annie said, jokingly.

"And she really believes that mess?" Elaine said, in a belittling manner.

"Of course, I do, Elaine, why wouldn't I believe it?" Annie asked just to irritate her.

Later that evening at dinner, Annie sat on Elaine's right side, and another person sat on Annie's right side. Elaine spoke across Annie to the person to start a dialogue. Annie made a general comment to add to the conversation.

"Who asked you anything? I wasn't talking to you. This is an A and B conversation and when I'm ready for C, I'll let you know." Elaine firmly told Annie.

Annie was surprised by Elaine's rudeness and the other person appeared to be also. The conversation was cut short. However, Elaine continued to make subtle insults to Annie throughout the trip. One of the group members noticed the hostility and asked Annie,   "What's up with your sister?"

"Oh, she's just feeling a little under the weather," Annie lied.

The group rode a train to Xi'an, China. Annie shared a room with bunk beds on the train with Elaine and two others in the group. The group toured several places including the Terracotta Warriors of the Qin Dynasty, the Great Mosque of Xi'an, and Xi Ming Temple.

After three days, the group flew to Shanghai. They visited another educational institution and later toured a few places, including a silk factory. Annie saw several items she wanted to buy for gifts. The best price for the items would have to be paid in cash. She didn't carry much cash. So she asked Elaine.

"Would you please loan me the money until we return to the states?"

"You better pay me back. I mean it." She snapped at Annie.

"Elaine, you don't know how difficult it was for me to ask you. I don't like to ask people for anything. If you don't think you should, then don't loan it to me."

Elaine lent the funds to Annie. But, after another incident of belittlement, Annie had had enough. Annie clearly understood that it would not be difficult to embarrass Elaine without a direct attack on her. Annie had observed Elaine's values as a person were measured by who she associated herself with. If a person Elaine knew did something silly or unprofessional, it would embarrass Elaine. Annie couldn't understand this, because she was not embarrassed by others' acts that may seem foolish as long as it was not a direct attack on her.

When the group boarded the bus to go back to the hotel, Annie sat near the front. Elaine walked passed her and sat in the rear. When the driver started to drive, Annie grabbed the microphone.

"I want everyone to sing along with me." Everyone smiled and looked forward to a little fun.

"This is a little song I wrote for future educators, so just repeat after me."

"Oh, Lord! Oh Lord, won't you hear my cry?

I want to be a teacher, please tell me why.

Long hours, hard work, and paper piling high.

Children on my nerves, but I still want to try."

Annie sang in a very poor pitch and tone. She looked back at Elaine who wasn't singing along. Instead, she seemed embarrassed. She was shaking her head and talking to one of the ladies, pointing her finger toward Annie.

Annie continued in her worst tone.

"One, Two. I know what to do.

Three, Four. I'm out the door.

Five, Six. Get ready for the tricks.

Seven. Eight. I get home late.

Nine, Ten. I'll do it again."

By the time Annie finished the verse, Elaine was furious. She continued to shake her head, and she fussed.

Annie finished the song.

"Will someone tell my sister back there to stop talking when I'm trying to sing?" Annie announced.

Everyone laughed. Annie felt that she had gotten a little retribution. She knew Elaine would have a lot to tell others when she got back to the states.

When they arrived at the airport to return to the USA, Elaine asked Annie if she would purchase a snack. It was only $3.00, normally, Annie would not have thought anything about it. But when she wrote a check out to repay Elaine for the loan, she deducted the $3.00.

Annie never understood the resentment her sister felt for her. But not too long after Elaine's gruesome behavior towards her, Annie accepted the fact that she had to let Elaine go.

Yet, through it all, Annie was able to capture the beauty of China and its people. Her interaction with educational personnel and students was an honor and all were hospitable and generous. The people and tours were magnificent. The experience was memorable and educational. Annie shared a lot of it with her students.

CHAPTER 62

Mother

Shortly after Stanly's medical ordeal, Annie's mother's health deteriorated rapidly. Margaret had a mild stroke and was hospitalized but was soon released to go home. Annie was able to get family sick leave from work and returned to Memphis to help her mother. Margaret wasn't able to speak clearly, and Annie noticed that her mother became very agitated when she couldn't be understood.

Soon Margaret had another stroke and she was readmitted to the hospital, where she stayed for weeks. The doctor recommended that Margaret move to a nursing home where she could receive twenty-four-hour medical assistance. Annie found a home for Margaret, but she was not overly satisfied with the conditions there. It wasn't a bad place, but Annie knew of one that was better. Margaret was placed on a waiting list.

Annie visited the home every day. It was shocking to her to discover that one of her dearest high school classmates was also a resident of the home. Rosa was a beautiful girl. She was popular in school and had the most exotic hazel eyes. Annie visited Rosa a few times. Even with the unfortunate health conditions that she faced, Rosa remained positive. Annie was inspired by her.

Margaret was soon transferred to the better nursing home that she had been waiting for. Annie became familiar with the nurses and staff. Since she was at the home every day, Annie taught Zumba classes to the staff during their lunch breaks.

About a month later, Annie was feeding her mother, but Margaret couldn't swallow the food.

"Swallow, Mother," Annie pleaded.

Margaret continued to chew the food, but the food remained in her mouth. This went on for a couple of days. The doctor finally decided to insert a feeding tube into Margaret's stomach. Annie stayed with Margaret and witnessed the entire procedure. She felt so helpless, and her heart ached to see her mother suffer. Margaret continued kidney dialysis but pleaded with Annie in her nonverbal communication that she had had enough.

"Mother, do you think you can handle dialysis twice a week, instead of three times?"

"Yes." Margaret nodded her head.

Margaret received dialysis on Mondays and Fridays.

Annie had spent several months in Memphis and realized that she had run out of leave time and would have to return to work. Margaret raised eleven children, five of whom lived in Memphis. For the last couple of years, Margaret had tried to get all of her children under one roof. It saddened Annie that Margaret's convalescence wasn't enough to pull them all together, or for them to schedule the regular sitting time that Margaret needed.

Annie sent an email to a few of her siblings listing all the things Margaret would need and asked if they would set aside some time to visit Margaret. Only one brother responded to the email, but he lived out of state. Annie asked one of her sisters to cut Margaret's nails while she was away.

"I can't do that. Mother sticks her hand in her butt," Daisy told Annie.

On Annie's last day in August, she went around to the staff at the home to bid them farewell and pleaded with them to check in on her mother. It was difficult for Annie to say goodbye.

Annie sat in her mother's room for a moment, as Margaret lay in her bed. It was a two-patient room, but the other bed had been vacant for a while. Margaret was calm and was gingerly picking lint off her blanket. Annie felt a moment of solitude and recalled her mother was always doing something with her hands such as sewing, picking peas or greens, cooking, cleaning, or folding clothes and towels with precise details and patience that none of her children could emulate. Margaret's hands were always busy. Annie watched her mother and thought about the places they had traveled together and heard her laugh. She also remembered many of her mother's tearful situations and disappointments. But what stuck in Annie's mind was that despite all her mother's tribulations, she was 'never bitter'. Instead, Margaret was always forgiving.

Finally, Annie stood and walked toward Margaret.

"Mother, I will be gone for a little while, but I will be back as soon as I can. I love you."

As she hugged and kissed Margaret, she felt her mother's frail body and thin cheeks. She wondered if she would ever see her mother again.

****

After returning to Tallahassee, Annie continued to call the nurses' station to check on Margaret. Annie was saddened to hear that Margaret received very few family visitors. Annie had planned to return to Memphis on the Friday before Thanksgiving and to stay until after the New Year holiday. But Margaret's kidney failed her, and she passed away the day before Annie was to return. Annie believed it was God's Plan, and perhaps His way to shield Annie from the additional pain of seeing her mother suffer.

"He built a fence all around me," Annie sang.

Annie was the executor of Margaret's will, and she made Margaret's funeral arrangements. Annie received very limited support from her siblings. But the funeral was beautiful. Margaret

249

looked like a queen and the church service was superb. It was hurtful to Annie to see that only eight out of eleven children attended Margaret's funeral. Even her death wasn't enough to bring all of her children together. Margaret was buried next to her first and only love, Jessie.

After Margaret's death, Annie gradually weaned herself off the anxiety meds that she had been taking for years. She also stopped taking any over-the-counter meds including aspirins and pain relievers. Annie didn't want anything to prevent her from grieving her losses and feeling the realities of life. Annie remembered one of her last discussions with her mother:

"I wish all my children would get together and enjoy one another. Before my mother died, she asked me to see that my sisters and brothers kept in touch. I did the best I could but, there were a couple who wanted very little to do with the family. I know that it is a lot to ask any child in a large family. But do your best Annie. You have a kind heart. I'm sure Samantha and even Daisy will help you." Margaret pleaded.

To reach out to her siblings, Annie fell short.

"I don't want to talk to you. I have nothing to say to you." Claudia told Annie without any explanation.

Others felt the same, the only siblings that continued communications with Annie were her youngest brother, Aaron, and three of her sisters, Samantha, Daisy, and Janis. But she also realized that there was strong rivalry among the other siblings.

Annie regretted not being able to fulfill her mother's last wishes. However, to maintain a healthy emotional lifestyle, Annie decided to distance herself from family members and acquaintances who wanted to bring misery into her life.

CHAPTER 63

Conquering Fears

Annie was no different than most people who may be consumed with fear of various things and circumstances. However, during Annie's earliest fears, she felt that she had to face them alone because there was no one she could go to for comfort or protection.

Fear of abandonment was Annie's earliest memory as a child when she had reoccurring dreams that her mother wanted to give her away to a stranger. Even though Annie learned to become self-reliant early on, she indirectly clung to her mother and sought acceptance until her mother's death. Later, Annie felt perhaps it was a sign that her mother was trying to protect her from the dangers in life.

Annie's fears of animals such as chickens, dogs, and horses were caused by the actual attacks and bites from them during her childhood. She overcame one fear later in her life by chasing the chicken, instead of allowing it to chase her. She bought and raised a puppy to overcome her fear and soon became very fond of dogs. When she was bitten by a horse while feeding it, she thought of it as a large mean dog and was terrified of it. Much later in life, Annie decided to take her daughter, Whitney, horseback riding as a birthday present to her. She never shared her fears with her daughter. After the riding lessons, Annie overcame her fear of horses.

At one time, Annie could never imagine living in the Deep South, especially since the thought of the region consumed her with horrific fears during the earlier years of her life. When she moved to the Deep South, the only time she felt similar fear, ironically, was when a few of her coworkers freely used the "N" word and other racial degrading language. It caused her much confusion and anxiety. She couldn't understand why educated Black individuals used such inappropriate language. Eventually, it compelled her to confront each individual when she heard them.

"I would greatly appreciate it if you would please refrain from using profanity within my hearing. You truly can't change the meaning of the "N" word. There is no endearment, love, or fellowship in its use. Just ignorance and hate."

From that moment, Annie never again heard her coworkers use the "N" word or profanity. With the help of her mother, the Deep South became her home and there was no other place in the world where she would rather live.

People look at death in different ways. The fear of death was much more complicated for Annie to overcome. Her first experience with death was very frightening. When her father retired from the Army and the family moved to Memphis, Annie washed dishes and cleaned house for a neighbor, Mr. & Mrs. Little, who lived three doors east of her house. The Little's had two adult sons who lived out of state. But the youngest son, Alex, returned home to live with his parents.

One day, Annie was cleaning the Little's house. Not knowing anyone other than Mrs. Little was in the house, Annie rushed into one of the bedrooms to dust and froze at the sight of what was before her.

"Don't let her see me like this, Mamma," Alex pleaded to his mother in a very feeble voice.

Catheters were in Alex's nose and arm, while his mother was putting clothes on his frail nude body. Alex's sunken eyes of sadness frightened Annie.

"Annie, please leave the room. I will be with you in a little while." Mrs. Little gently whispered.

Annie rushed out of the room and closed the door. She was terrified and embarrassed.

Annie remembered Alex as a kind and gentle person, and he was a strong handsome athlete. Seeing him like that, made her very confused.

Two days later, Alex died from cancer. Annie cried and became afraid of the idea of death. She saw it as painful.

If that can happen to a nice person like Alex, it can happen to me, Annie thought.

Sometime later, Margaret's oldest brother, Uncle JB, died. Annie had never been to a funeral and had never seen a dead body before. When she got in line with her family to view the remains, the sight of them caused her to faint. Jessie rushed to Annie's side and carried her to another room in the church. When Annie regained consciousness, she could hear her father speak.

"I was so afraid that we had lost you," Jessie said.

Annie didn't understand what her father meant by it. But she later learned that Jessie had witnessed someone who died during a funeral. Annie didn't like the idea of scaring her father, so she made up her mind that she would be much braver when she had to attend other funerals.

As an adult, seeing death firsthand when her boyfriend was killed and having been threatened with weapons pointed at her, caused Annie more confusion and anxiety about death. But strangely, during those moments, she never thought about pleading for her own life because she truly believed that the situations were in God's control. Annie witnessed her parents suffer in agony for many years from their illnesses. When they died, Annie then began to see death as a blessing.

Although Annie was not fearless, she did not allow fear to control her. She was grateful to God for helping her to face and conquer those fears that once had power over her.

CHAPTER 64

Gone

During the following spring break in 2010, after Margaret's death, Annie accepted an invitation from Whitney to go with her on a five-day Western Caribbean cruise. It was well needed by both of them. Whitney had been working long hours and had recently completed her second master's degree. Annie was also feeling stressed and a bit depressed. In addition, the trip would be a celebration of a major event for both. It was Whitney's belated fortieth birthday and Annie had turned sixty. The grandkids spent the break with their father and paternal grandparents.

Annie was excited about spending some alone time with her daughter. Fortunately, the cruise did not include many teens or younger children. Annie enjoyed singing a karaoke song with Whitney and dancing. They toured Belize, Cancun, and Costa Maya, Mexico. The food was good and the weather was excellent. It was a relaxing and fun trip. Annie wished that she and Whitney could spend more quality alone time together.

About a month after Annie returned from the cruise, she received a call from her ex-husband, Rick. When she saw his number on the caller ID, Annie thought Rick was calling to give late condolence for the loss of her mother.

"Hi, Annie, how are you?"

"I'm better than good, Rick. How are you?"

"Well, I have a little problem… uhh… IRS has garnished my monthly pension because I owe them income taxes… so I haven't been able to pay the mortgage," Rick said.

"How far behind are you?"

"Pretty soon, it will be two months."

"What do you want from me?" Annie asked

"I was hoping that we could refinance the house to pay off the taxes I owe to IRS and that way I can continue to make the mortgage payments.   If we let it go into foreclosure, we will lose everything. The market still isn't good and the bank could sell it at the loan amount that is less than a third of the appraised value." Rick explained to Annie.

"Let me think about it. Send me information on the mortgage and your garnishment."

"Okay, I will send all the information to you soon."

After receiving the information, Annie discovered that Rick had been gambling and had not reported all of his income. He owed about $25,000 in taxes between the federal and state governments. She decided to apply for the loan, but none of the financial institutions would include Rick on the loan because of his poor credit. Rick volunteered to transfer the property deed to Annie. He told Annie he just wanted to live on the property. Annie wasn't in any hurry to sell the property and as long as Rick paid the mortgage, she didn't see any problem with the arrangement.

Annie refinanced the property for $500,000 which was appraised at $1,450,000. She was able to receive enough proceeds from the loan to pay off Rick's IRS and State debts. She sent Rick an additional $10,000, and she had enough for what she considered a refund for the original divorce cost that she had paid.

It felt good to Annie to save the house and to get Rick out of trouble with the government. However, that feeling was short-lived.

About two months after the transactions, Annie received a subpoena in the mail that stated a person was suing her for fraud. The person had lived in Sacramento and was a former acquaintance of Annie and Rick. Annie had to find a California attorney to handle the matter. The attorney was a man, in his early forties.

After a legal investigation, the attorney shared information with Annie that was unsettling. When Rick retired from his state job, he went into private practice. In one of his cases, his client sued him, but Rick didn't show up for the hearing and the client won by default a $1,600,000 judgment. Rick did nothing to fight it. There was a lien on the property that the loan company had overlooked. Annie also learned that Rick had been disbarred because of a different case that he mishandled. Needless to say, Annie was floored.

Annie called Rick about the matter and asked him to help her save the house, but Rick refused. He didn't want to get involved and wouldn't offer Annie any support. She had to fly to California for meetings and depositions. She pleaded with Rick to help her, but he was adamant and didn't help.

What sealed the fate of failure was, that Rick had not protected Annie's interest in the property. Several years before, Annie had hired a California attorney for the divorce. After the divorce, her attorney had not completed the property issue, when Annie received a call from Rick.

"Annie, please get your attorney off my back. I will handle the property deed to secure your interest. Your attorney is going to charge you another $5,000 for something I can do."

Once again, Annie trusted Rick to take care of the matter. But, during the legal meetings, Annie discovered that Rick had not changed the deed, which allowed the plaintiff to sue Annie also. Over the years, with Annie's complex life with her job, her mother's illness, and other issues, Annie didn't think to check with Rick and confirm if he had changed the deed.

Annie's attorney advised her to give the plaintiff the property. Annie felt betrayed by everyone involved, especially her attorney. The dream home that she designed was turned over to the plaintiff. Rick was immediately evicted from the property and eventually, it was sold.

If that wasn't enough, sometime later, Rick sued Annie for her pension and retirement investments. Annie had to hire another California attorney to handle the matter. By this time, Annie had acquired a very strong dislike for attorneys. She had spent most of the year fighting legal battles. She was worn out and financially disabled. Annie felt that she had accomplished nothing and that all her resources had practically disappeared.

When there was a thunderstorm, somewhere there was a rainbow in the midst of it. Annie found an attorney who renewed her respect for the legal profession. Her attorney was a white female in her forties, who was direct and professional. In no time, Rick dropped his lawsuit against Annie.

Although Annie had lost about a million dollars in the legal battle, ironically, she felt very relieved that it was over. Sometime after the legal cases, Annie received a call from Rick.

"I just want you to know I'm not mad at you and I'm not saying anything negative about you." He said to Annie.

Annie was in disbelief and couldn't respond to such a delusional comment. She believed that his purpose was selfish and that his only concern was that Annie did not speak negatively about him in public. She hung up the phone and never spoke to Rick again.

Annie felt no bitterness for the marriage and material items that were gone. Instead, she was thankful and relieved that that episode of her life was behind her. Annie shared some of her life and work experiences with her daughter, Whitney.

"Mom, you need to write a book."

CHAPTER 65

Rhine River

About a year later, in 2011, Annie retired from the university as a fully honored professor. To celebrate her great accomplishment, Annie planned a tour of Egypt. But months before the trip, there was political unrest in Cairo that had a devastating effect on the country as well as worldwide. This was the second time that a planned trip to Egypt had to be postponed. Annie wondered if she would ever see Egypt.

Annie changed her travel destination to a European cruise along the Rhine River. Stanly and two of Annie's closest friends, Ashni and her mother, Mary Sue, decided to join her.

Annie's retirement felt surreal. She was blessed to be able to retire while still in good health. She did not have any regrets about her decision to retire early and looked forward to new and exciting experiences.

The first thing Annie did to celebrate her retirement was clean out her closets and drawers. Annie donated over sixty business suits, fifty-five pairs of shoes, other clothing items, and several household items. Many of the clothing and shoe items were sent to one of her former colleague's family in West Africa. But most importantly, she told her relatives and friends, "Do not buy me anything for any occasion. But, if you insist, let it be toilet paper and paper towels—I can always use those items."

Many laughed at Annie, but she remained very serious about it. Positive interactions at gatherings with family and friends had always been a more valuable gift to Annie than any wrapped presents.

Annie knew that she had ended another journey and had begun a new one that would take her to a different place in her life.

259

About two months before the planned cruise, Annie drove to Memphis. She hadn't visited Memphis as much after her mother died. She decided to stay with Samantha for a while and then visit Stanly. Within three days at Stanly's house, he became very ill. Annie drove him to the emergency. As a result, Stanly had major surgery. Annie stayed at Stanly's home but his relatives didn't visit him during that time. Instead, they called and sent gift baskets to Annie to thank her for being there. Even though at times, Annie felt misused and taken for granted, she believed that every time Stanly had medical issues, God had placed her with him, perhaps to be his support.

Annie, as she did on every visit, cooked large portions of Stanly's favorite dishes. He loved her homemade recipes for black bean turkey chili, ground turkey sausages, and walnut raisin oatmeal cookies. Annie would put them in small storage bags and place them in the freezer for him to prepare for work.

Although not fully recovered, Stanly decided he was well enough to make the nineteen-day cruise. The Rhine River cruise included five countries: Switzerland, Germany, Frances, Netherlands, and Belgium.

Annie had visited four of the five countries before, but Stanly had not visited Europe at all. Annie hoped the trip was a good idea to help boost Stanly's spirit and distract him from his medical issues.

The riverboat was nice and the personnel was pleasant, but Annie wasn't too happy with the scheduled activities. Although most of the travelers were over sixty-years old, Annie felt they were not mobile enough. With a little persistence, the captain allowed Annie to teach dance fitness classes on the top deck every day at 5:00 p.m., whenever possible. Although the weather was chilly on the top deck, several people joined Annie, and Ashni never missed a class. Stanly took pictures and videotaped a class, while Annie's long locked hair blew in the wind as the riverboat cruised alone from country to country. It was an amazing sight, especially to see one country on the right side of the boat and another country on the left. The cruise ended where France, Switzerland, and Germany bordered.

Ashni's mother, Mary Sue, was in her seventies and she kept up with all the cruise activities and tours. She had a magnificent trip, but agreed with others, that they looked forward to sleeping in their beds.

Annie flew back to Memphis with Stanly and stayed a couple of days to overcome the jetlag and then drove back to Tallahassee.

CHAPTER 66

India

No more than two days passed before Annie received a phone call from her sweet niece, Charu. They had developed a close bond.

"Hey, Auntie, how ya do'in?"

"I'm better than good, and you?" They laughed.

"I'm good. Mom and I are planning a trip to India. We would love for you to come with us."

Charu knew how much her aunt loved to travel.

"You know I will," Annie said with delight.

"Great, I will send you the details. I know your passport is always ready." They laughed again.

VanLila had planned to stay in India for six months. She had not been home for over twenty years and her father had been hospitalized. Therefore, she arrived in India about four months before Annie and Charu. She had already visited her family in Mumbai/Bombay and was staying with a younger sister in Belgaum, where her father also lived. VanLila grew up in a large family, similar to Annie's, with four boys and six girls. She was the fourth oldest child.

Annie drove to Memphis for the Christmas and New Year holidays. She stayed until her departure to India, in February. Charu departed the same day from San Francisco, but she arrived in India about nine hours before Annie. When Annie arrived in Mumbai, a host of her in-laws were waiting for her. Charu, Panita, (VanLila's youngest sister), her husband, Baneet, and two of Charu's, first cousins, Fadi and Rahil were there.

Fadi lived in Belgaum, India. His late mother was VanLila's oldest sister. Rahil was visiting from Australia and his mother was also VanLila's sister.

Annie felt so welcomed. They were pleasant and they all hugged Annie. As Annie rode along the roads, she noticed that there were a lot of small vehicles and some looked like golf carts. They drove on the left side of the road which made Annie very nervous. It looked as if the oncoming car was going to hit the car she was riding in. There wasn't much order on the street, Some drove down the centerline, on the sidewalk, bumper to bumper, and car horns were blowing constantly. The buildings looked old and worn but some with unique architecture. There were a lot of people on the streets begging. The air was thick with pollution, even on a sunny day, the sky was not clear. Fadi drove by the Gate of India in Mumbai. Annie had decided to tour Mumbai on her way back to the states.

Panita and Baneet were medical doctors. They had a twelve-year-old daughter and a six-year-old son. They lived in a four-story apartment building with only two rooms and a small kitchen. They had been building their new home for a few years. Annie was told that, in most cases, in India, people can't get mortgage loans. Instead, they have to pay cash. Most people would buy the land and build one room at a time.

The two-room apartment accommodated eight people that first night. The arrangement reminded Annie of her childhood in Memphis when her mother always managed to find space for guests.

Early the next morning, Fadi drove Annie and Charu to the airport where they flew to New Delhi. Fadi and Rahil agreed to meet them, in a few days, in Goa.

Annie and Charu spent a day sightseeing in New Delhi and the next morning, they caught a train to Agra. The train ride was comfortable. After settling into a hotel, the next morning, they took a shuttle to the Taj Mahal. When they finally reached the Taj Mahal, Annie and Charu were speechless. The entire tour was awesome.

Wow, this is special. All of this, he built for his wife, just to show his eternal love for her. Annie thought.

Annie and Charu also toured the Fort of Agra. After three days in Agra, they flew to Goa. When Annie and Charu arrived at the airport, VanLila, Fadi, and Rahil were waiting. VanLila had been staying in Belgaum but wanted to drive up with her nephews to be with her daughter and Annie.

Everyone had rented a hut on the beach. It was a new concept for Annie and Charu. The three ladies stayed in one hut and the two guys stayed in a hut across from them.

After getting settled in, they all walked along the beach. It was beautiful but still, the sky was hazy. The pollution hung over the country. Annie noticed a lot of stray dogs and animals everywhere she visited, but they kept their distance from people. There were a few shops and restaurants on the beach.

They all stopped to get a snack and returned to the huts. Everyone decided to sit outside on the porch swings. Annie was tickled to hear the three first cousins from three different continents discuss, in English, various topics. Charu talked like a California valley girl, Rahil had a deep Austrian accent, and Fadi had a strong Indian accent.

The next couple of days included swimming, touring local spots, and relaxing. Then, everyone loaded up in the van and drove to VanLila's hometown, Belgaum.

Three hours later, they arrived at another aunt's home. VanLila's younger sister, Jameela, was very sweet and kind. She was married to a medical doctor and had three lovely daughters. One was in college and the other two were in high school. They had recently completed building their new home. It was very spacious and stunning. Annie and Charu shared a bedroom.

Later that day, Fadi, drove everyone to the hospital to visit VanLila's father, Nana. Although he was over eighty-years old and frail, Annie was amazed at how handsome and youthful he looked. He had very few wrinkles and a smooth olive complexion. He hugged Charu and cried because he hadn't seen his granddaughter since she was a very little girl. He shook Annie's hand and smiled. Nana turned his head and spoke in his dialect to Jameela. He told her to buy Annie and Charu Indian clothes. It was a hot day and apparently, Annie and Charu were showing too much cleavage. Annie's long locks were also a discussion among the family. They wanted to touch them, and asked if her hair was real, and how did Annie maintain them.

There were a lot of shops and street vendors in Belgaum. Annie shopped 'til she dropped. She had about twenty outfits made and purchased several pieces of costume jewelry, fabric, and shoes. After her shopping spree, she had to purchase an extra suitcase that only cost her five dollars.

Annie was happy to see that everyone ate fresh vegetables. The carrots were a rich red-orange color and tasted great, and the red onions were sweet. Not too many green leafy veggies to select from, but there were various roots.

During meal times, Annie was limited in what she could eat. Some of her extended family members pressured her to eat more than she did. The meals consisted of oily and starchy items. Most of their plates were filled with white rice, white potatoes, roti (bread), oily meats, and very few green veggies. Annie brought some protein powder that she used to make smoothies in the morning. They were surprised that Annie was not taking any medication and was not diabetic, since most of them had been diagnosed with the illness. Annie enjoyed the spices that were used in the foods. Jameela went out of the way to accommodate Annie with special meals.

One evening all the ladies dressed up in sarees. Charu selected a beautiful bright yellow, VanLila selected white, and Annie selected red. The sarees belonged to Jameela's daughters. Photos were taken and Annie decided to have a red saree made to take back to the states.

Charu had to return to San Francisco for work. Annie remained at Jameela's house. One day, Jameela asked Annie to teach an exercise class. Annie had traveled with her exercise music and equipment and one of the daughters joined the class. Jameela caught on pretty fast, but the daughter disappeared after a short time.

Nana got stronger and was released from the hospital. He lived only a block away from Jameela. VanLila and Annie walked to his house to visit. All of the family came over to Jameela's house for a gathering. Annie had the privilege of meeting all the siblings, except the sister in Australia.

About a week later, they all returned to celebrate Annie's sixty-second birthday. Annie and some of the other ladies dressed up again in sarees. Jameela bought a delicious cake and some coconut cookies. The food was plentiful and very tasty. When it was time to blow out the candles, Annie asked Nana to help her blow them out.

"Okay, Nana, on three we will blow them out together." Nana nodded his head in agreement.

"Okay, one, two…" Nana blew out the candles. Everyone laughed.

Someone relit the candles. Annie started again.

"One more time, Nana. On three. One... " Nana blew them out again. Everyone laughed. It was a wonderful evening.

At the party, VanLila's older brother, Shrey, and his wife, Geeta, who lived in Nipani, invited VanLila and Annie to their house. After the party, they all drove a few hours to Nipani.

Shrey and Geeta were dedicated school administrators. They founded and managed a private elementary school. Annie and VanLila toured the school and took pictures with the children and teachers. During their three-day stay, Shrey drove Annie and VanLila to tourist sights. One day, several family members from Belgaum drove down to join them. The large group visited other popular places, including a Holy Land place, and had lunch at a very nice restaurant. Annie bonded with Geeta and they stayed in touch.

Annie and VanLila returned to Belgaum and later boarded a bus to Mumbai. They spent another two nights with Panita, Baneet, and their children. They toured a few locations and another Holy Land place. The next day, Annie caught her flight back to the USA.

Annie's stay in India was humbling. It was another life lesson she learned about people. No matter where she traveled, Annie learned that all people wanted the same things in life. Besides the necessities, such as adequate shelter, and food for their family, earning a living, and feeling safe, they wanted to be free, loved, and respected.

Annie returned home with a newfound perspective on how blessed she truly was. She wanted to make a difference in other people's lives and to use her talents to give back to society. Her energy immediately began to focus on special projects that had been close to her heart for many years such as starting a boarding high school. She began to research and write, and she continued fitness activities.

Annie's life felt, "better than good."

Chapter 67

No

Annie and Stanly spoke on the phone regularly. One time, in just a general conversation, Annie asked him a question that she thought she already knew the answer to.

"Stanly, who is your best friend?"

"Well, uh, I have to think about it. I would say maybe, Mike or Johnnie."

Annie knew he was kidding and waited for him to say that she was his best friend, but he never did. That was difficult for her and a turning point. It forced her to reassess their relationship.

Stanly visited Annie in Tallahassee during the Thanksgiving holiday and he stayed about a week. To make her guest feel comfortable, Annie kept a very nice and organized guest bedroom. On each visit, Stanly complimented Annie on how nice her home was and how comfortable the bed felt. It was quite a contrast to what Annie experienced when she stayed at Stanly's house. She had to make major adjustments before she could settle into his guest bedroom. Although he kept a very clean house, in most cases, it seemed that Stanly didn't plan for her visit or just didn't care.

The following summer of 2013, Stanly turned sixty-three-years old. His family in Atlanta had planned a birthday party for him and Annie agreed to meet him in Atlanta. After the party, she left her car at his brother's house and rode with Stanly to Memphis. Stanly agreed to drive Annie back to Atlanta after her stay in Memphis.

Annie had arranged to volunteer at two centers in Memphis to teach dance fitness and ribbon dancing for six weeks. Annie planned one of the activities through her former classmate and close friend, Rhonda, who had returned to Memphis after graduating from college.

Rhonda was a pretty girl and was voted the most attractive in the high school class. Although she was a very cute girl, Annie thought Rhonda's inner beauty was /and remains/ what people were mostly drawn to. Annie, Rhonda, Marie, and Leola played flutes in the school's band and were close friends. When Annie returned to the south and made more trips to Memphis, she and Rhonda reconnected. Now, Annie had two close friends that she could visit, Rhonda and Marie. Rhonda invited Annie to various events, including an exercise class held at a church. Since Annie was a certified aerobics and fitness instructor, the group instructor invited Annie to teach the class each time she visited Memphis. Annie enjoyed the interactions with the ladies and looked forward to each visit.

Annie had also been appointed Chairperson for her high school's forty-fifth Class Reunion that would be held in Memphis at a hotel. She had been preparing and had discussions with the reunion committee members while in Tallahassee. She planned to stay in Memphis until after the class reunion. With all the activities planned, Annie had more clothes than she usually traveled with. Stanly had driven his truck to Atlanta that could accommodate her luggage.

After his birthday dinner, Annie and Stanly headed to Memphis. Annie drove four out of the five-hour distance and was extremely tired when they arrived at Stanly's house. She just wanted to take a shower and lie down for a moment. Stanly pushed the remote to raise the garage door, jumped out of the car, and opened the house. He returned to the truck and grabbed Annie's luggage. Then, he put them in the garage, instead of the guest bedroom.

"Why are you leaving my luggage in the garage?" Annie asked.

"I'll get them later." He walked into the house.

Annie picked up one of her suitcases and went into the house. Stanly was in the den flicking the TV channels to catch a game. Annie continued to walk towards the back to her bedroom with her suitcase. When she opened the door to the bedroom, she could not believe her eyes. Stanly's clothes were all over the bed, books, and mail on the floor and dresser, the closet was full, and the drawer that was once emptied for her use was filled. Without skipping a beat, Annie began to straighten up. She had to pick up clothes off the bed, reorganize the closet to hang her clothes, find a drawer in another room to place her items, and vacuum the room.

About thirty minutes later, she was too exhausted to go on. She was so tired that she began to cry. Annie walked past Stanly, who was watching the game, straight into the yard where she continued to cry from her exhaustion.

What am I doing here? Why am I crying? She thought.

After a few minutes, Annie gathered herself. She walked into the house and approached Stanly.

"Stanly, I need your help. I'm so tired. I just want to settle in. Will you help me with the luggage?"

"No, not now, I'm watching the game. If you are so tired, just take your tired self and lay down in my room," he said, annoyed.

Annie was in shock. All she heard was the word, "No."

How can he say no to me when I have always been there for him? I have never asked him for help before and when I did, he said, 'No'. Annie thought to herself.

Annie made two phone calls while Stanly was still watching TV. When she finished, she stood at the den door, where he sat.

"Someone is coming here to take me over to my sister's house. Since your brother had planned to come to Memphis in a few days, I've asked him to drive my car here so that I will have transportation."

"I don't want you to go, but you do what you have to," Stanly said to Annie, barely looking at her.

"I just broke up with you and that is all you have to say to me. You don't care about me. Why do you think the world should always revolve around you?"

"That's crazy," Stanly said and said no more.

Within an hour, Annie left Stanly's house. Again like a fish, she swam away and never looked back.

Annie had dated Stanly for five years and had been celibate for four-and-a-half years during their relationship. At the age of fifty-nine years, when Stanly was undergoing surgeries, she stopped thinking about sex and felt satisfied with his companionship. She enjoyed sharing traveling, laughter, and new experiences with him. As she looked back on their relationship, Annie tried to place a title on it. They weren't lovers and apparently, not best friends. Annie always believed that a true friendship had to be tested. In this case, they failed. No matter what type of relationship had existed, it seemingly wasn't important enough for Stanly to fight for.

Surprisingly, she was not angry, instead, she felt relieved that it was over. She did, however, incur separation anxiety from her sweet canine friends, CiCi and Moe.

About two months later, Annie attended her forty-fifth high school reunion. As chairperson, she facilitated the banquet program.

It was a nice turnout and the class members were kind and delighted to see one another. Annie received many praises for the affair. Annie and Stanly cordially spoke to one another during the event, but there were no sparks for her.

Despite Stanly's cards and phone messages, which never offered an explanation or an apology to her, Annie soon stopped thinking about him.

****

In the late fall of the same year, Annie made a last-minute decision to get away on a four-day cruise along Mexico. During that cruise, Annie had moments of solitude while standing on one of the upper decks looking out into the wide ocean. The sky was blue with beautiful white clouds and the ocean was just as blue. She reflected on her life.

While approaching her sixty-fourth birthday, Annie decided to not act on her sexual desires. Moreover, she didn't need to get involved in another relationship. Her thoughts were,

Available men, my age are usually sickly or needy with lots of baggage and/or want a woman to nurse or care for them. On the other hand, younger men are usually looking for finance or a sponsor to ease their financial needs. These are unacceptable. An ideal relationship at this stage of life would be a traveling companion who is a true friend and has strong moral and spiritual beliefs. But surprisingly, I feel good just as I am.

God granted Annie's prayer to remove her sensation of sexual needs and to free her from ever feeling any desperation to be with a man. Instead, she continued to explore her creative talents, maintained a spiritual and healthy lifestyle, and did other ventures. Annie further examined the life lessons she learned.

CHAPTER 68

Life's Lessons Learned

Throughout many years, Annie had been tormented, bullied, and undermined by various people whom she loved and trusted. Annie wasn't sure, but perhaps she had restrained herself from calling attention to the perpetrators' intimidating and belittling acts against her, especially those closest to her because she feared they might detach themselves or even terminate the relationship.

Although late in life, Annie no longer knowingly placed herself in harm's way of her bullies and perpetrators. She also didn't hesitate to defend herself when necessary. In some cases, she felt relieved that those people were no longer a part of her life.

Yet, Annie felt that God placed just enough of the right people in her life at the right time. They encouraged her, and they didn't feel the need to dominate her emotionally, socially, or physically.

Annie accepted the fact that no matter how hard anyone tried, there was not a "Perfect" parent—and that one can only work with what they know. For clarity, she clung to the words of a writer, Kalil Gibran, on his assessment of parenting.

"Your children are not your children. They are sons and daughters of life's longing for itself. They come through you but not from you. And though they are with you, yet, they belong not to you. You may give them your love but not your thoughts. For they have their own thoughts..."

Annie realized that along her journeys she had made mistakes and done things that were inappropriate and sinful. But she felt assured that she had never willfully harmed anyone.

Those life experiences had taught Annie to view herself in a dissimilar way. She learned to ignore others' perceptions of her. She likes who she is and what she has accomplished in life, and won't apologize for them. She will no longer feel guilty for taking good care of her health and her body, and for being a charitable person. Annie no longer worries about being loved by anyone, because she knows that she is loved by God. Despite her perpetrators' deliberate attempts to break her spirit, Annie endured and rose above them.

On the day of her sixty-fourth birthday, Annie walked into her kitchen. She sat on a stool at the kitchen island with her laptop and began to summarize the lessons learned during her journeys over the sixty-four years of her life. She wrote:

Cons: There are those who-
- *you may love, but they are not capable of loving.*
- *confuse love with possession.*
- *enjoy seeing you in pain.*
- *find it difficult to say thank you.*
- *don't want to give you anything for fear that you may have a moment of pleasure.*
- *won't give you compliments or encouragement for fear that you will feel better than they feel about themselves.*
- *want you to feel the pain that they feel.*
- *take from you, only to exploit you.*
- *won't trust you, because they can't be trusted.*
- *will lie about you for envious reasons.*
- *will oppress you for fear you might learn what it means to be free.*
- *turn their heads when you are in harm's way.*
- *will bully you to gain emotional rewards.*
- *see your success as their failure.*

- *can cite and preach the holy scripture, while carrying out evil deeds.*

Pros: Yet, few will --
- *give you unconditional love.*
- *feel your pain.*
- *magnify your simple kindness.*
- *reach out a hand to you when you stumble or fall.*
- *be your family, when yours disown you.*
- *show concern about your welfare.*
- *support you through illness or hardship.*
- *give to you out of kindness.*
- *praise your accomplishments.*
- *open their hearts for mutual trust and respect.*
- *pray for you when you feel hopeless.*
- *hug you back with passion - or better, hug you first.*
- *protect you when you are in harm's way.*
- *encourage you when you are doubtful.*
- *pass the test of a true friend.*
- *uplift you and live by the holy words.*

Annie closed her laptop and returned to her comfortable chair in the living room. She realized that the long rugged journeys were behind her. Annie believed that what she had learned from all of her life experiences was truly a blessing. Those experiences had made her the strong and confident person that she had become. Annie is thankful to God that she has no bitterness or malice in her spirit, and her arms remain open to embrace those whose intent is to embrace her with the respect and the love that she is worthy and justly deserves.

CHAPTER 69

Joy Joy

Before Annie closed the last family photo album in her lap, she stared at a recent photo of her daughter, Whitney, and her two grandchildren. She expected a visit from them, later that day. Annie was thankful for each of them.

She closed the final photo album and reflected on the life lessons that had taught her so much and had led her to this day, time, and place, her sixty-fourth birthday.

There, on the coffee table, sat an empty album. Annie thought about her future journeys and the good memories that would fill the pages of that album.

Annie had always planned her life and now she is living it. She continues to pursue her dreams and maintains a strong faith that God is not through with her yet. Angel Candice is always with her and sends messages from God to guide Annie along the way.

Each day Annie awakes with excitement and joy and welcomes any surprises. She feels full of life -- without pain or sorrow.

With a new song in her heart- "Joy Joy in My Soul" by Rance Allen, Annie gives daily thanks.

"Thank you, God, for blessing me with a life that is truly **"Better Than Good".**

The End

About the Author

Taj Shotwell

Born Theresa Ann James, "Taj," in Ft. Eustis, Virginia. She is the sixth child of eleven children raised by a mobile career Army sergeant and homemaker. Many of her adolescent years were spent in Memphis, Tennessee.

Spent over 20 years in the San Francisco Bay Area and later moved to Florida where I reside now. Although started my career in accounting, taught for over 30 years at colleges and a university in business and education.- Teaching in bachelor's, Master's, and PH.D. programs. Now retired as Full Honored Professor. Since then, Shotwell has written and published six books of nonfiction and fiction including over 50 poems. She has written 16 songs, (the album is expected to be released in late September 2022), a musical play, and a screenplay.

As the founder and president of a business and performing arts boarding school for students in grades 7-12th, Shotwell completed the business plan and budget for the school. Also have written the school's anthem for the school at tajshotwell.com/BAAI. She played the concert flute and piano, lives a healthy lifestyle, and currently volunteers by teaching the community members a weekly dance fitness class.

MIDDLE CHILD: Build A Fence All Around Me

As the middle child of eleven, raised by a career Army sergeant and homemaker, Annie struggles to survive her dysfunctional family, a brutal Deep South transition, and ultimately an abusive relationship. 246 pages, 45,211 words.

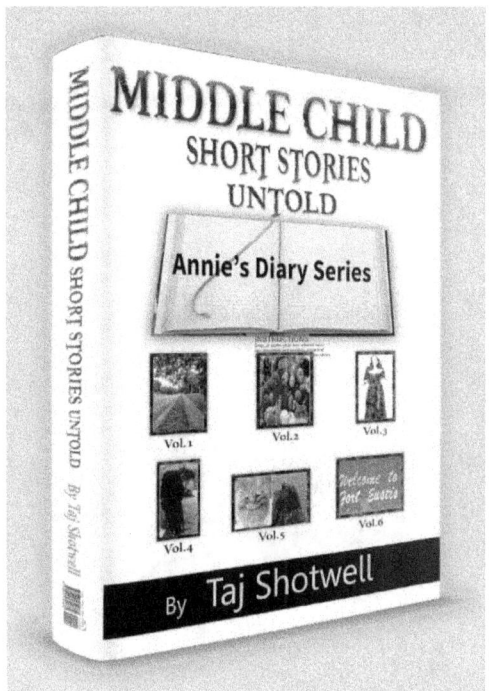

MIDDLE CHILD Short Stories Untold: ANNIE'S
DIARY SERIES. This collection of family-historical-fiction
short stories is based on true stories beginning in the mid-
1950s-2015. The series is an extension of the author's novels,
*"Middle Child: Build a fence all around me", and "Middle
Child 2: Better than good",* and consists of inspiring untold
stories that are appropriate for all readers. 79 pages, 14,225
words.

www.ingramcontent.com/pod-product-compliance
Lightning Source LLC
Chambersburg PA
CBHW070854180626
46817CB00003B/771